LOOKING INTO THE SUN

A NOVEL OF THE SYRIAN CONFLICT

by Todd Tavolazzi

This book is a work of creative fiction that uses actual publicly known news reports, history, events, situations, and locations as background for the storyline with fictional embellishments as creative license allows. Any similarity in this book to a living person is unintentional and the author has made every effort to not identify or defame any party. Although the publisher has made every effort to ensure the grammatical integrity of this book was correct at press time, the publisher does not assume and hereby disclaims any liability to any party for any loss, damage, or disruption caused by errors or omissions, whether such errors or omissions result from negligence, accident, or any other cause. At Pandamoon, we take great pride in producing quality works that accurately reflect the voice of the author. All the words are the author's alone.

www.pandamoonpublishing.com

Jacket design and illustrations © Pandamoon Publishing.
Cover Art Direction by Matthew Kramer, Pandamoon Publishing
Cover Illustration by Fletcher Kinnear, Pandamoon Publishing
Editing by Zara Kramer, Nicole Tone, and Daphne Tuccitto, Pandamoon Publishing
Author Photo by Danielle Caceres

Pandamoon Publishing and the portrayal of a panda and a moon are registered trademarks of Pandamoon Publishing.

Library of Congress Cataloging-in-Publication Data is on file at the Library of Congress, Washington, DC

ISBN-10: 0-9908709-8-7
ISBN-13: 978-0-9908709-8-2

Author's Note

I wrote *Looking into the Sun* in my off time while I was assigned as an operational planner to the U.S. Sixth Fleet staff in Naples, Italy, from April to August 2014. When I arrived at my new assignment, in September 2011, the Arab Spring was well underway. Syrian protestors had joined Tunisian, Libyan, and Egyptian protestors in voicing their displeasure with their government. The resulting unrest in Syria became a serious concern for the U.S. Central Command, as well as the U.S. European Command and its naval component command, the U.S. Sixth Fleet.

I was one of many operational planners to study the effect the Syrian conflict was having on our European partners. During my research, from unclassified open source material, I was appalled at the deteriorating situation in Syria and particularly its effect on Syrian civilians caught up in the violence. For the most part, there was only mainstream news coverage when chemical weapons were found to have been used in the conflict (which tapered off after only a short time) and when ISIS began to gain ground in northern Iraq and northeastern Syria.

In the course of my research, I found that there were many freelance journalists who had smuggled themselves into Syria to bravely report what no one else could, after Bashar al-Assad closed his borders to foreign correspondents soon after the violence began. The stories by freelance journalists working for *Vice News* or on their own were astounding. The video proof of the suffering of the average citizen in Syria was heart-wrenching, especially the awful plight of the children. I saw video reports of children that were blown up by the Assad regime in their indiscriminate bombing where helicopters would push barrels packed with explosives out of their cargo bays on neighborhoods suspected to be rebel strongholds. There were also video reports of starving families who could not be resupplied because the regime had cut off all services to their neighborhoods in a cruel play to starve out their own people who they perceived were harboring rebel groups.

The videos of the innocent children who were being shot, starved, gassed, or blown up drove me to write *Looking into the Sun.* I knew there was not much I could do in my position as a U.S. military officer to effect any real change, so I decided to compile my research and weave real case studies into a novel. Through that effort, I would attempt to put a coherent face on the horrible situation the world seemed to be ignoring. Only recently, with reports of refugee drownings, their push across Europe, and potential ISIS terrorists hiding amongst the fleeing masses, has the refugee problem been addressed in the mainstream media, despite the fact that the situation had been going on to some extent since the fighting began in November 2011.

My focus in *Looking into the Sun* was intentionally narrow. I had three simple goals: (1) raise widespread awareness of the sacrifices and risks freelance journalists take to bring us the stories the mass media machine doesn't seem to have time for, (2) acknowledge the ongoing child suffering in Syria since November 2011 and, most importantly, (3) remind the average reader that there are credible and effective ways to help these innocent children.

My publisher, Zara Kramer at Pandamoon Publishing, and I discussed what we could do to directly help the Syrian children. We mutually decided to each donate a percentage of the profits of the sale of this book to the most important organization providing real relief in the area. I am honored to support the selfless souls at *Save the Children* as we all work to provide Syrian children (and all suffering children throughout the world) the tangible, loving care they need and deserve. I thank you personally for contributing to this effort by purchasing this book. If you would like to make an additional donation, please visit www.savethechildren.org. Remember, every little thing we do makes a difference, but you first MUST ACT. Please make a difference today!

Todd Tavolazzi
U.S. East Coast
November 2015

Dedication

For the innocent children of Syria and the fearless journalists who risk their lives around the world to bring us the truth.

LOOKING INTO THE SUN

Amanda,

Thanks for being such a fantastic friend! Looking forward to hanging with you again in sunny California!

Todd

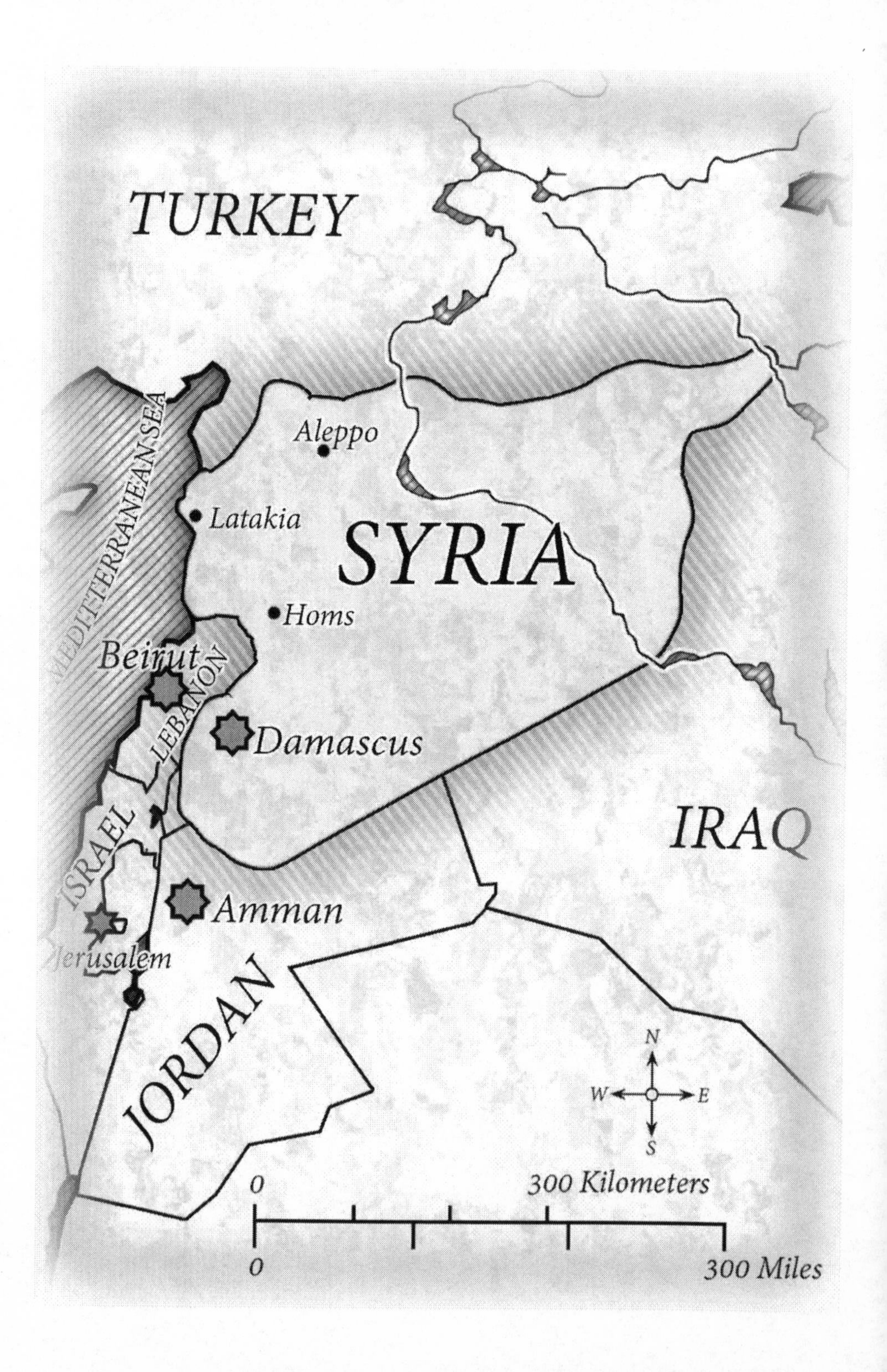
TURKEY
MEDITERRANEAN SEA
Aleppo
Latakia
SYRIA
Homs
Beirut
LEBANON
Damascus
ISRAEL
IRAQ
Amman
Jerusalem
JORDAN
N
W
E
S
0
300 Kilometers
0
300 Miles

Chapter 1

Al Assi River
Syria-Lebanon border
May 2, 2013

I felt the shock wave of the bullet that snapped so close to my head it singed my scalp. A quick succession of several more bullets impacted the dirt a few feet to my right. The moonless night made it impossible to see Rafi only a foot to my left. The same darkness that disoriented me also kept us invisible to the men shooting at us.

The night resembled a black canvas splashed with the disciplined single file of green tracer fire. The mesmerizing beauty of the night was shattered by indiscriminate sparks spewing from the heavy weapons firing from a few hundred meters behind us. The tsunami of adrenaline that saturated my blood made my eyes shoot their own white tracers that ricocheted inside my eyeballs. I strained my vision to pick out the next spot I would aim for when the shooting let up.

A bright flash illuminated the ground in front of us like a flashbulb, and I chose the base of an olive tree ten meters away as my next target. The flash disappeared but its ghost lingered in my vision and made it even harder to see.

"Rafi, that tree. Follow me."

"Okay," he said from the darkness next to me.

I shot up the instant the firing stopped and pumped my legs until I felt I had covered the distance to the tree. I held my hand out in front of me when I figured I was close, but managed to find the tree with my face. The force of my momentum knocked me flat on my back. I actually thought for a second that I'd been shot.

I heard Rafi hit the ground next to me.

"What are you doing on your back?"

"I ran into the damn tree. That last burst half blinded me."

I heard him chuckle in the dark. "You okay?"

I rolled over onto my stomach and maneuvered to get the tree between me and the onslaught of bullets I knew were coming.

"Yeah, thanks for asking. Where's the damn car?"

"It's at the end of this olive grove, about fifty meters."

The guns cranked up again and we buried our heads in the dirt at the base of the olive tree. I heard the bullets passing through the leaves over our heads seconds before the ground turned to gelatin from a massive explosion. I turned over and saw the flaming wreck of what used to be the car Rafi borrowed to get us to the Syrian border.

"They got the car. What the fuck do we do now?"

"Plan B, my friend," Rafi said.

"What the fuck is Plan B?"

"The river."

"Where is it?"

"It's over there about a hundred meters," he said pointing to our left.

His face and pointing hand flickered red from the reflection of our burning car fully engulfed in flames as more bullets chewed up the ground around our olive tree.

"Fuck, the fire's painting us. They can see us."

I was talking to myself. Rafi had bolted up and had a three-step head start in the direction of the river.

"Come on, Angus, we can make it!" he yelled over his shoulder.

Rafi maintained a full sprint three meters in front of me. Bullets chewed up our footprints as soon as we made them, all the way to the river. Rafi slowed a bit, and then disappeared through a stand of trees that lined the riverbank. I kept up my own speed and felt the prickly slap of branches on my face as I busted through. Then I was falling.

The riverbank wasn't high above the water, but the situation had slowed my perception and it felt like I was falling from a tall building. I hit the cool water and clutched my twenty-pound backpack with an iron grip. I thought of my video gear, iPad, and iPhone. I had packed it all in plastic just as Rafi had suggested, but I couldn't help worrying that all the footage I'd risked my life to get might be ruined.

I put the thought out of my mind as my head broke the surface of the water. I looked around for Rafi and saw his wet curls disappear under the water in front of me. The fire from our car made distorted shadows through the trees as we floated by them. I took a deep breath and dunked my own head as the first barrage of bullets skipped off the water. All we could do was hold our breath and hope they couldn't get a bead on us.

I positioned my backpack between my legs and hugged my knees as my body floated down the river at a frustratingly slow pace with my back barely cresting the surface. I figured if I got shot, it probably wouldn't be in the head.

I leaned back and took a breath of air every ten count as I went through a brief mental checklist and couldn't come up with one thing I could do to improve my situation, except maybe rub the fur off a rabbit's foot. But I didn't have a rabbit's foot. All I had was a two-thousand-year-old gold statuette in my pocket. So I rubbed that instead. Mostly just to make sure it was still there. I figured if it was still in one piece after two thousand years, there had to be some luck left in it somewhere.

* * *

Our pursuers didn't chase us into Lebanon. They stopped firing at us a couple of minutes after we hit the water. Rafi and I floated down the river for about twenty minutes after we had crossed the border from Syria into northern Lebanon. Rafi grabbed ahold of a rebar ladder rung embedded into a cement piling at a small pier we floated toward and reached out to grab me as I came by. We pulled ourselves from the water and walked down an adjacent dirt road, leaving wet footprints behind us.

The Assad regime had kicked out all foreign journalists in November 2011 and had not issued any press visas since then. The only way in or out was by smuggling routes. Journalists, along with western aid workers, faced kidnappings, mortars, barrel bombs, and possible beheadings. The country had earned its gruesome reputation as the most dangerous place in the world for journalists and aid workers alike. Rafi and I had just experienced some of that danger first hand.

"What the hell do we do now?"

"Do not worry. I've got you covered," he said.

Rafi pulled his cell phone, wrapped in a plastic bag, from his pocket, checked to make sure it still worked, and was soon speaking to someone in Arabic. He ended the short conversation and pocketed his phone.

"Okay, we have someone coming for us. He'll be here in a few minutes."

"Damn, Rafi, you know everyone in Lebanon."

"Whenever I make these runs, I always have someone waiting for me on the other side in case of this very circumstance. How is your camera? Good idea to wrap it in plastic?"

"Yeah, the camera, phone, and iPad all survived. Good call on the plastic," I said and pulled the gold statuette from my pocket. "And I didn't lose this either."

I handed the artifact to Rafi. He took it and illuminated it with his cell phone's screen to get a close look at it.

"It's a nice example. Do you have someone who can authenticate it?"

"Yeah, I know a guy in New York who would know all about it and I'm sure he'd love to salvage as much as he can from the fighting."

"You must be careful," Rafi said, handing me back the artifact. "There are stiff penalties if you're caught with that. Someone would love to snag a hotshot journalist trying to smuggle that out of the country."

"I know, don't worry, I've got a plan."

"Yeah, but do you have a Plan B?" Rafi chuckled.

Chapter 2

The Metropolitan Museum of Art
New York
May 6, 2013

"Where did you say you got this?"

"A Syrian man who said he was a museum curator had an intermediary give it to me to get my attention and lure me to the story."

My friend, Paul, looked up at me and then went back to scrutinizing the small gold artifact in his hands with a jeweler's monocle. After a minute's inspection, he put the small statue of what looked to be a king sitting on a small throne on his desk and pulled back a few feet from it. We both stared at it for a few seconds.

"Well? Is it real?"

My friend didn't say anything, but wheeled himself in his office chair to a specific spot at his floor-to-ceiling bookcase behind his desk. He scanned the shelves, pulled down a large volume, and laid it on the desk so I could see it. The cover read: *Artifacts of the Middle East.* He flipped through the pages and stopped on a picture of the exact figure that stared back at us on his desk.

"That's him," he said, pointing to our old, silent friend.

"So this guy is legit, huh?"

"How many pieces did your guy say he had on offer?"

"He said he had a whole museum's worth of stuff, from big stuff like statues as big as horses to small stuff like this little guy."

"How in the hell would anyone get it out of the country?"

"I had to smuggle myself in and out and that was difficult enough. He was interested in contacting someone who could figure that out for him in exchange for weapons."

My friend looked at me for a second. "He doesn't just want to get the artifacts out of the country?"

"Yes, but he wants to trade them for weapons."

Paul put his hands on his head, leaned back in his chair, and stared at the ceiling for a second. "These guys are pretty desperate, huh?"

"It's unbelievable," was all I could say.

I didn't feel like getting into too much detail. I just needed his professional opinion.

Paul picked up a pen from his desk and jotted down a first name and a phone number from memory on a purple Post-it Note and handed it to me.

"What's this?"

"It's a guy I know who can probably get you in touch with someone who could get your friend's stuff out in one piece."

I looked at the Post-it: *"Bill,"* followed by a phone number. "The number's local."

"He knows people. He can get things done all over the world. He saved stuff from Afghanistan, Iraq, and Libya. I know he has contacts in Turkey and Lebanon, probably Syria, too. He just hasn't shared that with me. He's offered us stuff before, but we can't do business with him."

"Why not?"

"Because we're the freakin' Met. We can't be caught with hijacked artifacts."

"What makes you think," I waved the Post-it Note in my hand, "old Bill here will talk with a journalist about any of this?"

"It's his business. I'm sure if you promise to keep his anonymity, he'll set something up and you'll get a good story out of it. I assume that's what you're after?"

I folded and then pocketed the Post-it. "Thanks," I said and pointed to the statue. "So, I guess you don't want to keep him?"

"Of course I want to. But I can't. It's contraband. I can't get caught with it and neither should you. Give it to Bill as a down payment and proof of what he can expect. Tell him I sent you and it checks out."

I reached over, grabbed the statuette, and put it in my pants pocket. "Thanks for your time, Paul."

"Anytime. Thanks for letting me handle it. It's rumored that Alexander the Great had one just like it as a good luck charm. It's possible it could be that exact one. Either way, I hope it brings you luck while you have it. Be careful, some of these guys in this business don't seem dangerous but they are."

I headed for the door on my way out. "I think I can handle some art smugglers after the last few weeks."

"Yeah, I bet. How was it there?"

"It was more horrible than I'd ever anticipated."

"How so?"

"I guess I wasn't prepared to see all the civilian casualties. And not just civilians, but the kids. It was the kids. I spent some time in a neighborhood there and got pretty close with a few families. I saw a lot of people get killed and too many kids. I've seen a lot of death in my work, but I've never gotten used to seeing the tears and wailing when a five-year-old boy realizes his parents are dead and never coming back, or the pleading look an eight-year-old girl gave me as she was lying in the street, screaming for someone to help her after her legs were blown off."

As I spoke, I became aware that I was staring at a spot on the floor trying to block out the images of the rows of dead children lying in the dirty street, parents and siblings wailing over their little lifeless bodies.

"That's unbelievable. I empathize with their situation."

What a ridiculous thing to say. But what do you expect of him except to sit there and act empathetic. What else can he do?

"I do, too. But there's not much that empathy can do for these people. The only thing that can really help is to get as many of them out of there as possible. That's the only reason I'm going back. Maybe your guy, Bill, can help me trade these artifacts for some help with that."

"Well, if there's anyone who can work that out, I bet Bill can. Good luck, my friend. Stay safe."

I've got to go back. I can't be one of those people only offering useless empathy. They need real help.

Chapter 3

New York City
May 8, 2013

I spent two days editing and then selling the footage that survived the Syrian ambush and my trip down the Al Assi River with Rafi. I told the producer who bought it that I'd be going back for a second part. He seemed interested enough in a continuation and said his network would buy it if it was as good as what I had just given him. I didn't tell him about my plans to do business with Bill, but figured he'd be thrilled to have an inside view of what was going on in Syria, no matter the subject, since there hadn't been any network journalists there since Assad kicked them out almost a year and a half prior.

Bill was as shady as Paul had described. He never answered his phone when I called him. He always had me leave a message and called me back from a different phone number each time we spoke. But he was able to confirm that he had buyers for any Middle Eastern artifacts I could get out of Syria. He also assured me that, with twenty-four hours notice, he could have whatever I needed in the way of medicine, food, water, and transportation for a few hundred kids from Al-Waer at the Lebanon border to trade for the delivery of the artifacts. The good doctor wants guns, but he's going to get aid instead.

Of all the things Bill and I tentatively arranged, the one thing that kept replaying in my head over and over was his final comment to me, "These supplies you requested in return for artifacts are very expensive. The people who get things for me at the other end don't run a charity organization. They play hard ball, Mr. Conn. If you can't get the artifacts to the border, you get nothing. No trucks, no supplies, no security."

***

I was on my computer booking my one-way coach ticket to Beirut when my cell phone rang. I didn't recognize the number, but I answered it anyway. I should have known better.

"Is this Angus Conn?"

"Who's calling?"

"I'm Bernie Sheffield, a talent agent."

"Who gave you my phone number?"

"Let's just say a mutual friend."

"I don't have any friends. Who gave you my number?"

"Bobbie."

"Why would she think I need a talent agent?"

"No, it's nothing like that. She and I were at this thing yesterday and she said you'd be a good choice for prepping my client for his next role."

"Oh yeah?" I chuckled. "Who's your client?"

"Jake Westin."

"Jesus Christ."

"Not quite, but he thinks he is sometimes. Anyway, he's just agreed to take a role about a badass foreign correspondent in the Middle East."

"A badass, huh? Did you tell him that they don't exist, except in the movies?"

"Come on, you're one of the most successful freelance journalists with over twenty years of experience, covering hot spots all over the world, and the Pulitzer for your reporting on the Israeli invasion of southern Lebanon in 2006. Those credentials definitely put you in the badass category whether you admit it or not."

"I think you ought to try somewhere else. Besides, I have an assignment. I'm leaving the country in the next couple of days for about a month."

"The timeframe's perfect. Where are you headed?"

"I don't typically talk about my works in progress and getting to where I'm going may not be exactly legal."

"Well, I'm in a big bind here. I've contacted producers from all the major networks and none of them are able to accommodate our request. The security requirement to send a celebrity anywhere remotely dangerous is just not feasible and they wouldn't even begin to discuss footing the insurance cost they would need to have in place for the preparation Jake needs."

"And what preparation does Jake think he needs?"

"He needs to shadow an experienced journalist on overseas assignments, preferably someplace hot but not too hot, if you know what I mean."

"Well, hot and too hot is usually not in anyone's control."

"All we need is Jake getting an appreciation for the risks you take in the normal course of your job, but I don't want him to get killed doing it.

Anyway, all the networks suggested I get in touch with a freelance journalist who may be able to access places that are a bit too dicey for the networks to cover. And then I met Bobbie, and she mentioned that you were putting together a plan that needed some funding and may be interested in showing my guy the ropes for the right price."

"Well, that was nice of her to think of me, but she was wrong."

"I get it, Mr. Conn. No one wants to babysit some prima donna, but he made three movies last year. They all sucked, but they each made him a lot of money. He's interested in changing his image. He's willing to work and get dirty to prepare for this next role."

"Look, I have a very specific story I'm running down that begins in Lebanon and will require me to cross a certain border to the north for most of it."

"Sorry, my geography is a little sketchy outside of L.A. or Manhattan. What country is it exactly?"

I rolled my eyes. "It's Syria, Bernie, and it's probably too hot for a celebrity right now."

"It'll be a game changer for him and he's willing to pay top dollar. One month getting an appreciation for what you do in a real-world dangerous setting is all he needs."

"Bernie, if someone like him comes along, I can't guarantee he can cross the border with me."

"This deal has to be all or nothing, Mr. Conn. He needs the full experience. I trust you can keep him safe. Get him some body armor and a helmet like those guys on TV, take a few pictures, write a few stories and then get out of there. In turn, your bank account will thank you for your efforts."

"It's not exactly that easy."

"Come on, it's not every day a movie star calls you up and begs to pay you for doing what you do anyway."

It sure would make it easier to get those kids out of Syria if I had a little "fuck you money" if this deal with Bill goes south. But dragging some ignorant young celebrity around probably isn't worth it. I'll throw out a ridiculous number to discourage him.

"Well, my fee for a month of being my shadow is half a million, plus expenses."

"Done. When and where should he meet you?"

Shit. I should have asked for more.

* * *

After I hung up with Bernie, I cleared out the coach ticket I was in the middle of booking and reserved two First Class tickets from New York to Rome and two more for the following day from Rome to Beirut.

I've never traveled First Class to a war zone. But why not, this trip could be my last.

Chapter 4

John F. Kennedy International Airport
May 10, 2013

I looked up from my phone and scanned the throngs of people hustling past one another on the way to catch their international flights. Travelers glided over highly polished white floors under a latticework of immaculate white exposed girders fifty feet over our heads. I tried to ignore the constant cable news reports from the half dozen extra-large flat screen TVs in view from the faux black leather seat at my departure gate.

A wave of turned heads followed Jake Westin as he approached a few gates down. He was difficult to miss despite the hat, sunglasses, and face buried in his iPhone. He was following Bernie like a little duckling through the throngs of travelers. Most people took double-takes and whispered to their friends and family to look as he walked by, not sure if they were really seeing one of the hottest young actors to grace the recent Hollywood scene sauntering through the JFK departure gates with the common folk.

Bernie recognized me and gave me a subtle wave. I put my phone away and watched the pair approach. They looked like Laurel and Hardy, Bernie being the larger Laurel and Jake the thinner Hardy. I've been told that being six feet tall with a lean build and a chiseled jawline gave me a rugged look that the media liked for my average-guy-off-the-street look in front of the camera, but Jake Westin was something else.

Jake was bred not only for TV, but also the big screen. He was slightly shorter than I, but solidly built, like he'd just come out of Gold's Gym. You could see the masculine utility of his face. He was a Hollywood publicist's dream client who could portray a tough guy one day and every woman's fantasy guy, with a tough and tender side, for the romantic comedy circuit the next day.

Jake was exuding the epitome of casual with black slacks, a plain white T-shirt, a few gaudy chains around his neck and a ridiculous tweed eight-point Gatsby cap with sunglasses. I had to laugh. Then there was Bernie. He was slightly overweight with a soft pink double chin and slightly long, unkempt reddish brown hair, but he was dressed well in a gray suit and expensive black shoes.

Bernie held out his hand. "Thanks for the work, Angus."

"My pleasure, Bernie," I lied.

Jake was still texting away with one thumb while he pulled his carry-on luggage behind him as he walked up. I refused to acknowledge him until he at least recognized my presence.

"So, what time's the flight?" Bernie said, trying to cut the awkward silence.

"We board in ten minutes."

"Good. Well, you have all my numbers, so call me if you need anything. Be careful over there," he said more to Jake than to me, but Jake was still texting.

I couldn't take it. I leaned down to catch his line of sight between the brim of his hat and his iPhone. "Hey, Bernie's talking to you," I said to Jake.

Jake looked at me and then at Bernie. "Okay, see ya, Bernie," he said, as he looked up quickly and then went back to texting.

"I'm sittin' over here. We can talk when you're done," I said and turned back toward my seat.

"Okay, I'll be one minute," he said.

Jake began to shuffle in my direction but never stopped texting.

"Jesus, this is going to be a long month," I said under my breath.

* * *

Four minutes later, when Jake finished his texting and sauntered up to where I sat, he moved the newspapers from the seat next to me and plopped himself down.

"Sorry about that. I have a couple contacts I really need to keep up with or the well will dry up, if you know what I mean."

"Look, Jake, I know you live in a different world than mine," I said as I kept acting like I was reading the newspaper and flipping through the pages, "but when you meet someone for the first time, you have to make eye contact, kiss, bow, or shake their hand, depending on the custom, and give them your full attention. Anything else is just rude." I put the paper in my lap and offered my hand. "Angus Conn, pleased to meet you."

"Jake," he said. "Sorry, I didn't know it was such a big deal."

"It's not that big a deal if it only happens once," I said as I returned to the newspaper. "You will be talking with real people in the real world on this trip."

"I know that—" Jake interrupted.

"Don't talk, just listen. It is likely that where we are going no one will know who the hell you are. The thought of that may be horrifying to you or you may love it. Either way, I don't care. Bernie wants me to show you how I do my job and the first step is to be polite and listen to people," I said as I put my paper down again and looked at him. "Got it?"

"Yeah, I got it," he said and went back to his phone.

We both sat in silence as I read the paper and he tapped on his iPhone. I wasn't really reading the paper, but thinking of the next fundamental lecture I was likely to give. I looked over and watched Jake take a selfie before he began tapping his iPhone with a purpose.

"What are you doing?"

Jake looked over at me for a moment and then went back to typing his message. "Just keeping my fans up-to-date on what's going on with me."

I found Jake's Twitter page and saw what he had just tweeted. "Jake, you can't tell everyone where we're going."

"Why not? My fans need to know that I'm progressing into leading man material. That's what this whole deal is about. I'm shaping my image, my brand."

"Your brand could make you a target if people can pinpoint your whereabouts. When we get to Rome you need to tweet that you had a change of plans and you're staying in Rome."

Jake rolled his eyes. "Whatever."

This trip may be more difficult that I thought.

* * *

It was amazing how fast we were able to board the plane when with anointed Hollywood royalty. I had only taken First Class a few times in my life and it really was an experience that made you feel important. The only difference was that I knew I wasn't important.

We got to our seats and settled in. The flight attendant didn't waste any time recognizing Jake and asked him if he wanted a drink. He pulled his face away from his phone long enough to order a Long Island Iced Tea. The flight attendant looked at me as an afterthought and I ordered a ginger ale.

Jake looked at me for a second. "Is it like a cop thing or something? You're on the job so you can't drink?"

"It's a long story. I choose not to drink. But since you brought it up, I suggest you enjoy it because you won't be drinking at all after our layover in Rome."

"Why not?"

"You have to keep your wits about you. Things move fast in this business and you can't afford any unnecessary hindrances."

"This drink is gonna help me sleep on this flight so I can be fresh when we get there," Jake said.

"I'll go through your stuff when we get to where we're staying in Rome and I'll show you what you can keep. We'll get you anything else I think you'll need while we're there."

The flight attendant arrived with our drinks and asked for Jake's autograph as nonchalantly as possible, but it still came out awkward since she was obviously nervous to speak to him. Jake smiled and signed the piece of paper she handed him.

"You want a picture too?" Jake asked.

"Sure."

She took out her phone and looked at me.

Jake looked over at me. "You mind taking our picture?"

I tried not to look annoyed, but got up and had her sit in my seat and raise my ginger ale next to his Long Island Iced Tea as if they were chilling on a flight to Europe. She thanked him, ignored me, and ran up to the front of the plane to squeal with her colleagues that she got a picture with Jake.

Jake looked at me and sipped his drink.

"What do you know about what's been going on in the Levant?"

"Where's that?"

"Lebanon, Israel, Egypt, Cyprus, Turkey, Syria. All the countries that border the Eastern Med."

"Just what's in the news," Jake said and continued to sip on his drink.

I was pretty certain he wasn't familiar with the recent news. Another flight attendant came up to us and asked for a picture sitting next to Jake as well. I got up and took another photo on her phone.

"Do you want the others to get one while we're at it?" Jake said.

"Sure! Let me go get them," she said and scampered off.

I stood in the aisle and tried again to talk with Jake. "Do you know who the major players in the region are?"

"It's pretty much Israel against everyone else, isn't it?"

"In a nutshell, but that doesn't get you any compelling stories. Our first step will be to educate you about the area, the history, the people, and the background on the current conflicts, and so on. As a freelance reporter, you need to have a firm grasp of what's going on and then look for what's not being reported and focus on that. Tell a compelling story that no one else has covered to bring to light what affects people personally. You have to make people care."

Three more flight attendants, two females and one male, and two passengers lined up in the aisle waiting to get a picture next to Jake. I smiled politely and had each person cycle through my seat as if it were theirs, getting the instructions on each iPhone and point-and-shoot camera they handed me. After I'd just pressed the last "big silver button on the top," the lead flight attendant finally shooed everyone back to their seats so we could buckle our seat belts and let the flight attendants do their jobs.

Once the ruckus had died down, Jake looked over at me and said, "How do you do that?"

"Do what?

"Make people care?"

I was actually impressed that he had been listening to me earlier. "That ultimately depends on how hard we work to get a compelling story and then how hard we work to get it out there. But first," I said as I fished through my carry-on bag at my feet and handed Jake two books, "you have to know a little about where you're going and what makes for a compelling story there."

"Is this homework?"

"You bet. Read the sections on Lebanon and Syria. Let me know if you have any questions. Our fixer is also a great resource for current information in the local area. He'll be picking us up from the airport in Beirut."

"What's a fixer?"

"It's a local contact in the target country that speaks the language and can help get you in contact with the people you want to interview. Fixers also help get a safe place to stay and arrange transportation, security, and visas."

"Have you been to Beirut?"

"Yeah, lots of times."

"What language do they speak there?"

I smiled. "Mostly French and Arabic."

"Cool, I studied a little French in school."

"Good, that'll help. Did you ever study any Arabic?"

"No."

"That's okay. I can get by in Arabic, but our fixer's my ex-brother-in-law, so we'll be pretty well covered."

Chapter 5

Rome, Italy
May 11, 2013

The flight went about as I had expected. Jake watched movies or slept most of the time and barely leafed through the books I gave him. We landed at Leonardo da Vinci Airport at seven in the morning. We collected our bags, cleared customs, and were met by a slim Italian man wearing designer jeans, a tight-fitting white button-down shirt, fashionably spiked hair, and sunglasses that looked like they once belonged to Bono. He held up a small white placard with my name on it.

I walked up to the driver and identified myself.

"*Buon giorno*, Signore Conn," he said and shook both our hands. "Welcome to Italy. Please follow me. The car you requested is just outside."

We followed him and he insisted on putting our bags in the trunk for us. Normally, I wouldn't splurge on a private taxi from the airport, but since Jake was picking up the tab, I figured I'd better make him feel like he was getting his money's worth.

Our driver was nice enough to point out a few of the sights once we got into the downtown Rome area. I grunted politely as if I'd never seen them. But even though I'd been to Rome many times, the fact that a modern city thrived in the midst of such historical significance everywhere one looked always put me in a sort of awe-inspired trance. I stared out the window as if it was my first visit. Jake, on the other hand, stayed in a sleeping trance of his own the entire thirty-minute drive from the airport.

We arrived at Piazza Ricci on a narrow cobblestone drive, only a few-minutes walk from the spectacular carved fountains and restaurants at Piazza Navona. I rent an apartment above the *Pier Luigi* restaurant at Piazza Ricci whenever I come to Rome. It's off the beaten tourist paths and the restaurant is a great neutral spot to conduct interviews with famous people because they go there anyway. I appear to be just one of their entourage, but really, I am doing business in plain sight.

One of the advantages of being a freelance journalist is that almost no one recognizes you unless they've worked directly with you in the past. Christiane Amanpour or Anderson Cooper would have no chance at doing anything like conducting an interview in a public place with the sort of international recognition they have. For me, anonymity is good.

We both took about an hour to settle into the apartment. I took a shower, put the BBC on mute, opened the windows, and listened to the city outside as I watched the headlines scroll by on the TV. The beating heart of a genuinely tight-knit community can be felt and heard right outside any window in Rome. The restaurateurs just below my window greeted both tourists and locals as they crossed the piazza. Vespas buzzed down the narrow, ancient cobblestoned street in the warmth of the fading afternoon sun.

The neighborhood sounds always reminded me of why I became a journalist. As long as I could remember, I'd always felt the need to explore other people's experiences and share their story and perspective. It all begins with listening. Listening to people also includes listening to the sounds they make as they live their lives right outside my window, wherever I may find myself.

After an hour of catching up on what's hot on the newswire while listening to my favorite city go about its business, I knocked on the door to Jake's bedroom.

"Yeah?"

"I need to see what you're bringing with you. And I'll let you see what I have so you can see how we journalists pack, whenever you're ready."

The door opened and Jake was in a black T-shirt, a pair of boxers, and flip-flops. "I'm ready now," he said and shuffled to his suitcase on the bed.

I picked up his suitcase and dumped everything out onto the bed.

"What the fuck? I gotta re-pack all that."

"No, you don't, because most of it isn't coming with us," I said as I scanned the contents on the bed.

We both stared at the pile of fashionable clothes and shoes. Not surprisingly, everything he had was meant to highlight him as an individual and make a poignant or cutting edge fashion statement. Everything you didn't want in a foreign correspondent's travel bag.

"Why? All I need to do is get in front of a camera and conduct an interview. Do I really need to be wrapped in a khaki vest with a bunch of pockets?"

"The on-camera interview is only a very small part of what a foreign correspondent does. Most of the time you're going to be chasing down the story and interviewing people off camera. What we choose to wear has little to do with style or fashion and everything to do with function and keeping a low profile, blending in with the population, especially if there is potential for hostility or violence. As a journalist, your job is to report the story, not be the story." I looked again at his clothes on the bed. "I see lots of clothes that say, 'Look at me,' and that's not good for us."

"Well, that's part of my job, to keep up my image. I can't be taken seriously in my industry if I look like I don't know how to dress. Or if I can't keep up with the fashions."

"Well, if you want to know how we journalists do things, I'm telling you right now, our aim is to blend in. Most of what we do is talk to people on their turf, in their cities and neighborhoods. You have to blend in and at least try to look local, even if you're not."

"So what do you suggest?"

"Well, you'll have to leave most of those things here. Our flight doesn't leave until three in the afternoon, so we'll go to a sporting goods store tomorrow and we'll get you the basics and you can get the rest in the street markets in Beirut."

"Sporting goods store? Street markets? This is a disaster."

"Yeah, street markets are where most of the world shops. Not everyone has a shopping mall around the corner. They'll have some good local shirts and scarves that are handy as well as gloves and cheap underwear and socks. You can never have enough underwear and socks."

"I can't keep my underwear?"

I looked at Jake and laughed. "Yeah, I guess you can keep your underwear, but get rid of any black shirts," I said and pointed to the black shirt he was wearing.

"Why?"

"Hezbollah and ISIS both wear black a lot. It's best to not be mistaken for one of them through a rifle scope if you can help it."

"Yeah, right."

"Come on, pour yourself some wine—I'm not gonna drink it—and I'll show you what I packed."

I spread my clothes and equipment out on the bed and placed a pair of brown suede work boots and a pair of running shoes on the floor.

Jake looked at my gear and then at me. "Okay, tell me how a world-class freelance journalist packs."

I smiled. "Well, like I said before, it's all about function. I stay away from cargo pants. That's a dead giveaway for foreign correspondents or foreigners in general. Normal everyday jeans are good because people all over the world wear them. I also have a few pairs of work pants I got here in Rome. They're like the European answer to Dickies work pants. They allow you to blend in well on the street or even in an upscale neighborhood if you're not too dirty."

"Dirty? Why would we be getting dirty?"

I just ignored Jake's comment for the moment and continued, "The shirts I got in Beirut at the markets, along with a wool watch cap if it gets cold in the mountains or deserts at night. I have lots of socks and underwear. Sometimes you won't be able to wash your clothes or even change them if you're down to your last set of things, so changing your underwear and socks after a good whore bath are all you got."

"A what?"

"A whore bath. You know. A washcloth and soap at a sink or a bucket, or even water out of a canteen."

I looked at Jake. He looked like he just realized that he signed up for the Marines and it was the night before boot camp and he couldn't back out.

"Don't worry, I don't have to do that all the time, but you never know when, so you gotta be prepared. I always pack several washcloths and a few bars of my own soap as a last resort. The washcloths are good for bandages in a pinch and the scarf can be used as a tourniquet."

"Bandages, tourniquets?"

"Yeah, most times you won't be near a hospital if you or someone else gets hurt. I always have a first aid kit, but you never know."

Jake pointed to my camera gear. "What's all that stuff over there?"

"I always have a mini commercial digital camera with microphone, an iPad with detachable keyboard, a point-and-shoot digital camera in my pocket, and an iPhone. I used to carry a satellite phone, but they're pretty expensive and they cost a lot to make calls. Most places are pretty well wired for cell coverage these days, so most of the time I just leave it at home. It's nice now, because if I have nothing else, I can do just about everything adequately with an iPhone, including writing and sending pictures, video, and a story."

"God bless Steve Jobs, huh?"

"You bet."

"What else is there?"

"External hard drive, power cords, batteries, and I even have a thin sheet of photovoltaic cells that can charge my iPhone in thirty minutes with direct sunlight. It rolls up as tight as a magazine. I don't go anywhere without it. Even first world countries, because you never know when you're gonna need to charge your stuff and the power goes out. You never want to be without any options.

"I also have power adaptors for the region we're visiting, ziplock baggies, a waterproof duffel bag, Gore-Tex pants and raincoat, warm gloves and fingerless wool gloves for tactile feel, and toiletries with an extra toothbrush."

Jake laughed. "Anything else?"

"That's pretty much it for the trip over, but I'll get sunscreen, bug spray, food and water, a multi-tool, and a couple small pocket knives when I get to my destination."

"It looks like you're going to war."

I looked at Jake. "I am."

Chapter 6

Rafic Hariri International Airport
Beirut, Lebanon
May 12, 2013

Rafic Hariri International Airport was no JFK, but it had gone through quite a drastic change since the 2006 conflict with Israel. It had polished white and gray floors and pristine white walls separating chic shops and cafes for travelers that hid the destruction of only six years before. It looked like most of the scars were patched up and out of sight. Not fully healed, just scabbed over to be ripped off later.

I pulled my bag behind me and headed for the street. I looked around and drew in a deep breath through my nose. The airport sat right next to the Mediterranean Sea, as did the city, and I could smell the fusion of cypress, kabob, and a hint of sea salt. I smiled and rang Rafi on my mobile phone.

"Rafi, we're here," I said into the phone when he picked up.

"I know. I see you," he said.

"Where are you?" I said, looking around.

"Look to your left."

He hung up. I pocketed my phone, looked to my left down the long sidewalk at people getting into buses and taxis with their bags, and immediately picked out Rafi's loping gait as he approached us. He seemed like he'd gotten a bit older even only after ten days. He caught my eye and waved as he approached with a big smile.

He was dressed like me in jeans and a collared Polo-style shirt. He was a little shorter than I with slightly unkempt black wavy hair and just a hint of gray on the sides. His build was like a tall barrel and his momentum was similarly hard to stop when he got rolling. His energy had always inspired me.

He approached with both arms open and gave me the traditional three cheek kisses reserved only for close family. "I'm so glad you're back. How was the flight?"

"It was fine. No problems at all."

"Good, good," he said.

Rafi looked at Jake standing a few feet behind me.

"Rafi, this is my companion on this trip, Jake Westin."

I looked over at Jake. "Jake, this is Rafi, the best damn fixer in Beirut, and my brother-in-law."

Rafi extended his hand and Jake shook it.

"Nice to meet you, Rafi."

"Good to meet you, too."

"Where's the car?" I said.

"Plan B, Angus," he said and smiled. "I was waiting here, but the damn police made me move and park the car so we have to walk a bit."

"That's okay," I said.

"Come, it's this way," Rafi said.

We turned to go back the way Rafi had come.

"How have things been?" I asked as we walked. "I noticed you're limping a bit. Are you still feeling our last trip?"

He looked at me and grimaced. "Angus, that last trip killed me. I was sore for a week after you left. We need to work on our exit strategy. I don't think I can take any more punishment like the last time. I'm getting old."

"Naw. That's all in your head, Rafi."

"Well, my head needs to tell that to my back," he laughed.

"Where did you guys go the last time you were here?" Jake asked.

"Syria. The government forces blew up our car and we had to jump in a river and swim back across the border."

"Wow."

"Yeah, sometimes you may get dirty. It's not all hotels and satellite broadcasts to the media machine at home," I said.

"Were you able to get the statuette looked at in New York?" Rafi asked.

I just shook my head. "I'll tell you about it later."

"Is he coming with us this time?" Rafi said and motioned toward Jake.

"We'll see," I said. "He's here to learn what I do."

"Learn what you do? Is he an intern or something?"

"No. Don't tell anyone, but he's a movie star."

"Like from Hollywood?"

"Yeah. I promised his agent that I'd show him how I work so he can prepare for his next role as a foreign correspondent."

"I thought you looked familiar," Rafi said to Jake. "What movies?"

"I'm kind of just starting out. I've only been in a few," he said, trying to be low-key.

"Like what? I watch many movies."

"My last big one was a spy movie called *Ghost Hunt.*"

"Who else was in it?"

"George Clooney."

"Oh, yes. I saw that one. It was really good. I don't remember you, though. Who did you play?"

"I was his partner. I got killed about a third of the way through."

"Oh," Rafi said. "I don't remember how it started."

We kept walking in an awkward silence.

Rafi turned to Jake, "I'm sure you were very good. I'll have to watch it again and look for you."

"Are we headed for Jafir's?" I said, trying to change the subject.

"Yeah, I thought we'd go there and get something to eat and then get a smoke at the Bay Rock."

"Sounds good to me," I said.

I tried to get Jake's attention as we walked but he had his head down, staring at the sidewalk in front of him as he pulled his bag behind him. I could tell he was a bit disappointed that Rafi didn't remember his performance. I tapped him on the shoulder and he looked up at me. I gave him a shrug and smiled. He appreciated my sentiment but still seemed disappointed.

Fucking movie stars.

* * *

Rafi and I talked about his family on the car ride from the airport. He had a teenaged son and daughter both within a few years of high school graduation. They were both doing excellent in their English classes. His son had just been accepted to the American University in Beirut and told Rafi that he wanted to major in journalism.

"I told him he could do anything he wanted. You know what he said?"

"What?"

"He wanted to be just like you."

I smiled. "What did you say?"

"I told him he should go be a taxi driver or open a damn falafel stand. Anything but a journalist," he laughed.

"Good advice. You think he'll listen to you?"

"He's eighteen. Of course he won't listen to me. He's gonna do what he wants to do."

"I bet you're regretting ever meeting me, huh?"

Rafi looked at me with a serious face. "If he becomes half the man you are, I'd be proud. Don't you forget that," he said and slapped me on the shoulder.

"Thanks, brother."

I love Rafi. He always tells me what's in his heart.

* * *

The streets were choked with afternoon traffic. White delivery trucks, new luxury cars, and a grab bag of colors on old and new Mercedes taxis all honked and jockeyed for position. Rafi chose to cruise north around the Rue de Paris that paralleled a wide pedestrian promenade called the Corniche with a spectacular view of the Mediterranean Sea on our left and luxury high-rise hotels and apartments on our right.

We sat in silence for a bit as I thought back to the first time I came to Beirut in the mid-eighties. Back then, the streets were littered with debris from burned out cars and buildings that were pummeled by small arms and artillery fire. One could hear gunfire down every street, not sure where it was coming from or whether it was coming for you. The bustle of traffic was a welcome change from the Beirut I met as a young freelance reporter a few decades earlier.

"A lotta memories here," I finally said.

Rafi looked over at me and smiled. "It's nice to have you home again, Angus."

We found a parking spot at the northern end of the Corniche and walked the wide brick public walk with a view of the Mediterranean Sea and the city on opposite sides.

Lovers walked hand in hand as they gazed at the sea, boys played pick-up games of soccer, and old men sat on benches that faced the water and talked with one another about the old days when they were young men and agile enough to play soccer. The Corniche seemed to me like a park stretched along the length of downtown Beirut, where anyone could come to enjoy the city and the water all at once. Being there always reminded me of walking with Lilya. The thoughts both comforted and pained me, much like the city itself.

"Every time I come back, Rafi takes me here to get some food and just soak in the city," I said to Jake as we walked.

"It's beautiful here," Jake said.

"It wasn't always like this." I pointed to a tall, gray and black building to our left, pockmarked with obvious war damage. "Check out that building right over there. That's the old Holiday Inn. You see the bullet holes and burned out rooms?"

"Yeah. What happened?"

"You seriously don't know?"

"No."

"This place was a war zone for sixteen years, from seventy-five to ninety. I had the pleasure of calling it home through most of nineteen eighty-seven. All of the foreign correspondents and news crews covering the civil war were hunkered down in the Holiday Inn until rival groups took turns kicking each other out and sometimes even off the top of it. Each group who dominated it used it as a sniper position from the roof. The Israelis did their best to demolish the place. They did a pretty good job of it too. But it's still here as a reminder to everyone what can happen if we choose not to get along."

"Wow," Jake said.

"Where were you during that time?" I asked Jake.

"I was born in eighty-seven," Jake said.

Rafi and I just looked at each other and laughed. "Don't worry, kid. You gotta start your career somewhere. In eighty-seven, I was a twenty-year-old journalism dropout who wanted to go see what the real world was like. I landed here not knowing a damn thing, trying to write stories for Reuters and trying not to get shot."

"I think I like the city a whole lot better now," Jake said.

"Me, too," I said.

We walked a bit farther up the Corniche and came to a street vendor's cart spewing steam from several stainless steel pots over open flames. We bought a few falafel wraps and fruit juices and strolled south along the water, watching the sun dip lower into the sky.

"My second wife, Lilya, Rafi's sister, and I used to walk down the Corniche at sunset every night that I wasn't away chasing a story. We'd walk and talk and enjoy the tranquility of the place. She worked as an administrator at one of the news bureaus. I managed to impress her with my terrible Arabic.

"She was always politely correcting my grammar mistakes or pronunciation, or teaching me new words and phrases you could only learn from a local. I never had to correct her English though. She studied English at the American University and was fluent in English, French, and Arabic. She'd help me with my reports and tell me where I could find the best stories. It didn't take long before I was spending more time with her than on my reporting, but I didn't care. I always feel her over my shoulder when I walk the Corniche."

"She sounds like an incredible woman," Jake said.

"She was."

"What happened to her?" Jake asked.

"Breast cancer, a couple years ago," I said.

"I'm sorry," Jake said.

"Thanks. I miss her every day, especially when I'm here," I said more to myself than Jake or Rafi.

Rafi patted me on the shoulder. "I do too, brother."

* * *

We finished our meal and watched the water for a bit until I noticed that Jake seemed a little bored.

"Thanks for dinner, Rafi. I think it's time we headed to the office."

"You have an office here?" Jake asked.

"It was more like his second home," Rafi said.

We walked a few blocks to the Bay Rock Café overlooking the Pigeon Rocks on the western side of Beirut. At the rooftop restaurant, I chose a spot near the floor-to-ceiling windows to watch the sunset unobstructed. The lounge was situated with a dozen sets of couches facing each other with soft cushions and a low table between them. A tall hookah pipe sat at each corner of the couches for our smoking pleasure.

Rafi and Jake ordered champagne and I ordered a pomegranate juice to go with my mango flavored tobacco in the hookah.

We watched a half dozen local boys with bronzed skin from the Mediterranean sun laugh and tease each other as they climbed and jumped from the Pigeon Rocks into the sea. They dared one another to jump from higher and higher up the rocks. The first boy who jumped from the highest point got a few cheers, but the first one who dove from the top earned cheers from the people next to us in the bar high above the rocks.

Our drinks and tobacco came and our waiter set up each of our hookahs for us. I leaned back on the plush couch and puffed on the smooth tobacco smoke.

"Well, welcome to my office," I said to Jake. "I used to have most of my interviews here. Sometimes you had to go out and get the story, but if I could have the story come to me, this was a great neutral place where people who shouldn't be talking to me, or were afraid to talk to the press, could come and feel comfortable."

I raised my fruit juice glass. "I propose a toast, to those who have given their lives for exposing lying bastards everywhere and trying to nail down that mysterious bitch, the truth," I said and took a long pull on my pomegranate juice.

"Here, here," Rafi said and slugged half his champagne.

Jake emptied his glass, fumbled with the hookah for a minute, and then got up for the bathroom.

As soon as Jake was out of sight, Rafi leaned over to me. "Okay, so what did the guy in New York say?"

"He said the statuette was real. The guy who gave it to us is legit."

"So what do you want to do?"

"I need to go back and get those Syrian kids outta that neighborhood and get this story."

"Are you going to take the movie star?"

"I don't want to. Can you arrange someone from Reuters or the AP to babysit him while we're gone?"

"Maybe, for a couple of days. How long do you think it will take?"

"I don't know. Maybe a week."

"Why did you bring him here, Angus? You know he can't go to Syria with us. If anyone recognized him, he'd get taken."

"You didn't recognize him," I said and puffed on my hookah.

"Angus, I'm as old as you. When's the last time you went to the movies?"

"A long time ago."

"Exactly. These kids in Syria, they love American culture. Even with what's going on now, someone's going to recognize him."

"Don't worry about it. Just arrange for him to shadow one of the local guys here in Beirut until we get back."

"Did he pay you to be here?"

"Yeah."

"If he paid, he's not going to like that plan."

"Well it's the only plan that will work if we're gonna go through with this."

Rafi took a pull off his hookah and gazed out at the setting sun for a few moments. "You don't have a Plan B?" Rafi said and smiled.

"Not this time."

"I would have a Plan B." Rafi sucked on his hookah and blew a perfect smoke ring into the air. "How much did he pay you?"

"None of your damn business, Rafi," I said and took a puff from my own hookah. "But it was a lot. All you need to know is that I'm paying you well to set things up. This is what I need, can you set it up?"

"Of course, that's what I do. But he's not gonna like it."

Well, fuck him, I thought, and took another drag.

* * *

We finished our hookahs and Rafi drove us to our hotel. I usually stay in Rafi's guest room when I'm in Beirut but I knew Jake would be more comfortable in a hotel suite, especially if I was going to leave him alone for a week.

Jake's payment not only got us First Class airline tickets but also a luxurious suite at the legendary Intercontinental Phoenicia Hotel, all lit up with exotic purple light. Our rooms had a spectacular view of the Med with the ghostly hulk of the old Holiday Inn behind it reminding me of tougher times.

I made it clear that Jake needed to be in the lobby at eight o'clock sharp so Rafi could take us to the local Global Reporters Live office where we could check in with the local journalists and get a feel for what's going on. It was important we were early before they got pulled out of the office chasing down stories for the newswire they fed later in the morning for the London and New York news bureaus.

I usually sleep well in Beirut, but I was up most of the night smoking on my balcony and talking with Lilya in my head. I always feel her presence the most when I'm in Beirut.

Chapter 7

Beirut, Lebanon
May 13, 2013
Morning

The sun came up over the Mount Lebanon mountain range east of Beirut, which always shadowed the Mediterranean Sea in the early morning. I rose with the sunrise and ran in the cool morning air along the deserted Corniche. It was nice to be in Beirut when it's peaceful. I've always drawn strength from the city. Its own strength lies in its role as a crossroads between many cultures, between Europe and the Middle East. It stands as proof that we can get along and thrive if we make the effort to compromise, embrace the similarities, and celebrate the differences. It was heartbreaking to see a city with such beautiful people and great potential for the cultivation of civilized existence violently stifled by racial, political, and misplaced religious hatred. It's always the innocents that suffer.

I felt the beating heart of the city getting stronger with the passing of every peaceful day. She would be strong one day to heal her people and embrace their appreciation. For now, my sights were set on helping other victims to the northeast.

I arrived back at the hotel after my run, showered, and met Rafi in the lobby at eight o'clock.

"Have you seen Jake?"

"Not yet."

I looked at my watch. "I'll ring his room. Go get us a coffee and I'll meet you at the bar."

I had to ring Jake's room three times before he answered and ended up pounding on his door after Rafi and I had finished our coffees and were still waiting on him. Jake answered his hotel room door with a towel around his waist, still wet from the shower.

"Listen, Jake, the first rule is that the story doesn't wait for anyone. If you're not ready to roll when it goes down, you'll miss it and then you're shit outta luck because there'll be a half dozen other guys taking your story and selling it while you're hittin' snooze and wondering what went wrong."

"Okay, okay, sorry. I just have a little jet lag."

"You gotta be able to fight through that and be where you need to be. One of the reasons we stopped in Rome was to get caught up a bit. But now it's time to work. I don't know how many stories I grabbed out from under people's noses because I was available and ready to move."

"Okay, okay, I got it."

"You gotta have a bag packed and be ready to move no more than a minute after you get an e-mail or a call. You got that?"

"Okay."

"Good. We'll work on it."

"Great."

I pointed to his towel, "Get dressed, you don't need anything but your wallet and your phone today. I'll see you downstairs. Don't be more than a couple minutes."

"Okay, okay," Jake said and shut the door behind me.

* * *

"What's up for today?" Jake said as he walked up to Rafi and me in the lobby and acted as if he was right on time.

"We're gonna check in with the local GRL office and find out what's been going on lately."

"What's GRL?'

"It stands for Global Reporters Live. It's an English speaking news service that takes freelance stories and helps us sell them to news agencies all over the world. It's a tight-knit community unto itself. Whenever I'm overseas, I'll stop in and let them know where I'm going and see what info they have on the local area at the time. They'll also check on you or make some calls if they haven't heard from you if you're going someplace hazardous."

"Chuck said Bobbie was here," Rafi said.

I acted like I didn't care. "So?"

"Come on, Angus. You don't have to act like you don't like her just because I'm your brother-in-law," Rafi chuckled.

"She's a pain in the ass."

"Yeah, just the sort of pain in the ass you need."

"Who's Bobbie?" Jake asked.

"Hopefully, you won't have to find out," I said.

"She's nice," Rafi said.

"In the last few years, she curiously seems to pop up right where I decide to go for a big story."

"She likes you, Angus. You should take advantage of that. Life's too short."

"There's nothing more annoying than a competing journalist."

"You should let her get the big stories. Let her get promoted and then she can support you once she's a big news anchor."

"Fat chance. She doesn't want any of that. She's an activist that got into journalism when the activists got too annoyed with her. She's trying to save the world."

"Look who's talking, Mister Philanthropist," Rafi said.

"Is the car here?" I said, trying to change the subject.

"Yes, it's right out front."

I headed out the front door. "Well let's go, then. We don't have all day."

"What's the philanthropist thing?" Jake asked Rafi.

"I'll tell you later," I heard Rafi say.

* * *

The GRL office was just a few blocks to the south of the Corniche on John Kennedy Street, near the tree-lined campus of the prestigious École Supérieure des Affaires, a world-renowned business school aimed at bridging the business gap between Europe and the Middle East. Unlike the respected business school, the GRL occupied a long, narrow renovated storefront next to a clothing shop and a small local grocery store.

As we passed a small fruit stand on the way to the GRL office, two boys of about eight or nine years old asked us in Arabic if they could shine our shoes for our change. Rafi asked them where they were from in Arabic. They both said they were from Aleppo, Syria. They said they were trying to save money to get the rest of their family members to move from a refugee camp up north to find work in Beirut. I gave them each a yellow ten thousand Lebanese pound note worth about seven U.S. dollars and wished them luck. Both of them thanked me profusely, kissed my hands, and smiled. I wished I could do more for them.

As soon as we walked through the door, the middle-aged guy behind the counter, with gray hair and deep crow's feet from a hereditary squint, looked up and saw Rafi and me and turned around to the several journalists jammed into the space at the desks behind him.

"Listen up everybody, you can all go home. Angus Conn will be taking all of your stories from you from here on out."

A few heads looked up, but the announcement seemed to fall on deaf ears as the journalists continued to type and make phone calls.

"Hi, Chuck," I said as I shook his hand over the counter.

"How the hell have you been?"

"I've been well."

"Rafi told me you were coming. You missed Bobbie by about a day," Chuck said.

"Don't tell me, she was headed northeast."

"How could you guess?"

"That's where the stories are."

"Yeah, if you're crazy enough to chase them there." Chuck looked at Jake. "What brings you out of Hollywood?"

"I guess I'm crazy, too," Jake said.

"If you're hangin' out with Angus, that's got to be true."

"He's shadowing me for a bit. He's researching what it is we do for his next role."

"Well, you couldn't have picked a better crew, that is, since Bobbie's not available."

"Can you please stop saying her name like she's the damn Pope or something?" I asked.

"Hey, it's not my fault she beats you to every big story. It's a good thing there's plenty of market out there for both of you or we may have to choose sides, and I gotta say she's a lot better looking than you, Angus. I don't care what those guys at the network say about your pretty face on TV."

"Yeah, yeah, my mom wanted me to be a girl too, but I don't really think this is the place to discuss it," I laughed.

Chuck had saved my ass almost as many times as Rafi, so I tolerated him giving me shit.

Chuck slid three forms across the counter. "Here you go, gents. Each of you fill these out with your updated info and don't make me come looking for you. When you're done, I'll be in my office and we'll talk."

* * *

A few minutes later, I sat with Rafi and Jake in Chuck's office as he reclined in his office chair and rested his arms across his slightly bulging belly with his fingers intertwined like a buckle.

"So, what's the pulse around here?" I asked.

"There's not much other than refugees and gunrunning up north at the moment unless you want to cross the border, and I don't recommend that."

I looked at Rafi and he just looked down at his shoes. "We have a contact that wants to meet with us to document the trade of Syrian artifacts for weapons," I said, laying it all out there.

"Now that's a good story. But what's it worth to you?"

"It's why I'm here. The refugee thing has been covered. This hasn't."

"Do you know why?"

"Yeah. Because it's dangerous as hell."

"Are all of you going?" Chuck said and pointed to Jake.

I looked at Jake and he looked at me. "We haven't made any concrete plans yet," I said. I could sense from Chuck's expression that a lecture was coming on.

"Angus, what's the golden rule?"

"Don't be the story," I said like a good student.

"That's right. Now you know that's what you'll be if you choose to go in there for some shit story people will only care about for the time it takes them to drink their morning coffee."

"I know. But it's all I got right now. The guy we've been talking to is adamant that he wants a journalist to cover this thing."

"Of course he does. They all want exposure. They're getting killed there and no one cares. You'll get yourself killed and become a story on the back page of the *New York Times*. And you know what people will say? He shouldn't have been there in the first place."

"I know, but I told them I'd be back. So, here I am."

Chuck took a sip of coffee and shook his head. "There's no getting through to you is there?"

I just shrugged. "I got nothing else, Chuck. I told them I'd come back."

"Well, you're a big boy. I've got your information. I'll be waiting for your stories. Make sure you check in every day. I don't want to have anyone else go looking for you."

"Do you have anyone else there?"

"Bobbie's there."

"What?"

"That's what I meant about she went northeast. She checked in yesterday. She's doing a few in-depth pieces with the refugees near the border. You know you'll never hear the end of it if I have to send her in after you."

"Tell me about it. Maybe I'll see Bobbie at the border and have her show Jake around for a few days, since she's the one who referred him to me."

"No shit," Chuck laughed.

"What's so funny?" I asked.

"You two have been competing for what, five years now?"

"Yeah, just about that."

"Two freelancers duking it out for who gets the next Pulitzer Prize? She gave you a pretty heavy anchor to lug around while she flutters off to get a story unencumbered. Well played on her part."

"You think she made that referral on purpose to get an edge over me?"

"I wouldn't put it past her. She knows how to get there first."

"I don't think it's like that. I think we both are pretty passionate about what we're doing."

"Well, you got that right. I couldn't talk her out of going up there either. She wants to be where the action is."

"That's where the stories are."

"Speaking of action, do you need any gear? A flak vest or helmet?"

"Naw. I got everything we need. Thanks, though."

Chuck stood. "Well, be careful, amigo. And keep this guy outta sight," he said and pointed to Jake. "I can keep him busy here if you want to leave him with me."

"I'm financing this thing, so I'm going," Jake piped up.

"We're still working out the details. I'll let you know if I need to take you up on that when we decide what we're doing for sure."

"Well, if you do go over the border, I hope your life insurance is paid up, kid. I'll sell the shit outta the story about the dumbass movie star who went to Syria and got himself kidnapped or killed, but I'd rather not."

Chapter 8

Intercontinental Phoenicia Hotel
Beirut, Lebanon
May 13, 2013
Afternoon

I had Jake come down to talk with me about going into Syria. I couldn't string him along any longer. I was sitting on a plush lobby couch going over a few of my notes in my notebook when Jake walked in.

I looked up at him. "Have a seat for a second, Jake."

I motioned to the couch across from me and he sat and waited for me to speak. I looked him in the eyes and told him straight.

"I've got to leave you here with Chuck for a couple days. He said he'd show you around with a few of his guys here just until we get back."

"Hell no. I came to follow you around. That was the deal."

"Well, things have changed. You can't come with us. It's too dangerous."

"The hell I can't. I'm the only reason you're here."

"That's not true. I was coming anyway. You're the reason we took First Class and are at the Phoenicia. But if you hadn't have come, I would have been in coach and stayed at Rafi's house like I usually do. So, you're not the only reason I'm here."

"This is fucking bullshit."

"You don't get it, do you? You could die doing this."

"How am I ever going to accurately portray your profession if I never experience it, or even better, see you reacting in a crisis. I won't know the nuance or the meaning to any of it unless I've seen it done and experience it myself."

"Well, not this time. When I get back, I'll take you to interview some refugees on the border or we'll go to Israel and hang at some Gaza checkpoints. There are plenty of other things going on that are dangerous without getting you into a war zone. One hundred and thirty-two experienced foreign correspondents were killed around the world last year. And Syria's one of the hottest places for us right now. It's no place for amateurs, and definitely no place for freakin' movie stars."

Jake got up, took a few steps, and then came back, pointing his finger at me. "I'm calling Bernie and telling him to cancel your payment if you can't deliver what you promised. This is bullshit."

"Do whatever you need to. You aren't going."

I can't blame him for being pissed, but there's no way he'd survive in Syria.

* * *

When I returned to my room, there was a message on my phone for me to call Bernie back as soon as possible. I knew he wasn't going to tell me anything new. But I knew it would come to this.

"Come on, I don't want to cancel the payment. Bobbie says you need the money," Bernie pleaded.

"Fuck Bobbie. Do you want your talent to get killed over here? He can't make movies if he's dead."

"Angus, if you really think there's that much danger, then you're right. I'll pick up all expenses through today, but I'll cancel the main fee."

There was a long silence on the phone.

"Angus, are you there?"

"Yeah, I'm here. Let me make some calls. I'll let you know tomorrow morning, Beirut time, whether to cancel or not."

"I'll be at this number, day or night. Just let me know. Give the kid a chance. He needs this, and according to Bobbie, so do you."

* * *

I knocked on Jake's hotel room door a few down from my own. He held the door open with his foot and crossed his arms across his chest.

"Did you talk to Bernie?" Jake asked.

"Yes."

"And?"

"Look, I can't have you going with me if you're not serious."

"I'm serious as a heart attack. This thing has my full focus right now."

"Did you read the books I gave you?"

Jake gave me a look betraying that he didn't want to tell me the truth. "Not all of them."

"Okay, I'll make you a deal. You answer eight out of ten questions correctly and you can come with me."

"How much time do I have to cram?"

I looked at my watch. "Be in the Cascade Lounge downstairs for a pop quiz in fifteen minutes."

"Okay, which lounge is that?"

"The one with the big fountain in the middle."

* * *

Jake walked into the Cascade Lounge exactly fifteen minutes later. He carried the books I'd given him.

"You won't need those," I said, pointing to the books. "This is a closed-book quiz."

"Fine," Jake said defiantly as he slammed the books down on the table and threw himself into a plush chair across from me.

The waiter appeared and I ordered us both an iced tea.

"Look, I want you come with me. It means a big payday for me. But I also need to know that you're serious and won't put us in danger because you're ignorant. Fuck your money. I care more about us staying alive than a bunch of money, okay?"

"Okay, fire away."

"Okay, first question. What religious sect are the government forces in Syria?"

"Alawite."

"Good. Number two. Name at least one country that is supplying the rebel factions in Syria."

"Iran?"

"Nope. Number three. What country is backing Bashar al-Assad?"

"Russia."

"Good. Anyone else?"

He shrugged.

"That's okay, number four. Why does Russia care about Syria so much?"

"Syria is a major trade partner with them, mostly arms, and Russia strategically wants to maintain their only access to the Mediterranean Sea at Latakia."

"Good. Number five. What countries border Syria?

Jake closed his eyes and recited, "Israel, Lebanon, Turkey, and Iraq."

"Almost, don't forget Jordan. Number six."

Jake closed his eyes and said, "Dammit," under his breath.

I continued, "What is the major anti-government faction that has ties to Al-Qaeda?"

"al-Nusra."

"Jabhat al-Nusra," I corrected. "Good. Is there another one?"

"ISIS?"

"Yep. Do you know what it stands for?"

Jake closed his eyes and concentrated again. "I can't remember."

"That's okay, number seven. What are the major religions fighting for control in Syria?"

"Alawite, Christian, and Muslim."

"Yeah, good enough. The Alawites are actually a Shi'a sect of Islam and the fighters are actually splinter Muslim groups. Everyone else is pretty much trying to stay out of the way. Number eight. What territory did the Israelis take during the Six Day War that Syria is still pissed about?"

Jake looked to the ceiling, trying to think of the answer. "Fuck, man, I don't know."

"Okay, number nine. What caused the United Nations to finally get involved in mediating the conflict?"

"The use of chemical weapons."

"Good. Last one. This one's for all the chips. If we're captured by government forces, do you say you're a journalist or a movie star?"

"Journalist."

"Wrong. If you tell them you're a journalist, they'll detain you and try you in a show trial as a spy. They believe all journalists are spies for the West."

"Okay, what if I tell them I'm a movie star?"

"That's even worse. They'll use you as propaganda and a bargaining chip to embarrass the U.S. government and probably end up killing you as an example to other non-believers."

"This is bullshit. That shit wasn't in your fucking books. You never intended on letting me go in the first place."

"Jake, I'm impressed that you did some homework, but it's simply too dangerous to take you on this story. I'm sorry. It's in the best interest of everyone involved that you sit this one out."

"Screw you, you pompous fuck. Just because I don't keep up on all the bullshit in the world doesn't give you the right to treat me like a child."

Jake got up and stormed out of the bar, like a grown child.

I drained my frosty iced tea, reached for Jake's untouched drink, and let out a sigh of relief.

That actually went better than I expected.

Chapter 9

Beirut, Lebanon
May 14, 2013

The next morning, Rafi pulled his old gray Mercedes he'd had forever up the palm tree lined front entrance at the Phoenicia fifteen minutes ahead of schedule. I looked at my watch, then out past the line of shiny new private hire Mercedes taxi cabs lined up at the curb, and then out to the luxury yachts moored at the marina across the street. I turned and looked one last time inside the marble-floored lobby to make sure Jake wasn't going to appear to try and plead his case one last time before we left. The lobby was deserted.

"Thanks for meeting me early," I said to Rafi as he helped me with my bags. "I didn't want Jake to meet us and demand to come along."

Rafi just smiled. "Okay, let's go then. I need to put your bags in the back seat," he said as he opened the rear door. "I have a bunch of toilet paper and gasoline in the trunk for bribes."

We loaded my stuff and Rafi drove us east out of Beirut on Highway One toward the mountains and the dangers beyond.

* * *

Scrub brush and olive trees dominated the drive until we climbed the foothills on the way to the mountains. Every ten minutes, the temperature seemed like it had dropped a few degrees. The hills were stair-stepped with small plots for gardens and orchards as far as I could see as we wound our way up the hills and into the steeper mountains. The thin, drooping branches of hundreds of green cedar trees, the same tree on the Lebanese flag, dotted the razorback mountain ridge. The western Bekaa Valley below spread out in a complex palate of several shades of green, brown and splotches of rocky white.

An hour into the drive, we decided to stop for a quick lunch in the small town of Zahle with stone houses situated on the cliffs over the Berdawni River in the southwestern edge of the Bekaa.

Rafi parked the car and I started walking up the cobblestone street toward the small square at the center of the ancient mountain city.

Rafi called after me, "Angus, wait, I need something from the trunk."

"What is it?"

I watched as he opened the trunk and helped Jake out of the back.

I ran down to the car. "You son of a bitch! What the hell are you doing?" I said to Rafi.

"I'm sorry, Angus, but he paid me a lot of money."

"I don't care, take his ass back right now."

"We can't, Angus. We're supposed to meet our contact this afternoon at four. If we're late, he's going to think we couldn't make it and you'll lose the story. There's no time to go back."

I turned to Jake and put my finger in his smiling face "If anyone gets hurt because of you, it'll be my mission to make sure you make it back so you can personally witness the suffering you caused."

"I understand. Can we go get a kabob? I'm starving."

"No, you can't get a fucking kabob. Get your ass back in the trunk where you belong."

"Okay, it's Plan B then," Rafi said and gave a thumbs-up to Jake.

"That doesn't help, Rafi. I should shove both you fuckers in there together. You're even guiltier than he is. Dammit."

I took out my cellphone and dialed Bernie's number. The voicemail picked up, just as I expected. "Hey, Bernie, this is Angus. Your boy's coming with me across the border. I'll have him call you as soon as we get back. A guy named Chuck will be in contact with us while we're there. He has your information and will let you know if things go sideways. Talk to you later," I said, disconnecting the call and pocketing my phone. "Come on, let's fucking go," I said to Rafi.

I got back in the car and slammed my door. Jake climbed back into the trunk and in the mirror I saw Rafi give him a fist bump before he gently pressed the trunk shut.

Rafi got back in the driver's seat. "How much did he pay you?" I asked.

"None of your damn business," Rafi said and smiled.

"Asshole."

Chapter 10

Bekaa Valley
Eastern Lebanon
May 14, 2013

We stopped and let Jake out of the trunk a few miles up the road and eventually got something to eat in Zahle at a roadside restaurant on the way to Baalbek. The restaurant was merely a small kitchen and a few white plastic tables and chairs in a dining room not much bigger than the kitchen. But the patio in the back offered a spectacular view of the patchwork of green and brown farmland several hundred feet below in the Bekaa Valley.

The naan with hummus, lamb, and brown rice with fresh olives and pine nuts was some of the best I'd ever had. The local villages served the most delicious food, even to outsiders like us.

For as much as I enjoyed the lunch, I still felt nervous about giving in to Jake. I should have turned around and made him stay in Beirut. It was bad enough for Rafi to be going back in with me, but going in with a complete cherry was worse than stupid; it was knowingly negligent. But five hundred G's was a lot of money. I guess I just didn't want to go down in history as the asshole responsible for snuffing the young life of Hollywood's next big star.

Highway One turned into Highway Four at Zahle. The road wound through eastern Lebanon and up the Bekaa Valley thirty miles from Zahle in the south through Baalbek and all the way north to the border town of Qaa. We turned west just before Qaa and headed for the town of Qasr, about six miles north of where Rafi and I had jumped into the Al Assi River a few weeks prior. The area was a known smuggling route both in and out of Syria.

We came to the town of Qasr where we were to meet Rafi's contact only a half hour before the 4:00 p.m. meeting. Rafi parked the car at his friend's house a few blocks from the meeting point. We stayed inside the house and out of sight. It was well known that the Syrian security forces, the *shabbiha*, employed shopkeepers and taxi drivers as informants all along the border towns to monitor smuggling. The last thing we wanted was for every local to notice the Lebanese man with two Westerners window-shopping in an out-of-the-way border town.

When the time came for our meeting, we all went directly to a small butcher shop a half block from where we waited. It had cured meat hanging in bundles from a small pergola that shaded the stone storefront from the afternoon sun. We entered and Rafi waited his turn behind a local man as he watched the young girl behind the counter weigh and wrap his order in brown paper. Jake and I browsed the prepared meats and goat cheeses in the single refrigerated case in the store as Rafi waited.

Flies buzzed everywhere and the whole place smelled of must, covered by a thin veil of disinfectant. I browsed the cans of beans and glass jars of pickled vegetables on the shelves. Everything had a fine layer of dust on it. It seemed the locals enjoyed the meats but saved the canned goods for emergencies.

The girl collected the local man's money and he looked each of us up and down before he stepped outside with his purchase. "Is Fadi here?" Rafi asked in the local Arabic dialect.

She nodded and looked at each of us just as the old man did and disappeared behind a small curtain in the back of the shop. A few seconds later, a middle-aged man appeared wearing a bloodstained apron, wiping fat and bits of bone from his thick hands on a filthy towel.

"*Salaam alaikum*," Rafi said to the man.

"*Alaikum salaam*," the man said in return.

"We are here to pick up lamb for our friends," Rafi said in Arabic.

The man looked at Jake and me and then at Rafi again as he untied his apron and tossed it on the counter behind him. "I'll be back in a few minutes," he said to the shop girl, probably his daughter, and motioned for us to follow him behind the counter.

We all followed him behind the curtain and around a corner to a small table next to a stove. He motioned for us to sit and offered us coffee. Rafi thanked him and we all sat around the table as the man prepared the coffee. Once it was on the stove, he joined us at the table and spoke quietly with Rafi for a few minutes. He was speaking too softly and too quickly for me to fully keep up, but I was getting some of it.

Jake leaned over to me and whispered, "What's he saying?"

"He wants us to pick up a few supplies from the market before we meet another contact who will guide us across the border."

The man stopped talking and looked at Jake and me. "Americans?" he said in English.

"Yes," I said.

"It is dangerous for you there. Journalists?"

"Yes."

He nodded as the coffee pot whined on the stove. He got up and poured us each a steaming cup and sat again. We sipped his strong, dense, and bitter brew from two short, thick glass teacups for a few moments as he and Rafi continued to talk. I missed a bit of what he said because of their whispering and his northern Bekaa dialect.

Rafi turned to look at me. "He wants to double the fee because you are Americans. It is dangerous smuggling journalists in, especially Americans. If we are caught it will be bad for us, but most likely mean death for his guide."

"Tell him it's okay. We'll pay whatever he wants."

Rafi turned to the man, nodded, spoke a bit more, and then looked at his watch. I understood a few key words of what he said next: weapons and ammunition. The man shook hands with Rafi and then they got up from the table. The butcher disappeared around the corner and rummaged through a few cardboard boxes.

"I guess we're done?" Jake asked Rafi.

"Yes, his son will meet us at a place not far from here at midnight tonight. But right now, we must go to the market and collect some supplies for the neighborhood in Syria where we will be staying."

"What did he say about weapons and ammunition?"

Rafi looked at me and shook his head almost imperceptibly, "I'll tell you later."

The man returned with two black duffel bags and handed them to Rafi who handed them off to me. The man then disappeared to the front of the shop and returned a few moments later with several neatly wrapped brown paper packages and set them on the table. He motioned for us to place them in one of the duffel bags.

"This is meat for the people in the neighborhood. He told me the town we are going to has been under siege by the regime for some time. Many are without food."

We all stood and each of us shook the butcher's hand.

"Thank you for coming, my friends," he said in English before he turned and led us out of the shop.

* * *

We made our way to the small open-air market and began collecting the items Rafi said the butcher wanted us to deliver, along with the meat in the duffel bags. The open-air market in Qasr was nothing more than a few dozen stalls with blankets, sheets, and canvas awnings to keep the sun off the patrons as they perused the goods on plywood tables set up on sawhorses.

Rafi was the only one who really blended in. Speaking a bit of Arabic and wearing local clothes only went so far to mask the fact that I wasn't from the Middle East. Every stall owner looked at Jake and I as if we had just arrived on a cruise ship from New York City. I tried to speak as much Arabic as I could to make it less obvious, but it seemed like everyone had already figured out we were westerners. We focused on gathering the supplies we needed so we could leave as soon as we could.

We spent the next hour gathering several bottles of wine, grape leaves, rice, coffee, tea, sugar, soap, duct tape, cigarettes, and hard candy for the children to add to the forty pounds of lamb and chicken he had given us. I also bought a couple pocket knives, a multi-tool, cheap flashlights, alkaline batteries, toothpaste, deodorant, scarves, and a few sets of bed sheets, pillow cases, and washcloths. All things you need when the stores run out with no possible resupply.

* * *

We ate a few kabobs from a market stand, then headed for Rafi's parked car and packed the supplies into the duffel bags until we couldn't possibly fit one more thing in them. I showed Jake how I packed my backpack, with everything I would carry in with me, and helped him repack the same way.

I looked over at Jake while we packed. "Are you nervous?"

"A little. It just hasn't really dawned on me what we're doing until now."

"Well, everything is set. Let's get this gear in the car and try to get a nap. We'll be up most of the night trekking in."

"Yeah, right. I don't think I can sleep."

"Me neither. I never do right before something like this, but at least lie down and close your eyes. I'll come get you when it's time."

Jake blew out a long breath. "This is kind of crazy."

"Hey, man, this is the job. You wanted to be here."

"I know," he said and took his bag out the door.

Chapter 11

Outside Qasr, Lebanon
May 14, 2013
2350 Local Time

We arrived at a small cinder block building a few hundred yards from the Lebanon-Syria border. Rafi parked the car under a nearby olive tree and we all got out to meet the butcher's son. We were careful not to make much noise as we each put on our bulging backpacks that stored all of the essentials we would need for what we anticipated to be a week-long stay in Syria. I helped Jake hoist the heavy duffel bag with the provisions from the market over his shoulders and Rafi did the same for me. Rafi had me follow him to the car and help him sling a large bag that I didn't realize he had.

"What is this?" I asked Rafi.

"I'll tell you later. It's just more supplies on their list I got for them from Beirut."

"Well, I'm glad you're carrying it. It's heavy as shit."

I helped him put the heavy bag's strap over his shoulder. We carefully made our way, loaded down with our kits, through the darkness to the front of the small building and entered the darkened doorway.

I heard, "*Salaam alaikum,*" whispered in the dark corner of the empty building.

Rafi quietly returned the traditional Arabic greeting, "*Alaikum salaam.*"

We shook hands with and kissed the cheeks of the butcher's son. Rafi talked quietly with the man in Arabic.

After a few moments, Rafi turned to give us the plan. "This is Asra. He wants us to follow him as quietly as possible outside to a manhole where he will lead us underground through a cement storm drain that empties out into a field where we will meet his friend, who is waiting with a truck to take us twenty kilometers to their village. We'll sleep there tonight and press on to the outskirts of Homs in the morning."

"Is it safe to travel in there in the daytime?" I asked.

Rafi asked the man my question in Arabic. He answered with a few words that I didn't understand.

"He said it is better to travel in the morning when the army is turning over their guard responsibilities. The regime has night patrols with night vision goggles and they have random checkpoints along the road we need to travel. If we go when they are turning over it is likely we can slip through."

"Likely or certain?"

"Nothing is certain. But he says that this is the best way."

I turned to Jake. "You ready for this?"

"This is what I'm here for, right?"

"Just making sure."

There was a moment of silence broken by our guide.

"What did he say?" I asked Rafi.

"He wants to know if I brought the weapons and ammunition."

"What?"

"I had to agree to bring him a few AK-47s as payment for his services."

"We're running guns?" Jake asked.

"This is how things are done here," Rafi said.

"What happened to not being the story?" Jake asked me.

"You heard the man. It's what we need to do to cross the border to get the stories."

"Do you have the weapons?" I asked Rafi.

"They're in my bag. You guys ready?"

"You fucker," I whispered to Rafi. I could tell he was giving me that sly smile of his even in the dark.

"Come on, Angus, they wouldn't take toilet paper or gasoline as payment. They wanted cash and a few weapons. We can all climb in the car and go back home if you want."

He knows I'm not going to do that.

"Nope. Calculated risk. Let's do it," I finally said.

Rafi told our guide we were ready.

The man led us out of the building and around the corner to an open manhole cover several feet from the building. He climbed down first into the pitch-black darkness, followed by Rafi.

"I can't believe we're doing this," Jake said.

"This is where it all begins, my friend. You ready to do this? There's no turning back once we get there."

"I know."

"This is where you catch the bug or you quit it forever. You good?"

I heard Jake take a few quick short breaths, like he was preparing to go on a long underwater free dive. "Yeah, I'm ready."

"Okay, after you," I said to Jake and heard him struggle under the weight of his gear and supplies as he descended rung by rung into the deeper darkness. I followed close behind with a big smile.

It felt good to be back in the action.

* * *

We made the slow walk through the drainage tunnel, only large enough for us to stoop down, making slow but steady progress one foot in front of the other for about a half hour. We emerged at the other end of the tunnel behind thick, six-foot-tall grass reeds and into fresh air. The stars above us blazed with effervescent glory against the black night sky.

"Wow, I've never seen stars shine that bright," Jake said as he scanned the sky above us, almost losing his balance.

I caught him before he toppled over backwards. "Easy now, it ain't sightseeing time yet."

We all doffed our gear and greeted the driver.

I heard the driver ask Asra, "Do you have the weapons?"

"Yes," Asra said.

"*Allahu akbar*," the driver said.

"Welcome to Syria," the driver said in English as we piled into the back of his pickup truck.

Asra and the driver pulled a heavy canvas tarp over us, cranked up the engine, and took us farther into the Syrian night.

* * *

After about thirty minutes of getting banged around over twenty kilometers of bad road, the driver stopped and pulled the tarp off us. Just like Jake mentioned earlier, the lack of ambient light in this remote part of Syria showed us layers upon layers of stars that made the sky look like an electrified George Seurat painting. There's nothing like the mesmerizing light from millions of light years in the past to make your efforts feel small.

We all got out at our designated overnight stop and slept on thin wool rugs in a single second floor room in a two-story cinder block house for a few hours until the rising sun lit up the one window in the room enough for us to see clearly. I actually managed to sleep a bit despite the adrenaline in my system. I smelled coffee and heard some muffled Arabic in the kitchen downstairs. I sat up, rubbed my eyes, and saw that Rafi was gone.

I put on my boots, went down the marble stairs, and found Asra, Rafi, and the driver standing in the kitchen, sipping coffee and chatting.

"Sabahul khayr," I said to the group. *Good morning.*

They returned my greeting.

"Hello, Angus. Do you want a coffee?" Rafi asked.

"Of course."

Tinny voices on a handheld radio on the counter let out a spew of fast-paced Arabic I wasn't able to catch.

"The boys here have just gotten word from their friends down the road that they heard the Syrian Army day shift replacements checking in on the radio for their patrol turnover. They said they would be busy for the next hour as the units switched over," he said as he poured me a steaming cup of coffee.

"Are we going soon?"

Rafi handed me the small glass cup. "Finish your coffee first. It will probably be your last luxury for a while."

I sipped it and immediately felt better. I loved the way they did coffee in the Middle East. I liked Italian coffee too, but the thick and potent coffee throughout the Middle East really kick-started my heart and elevated my mind to a highly efficient frequency in only a few sips.

I finished my cup as the trio talked. "I'll go get Brando outta bed and we'll be ready to go in a few."

"Brando?"

"Yeah, I was thinking we should have a call sign for Jake while we're here. I can take the chance that people may not recognize him but I don't want to make it easy for anyone by using his real name."

"You mean like in *Top Gun*?"

"Yeah. Like *Top Gun*."

Rafi nudged me. "Are you 'Maverick' then?"

"Hell no. I'm 'Iceman.' You know, 'ice cold, no mistakes.'"

"Stick with me and stay away from Plan Bs and we'll have no mistakes. What's my call sign?"

"I was thinking 'Merlin' because you're always working miracles."

"No. I want to be 'Viper.'"

"I don't know."

"Well, just don't name me 'Goose.' He gets killed."

"Good idea. I think 'Viper' fits you fine. Like a snake in the grass, I think that's perfect."

Rafi pushed me playfully and laughed. "Fuck you. Go wake Brando. We need to get going."

* * *

I went upstairs and rousted Brando from his nap. We collected our things and hit the bed of the truck for the final leg to Al-Waer, the neighborhood where we were set to stay, just outside Homs.

The road was just as bumpy as before but a little more nerve-racking. Every time the truck slowed down we thought it was a checkpoint where we could be found out and ultimately taken prisoner by the Assad regime. I'm not overly religious but I tend to agree with Reverend William T. Cummings, a World War II veteran of the Bataan Death March, who is attributed with the famous quote that "there are no atheists in foxholes." I was definitely praying to whatever supreme being that might be out there watching over us that we made it safely to our destination.

About twenty minutes into what the driver said would be about a thirty-minute drive, we slowed to a stop. I couldn't hear anything except the low idling of our truck's engine. My heart raced as I went through all of the possible actions I could take if our tarp were ripped off and I was face-to-face with Assad's security forces, the *shabbiha*.

I heard the passenger door open and someone get out and my pulse went through the roof. The tarp came back to reveal my face and I was relieved to see Rafi looking at me.

"What's up?" I said, trying to be calm.

"They see an armored vehicle just over the next hill, waiting. They're not sure if they saw us coming or not. But they have called some friends on the radio to expose themselves and hopefully, draw their attention away from the road."

"Do you think that's going to work?"

"I don't know. They don't seem too concerned. We just have to wait."

"Okay, I guess."

"How are you doing, Brando?" Rafi said to Jake.

"My name's Jake," he said.

Rafi looked at me. "You didn't tell him?"

"No."

"Tell me what?"

"We're going to use call signs so it's not so apparent who you may be."

"Why am I Brando?"

"What's wrong with Brando? Marlon Brando's a classic American actor. You should be proud."

"I don't like Brando. Every damn actor tried to impersonate Brando's style and failed. Any actor caught trying to do that nowadays is permanently seen as a douchebag wannabe."

I looked at Rafi. "In that case, Brando sounds perfect," I chuckled.

"Fuck you. I want a different one."

"You don't get to choose your call sign. Right now I think that 'douchebag wannabe' fits you perfectly."

"Fuck you, Angus."

"No, it's, 'Fuck you, Iceman,'" Rafi laughed.

"I did a piece on naval aviators once and just about every one of them had earned their call sign, good or bad, and it was mostly bad. And if they hated it, it was more likely to stick."

"Okay, fine. I love Brando."

"Brando it is."

Rafi laughed again. He was playing right into our joke.

"Fuck you guys."

Just then, a burst of heavy machine gun fire erupted in the distance.

"Here we go," Rafi said. "Hang on, it may get a little rough for a few minutes."

Rafi pulled the tarp back over us and I heard him get back in the cab.

The driver put the truck in gear and crept up the road. I couldn't stand it. I had to see what was going on. I pulled the tarp off me and put my head just over the edge of the bed on the driver's side.

As the truck crested the hill above where the armored personnel carrier was stationed on the road in the distance, I could see dirt flying up in small geysers. I saw the government troops in the distance take cover behind their armored vehicle as the bullets impacted all around their position. The soldiers endured the fire for a few seconds before they decided to get inside the safety of their vehicle.

The firing stopped and I saw the turret traverse in the direction of the hillside where the shots were coming from. Its cannon let off a burst of fire that impacted the hill well below the truck's position in the distance. I saw the truck disappear over the crest of the hill and saw the regime armored vehicle begin to lumber off the paved road and onto a dirt road to pursue their attackers.

The driver saw me in the rearview mirror, smiled, and gave me a thumbs-up. A few seconds later, he gunned the engine and worked his way through the gears to get up to speed. My hair whipped in the wind as we increased speed and raced toward where the armored vehicle used to be.

I could hear the thump of cannon fire in the distance as the government forces did their best to return fire and give chase. Our driver kept up his speed knowing that it was unlikely that the security forces would turn around to investigate a truck in the distance as it pursued a hostile threat. It was a brilliant tactic and I was encouraged to see that these guys with little help were able to circumvent such a formidable force. I lay back down and pulled the tarp back over my head, confident we'd be okay. I was wrong.

Chapter 12

Intersection of Provincial Highway and Western Ring Road
Seven miles south of Al-Waer, Syria
May 15, 2013

The truck was screaming at top speed down the dusty road that split the tan-colored desert with green knee-high scrub brush as far as the eye could see. I immediately poked my head out from under the tarp again and pushed my head into the breeze to see what was going on when I felt our vehicle absorb several sharp impacts. The government forces had left two shooters behind to cover the road and they were shooting at our truck as we approached. My eyes squinted against the wind when I felt a few more impacts as the fire burst from their rifles in the distance. I caught the eye of the driver, but he just smiled and gave me another thumbs-up.

As we approached, the fire got more intense and I had to put my head down.

"What the fuck is going on?" Jake asked.

"The government forces left two guys behind and they're shooting at us."

"What do we do?"

"Grab your duffel and hug it. Lie on your left side and put your back against mine," I said and did the same.

"Shouldn't we wear those flak vests you said you had?"

"I didn't bring 'em."

"What? Why not?"

"You could barely carry all the gear we have. Besides, a vest with PRESS in big white letters is as good as a bull's-eye around here. They don't stop rifle fire anyway, they're only for shrapnel. Just hug your bag."

I felt Jake nuzzle up to me and I closed my eyes and gritted my teeth as we got shot at. I talked tough because it had happened to me plenty, but I never did like getting shot at.

I heard the driver yell in Arabic, "Get down," from the cab.

The rifle fire continued as we sped down the road. I felt more bullet impacts and heard the Doppler shift of the gunfire as we passed through their position. They were now firing behind us. I couldn't resist. I pulled the tarp off me and poked my head up and looked behind us. Two regime troops had their rifles in their shoulders, one on each side of the road firing non-stop at us as we sped away from them. I flipped them off with both hands and laughed.

"Damn, Angus, you're gonna get killed doing shit like that," Jake said.

He looked over at me. I could see in his eyes that he was scared. The road guards began firing again and he went back to hugging his duffel bag. The rear window exploded as shots went through the glass and impacted the windshield. In the cab, it looked like no one was driving. Rafi, Asra, and the driver were hunched down below the dash as we drove at top speed. The truck never faltered, so I guess they didn't hit anything vital. And then the cannon fire began.

I looked in the direction the armored vehicle went and I saw that it had stopped and was firing at us from its position halfway between us and the crest of the hill where our friends on the ridge engaged them. They weren't going to let us off so easy.

Their cannon fire sent large explosions of sand, dirt, and asphalt in our path as they tried to lead us in their gun sights as the driver tore down the road. There was a small rise in the distance I knew the driver was gunning for to shield us from the gun fire. More cannon fire erupted right around our truck and I got a torrent of sand in my eyes and mouth from the bullets impacting the ground around us. The driver kept up the speed as we crested the hill and came down the other side, out of their line of sight.

I could hear laughter erupt from the cab of the truck. I looked ahead and saw a group of houses in the distance. If we made it to those, we would be okay. The armored vehicle didn't have the speed to catch us and wouldn't be able to track us once we were in the city.

I put my head back down and looked over at Jake. He looked at me and silently pointed to two bullet holes in his duffel bag from bullets that had managed to penetrate the truck's bed.

"This is the job, Brando," I yelled. "Ain't it cool?"

"This is fucked up," he yelled back and turned over and hugged the bag again. "And stop calling me Brando."

I just smiled. *There's nothing like chasing a story into the absurd. No place I'd rather be.*

Chapter 13

Al-Waer, Syria
May 15, 2013

I felt the driver down-shift the truck and heard a few people yelling as we passed by them. The driver yelled back at them and laughed. I couldn't hear what he was saying over the wind and engine noise, but it didn't sound hostile. The truck slowed to a crawl and then stopped.

The driver got out and slammed his door. Then the tarp was pulled off and I was looking at Rafi's face again. This time he was smiling.

"We're here," Rafi said.

The morning sun was bright and I squinted as I sat up and looked around. We were being protected from the searing sun by the shade of huge concrete hulks of bombed-out apartment buildings and ground floor storefronts that surrounded us. There were several dozen local people standing around the truck, mostly old men and women clutching young children, probably their grandchildren, watching us.

Jake sat up as well. "Where are we?"

I climbed out of the truck and grabbed my bags. "Welcome to the besieged neighborhood of Al-Waer," I said. "Come on, Brando, we'll put our stuff down and give these people their supplies."

Jake hopped out of the back of the truck and grabbed his bags. I followed the driver into a nearby building and thought Jake was right behind me. I heard two dogs barking and growling and then I heard Jake scream.

"Help me," Jake yelled.

I headed back outside and saw Jake on the ground in a ball with two dogs fighting over the duffel bag he had carried with most of the food for the neighborhood. I ran over and kicked both dogs away and pulled Jake's duffel from the ground.

Rafi helped Jake to his feet. We all looked around at the neighborhood people. They were smiling and laughing at Jake's reaction.

"What the hell is so funny? Those dogs attacked me for no reason."

Rafi looked at me as he dusted Jake off. "I guess we shouldn't have given Brando all the fresh meat to carry," Rafi laughed.

"You guys are assholes. You knew this would happen, didn't you?"

I dusted the dirt off Jake's shirt. "No, everyone here is starving, especially the dogs. Come on, let's go give this stuff to the patriarch and we'll meet everyone."

* * *

The driver led us to the second floor of a building that was partially blown apart. There were holes in the cinder block and tile walls and debris everywhere. It didn't seem like there was a clean place anywhere to be seen.

We arrived at the first room at the top of the stairs and the driver pointed inside. "There is only this room and the one next to it. I'm sorry, that is all we have to offer."

The room had a dark brown blanket nailed to the wall over the window to act as a curtain and a twin-size mattress in the corner that was once white but was now covered with random brown and black splotches. Someone had swept all of the debris into a heaping pile in the corner and stacked several demolished pieces of furniture along the far wall.

I looked at our driver, "It's great. Thank you for having us here." I dropped my bag in the first room. "Rafi, you stay with me, we'll give Brando some privacy in the other room."

Rafi dropped his gear as well. "Okay."

"When can we present the things we have for the neighborhood to the patriarch?" I asked the driver.

"Right now. Tamir is waiting to meet you."

We each grabbed our heavy duffel bags and followed the driver up another flight of stairs and down a long hallway to a lone door at the end. The driver knocked softly and a voice from inside grunted an incomprehensible reply. The driver opened the door slowly, asked in Arabic if he was ready to meet the visitors, and then gestured for us to follow him into the room.

The entire room was covered with several Turkish and Iranian rugs with soft pillows lined up along the wall. The patriarch, seated with his back against the far wall, was flanked by two of the largest pillows in the room. He was dressed in gray slacks and a loose-fitting white tunic that covered his knees. He looked to be in his mid-sixties and had a gray beard and mustache with thick salt and pepper hair.

He motioned for us to sit near him. The driver handed us each a pillow and we all sat in a semi-circle in from of him. Rafi knew the drill when he and I spoke with an Arabic speaker in this sort of setup. Rafi would introduce each of us and then let the patriarch know that he would be the translator.

Rafi began speaking to the patriarch and he nodded slowly and smiled as Rafi spoke. Rafi pointed to Jake and me as he introduced each of us. We nodded respectfully when the old man looked at us and smiled.

Rafi told him that we brought a small amount of aid for the neighborhood and hoped he would allow us to stay a few days to tell their story.

The patriarch replied to Rafi in Arabic, "I am Tamir, and I am honored to have you here and we are truly grateful for your gifts. As you know, it has been difficult for some time and we appreciate you thinking of our neighborhood. I would be proud to have you here so the world can know our sacrifice. I hear that you have brought food as well as medical aid and other useful things?"

Rafi pointed to the three large duffel bags we lined up near the door. "Yes, our only regret is that we could only bring as much as we could carry."

Tamir looked at the driver who was standing near the door. "Take the food to the women and have them prepare something for us and our guests."

"What about the fire?" the driver asked.

Tamir thought for a moment before he replied. "Have the young boys cut down branches from my olive trees. Only what we need for tonight though. I have someone bringing more gas for the stoves in a few days."

"Yes, Tamir," the driver said and had two other men help him carry the duffels away.

Tamir directed his attention back to us. "I want to thank you for having the courage to come here. I know it is dangerous for westerners to be here, but I admire your courage just as I admire the courage of my people who are standing up against injustice. With help from people like you, we will have a free country once again without extreme repression. There will be peace, *Inshallah*."

"*Shukran*, Tamir," I said and nodded to him with respect.

"I thank you again for your donation to our neighborhood and invite you to have dinner with us to celebrate our friendship this evening."

We shook hands, thanked Tamir again, and left him alone against the wall.

* * *

The driver met us outside Tamir's door, showed us around the building, and introduced us to a few of his friends. Rafi translated what the driver said for us since he was speaking so fast I could hardly keep up.

"There is a bathroom down the hall from your rooms but no running water. There will be a bucket of water refilled in there twice a day, but if you have bottled water or your own container, that seems to work well for everyone," Rafi said.

I looked at Jake. "Whore baths for everyone."

Jake rolled his eyes. "I can handle that, but if there's no running water, how do we use the toilets?"

Rafi asked the question and then translated the driver's answer. "There is a barrel cut in half on the ground floor with a makeshift toilet seat that both men and women use. It has a shower curtain rigged up for privacy."

"What happens when it gets full?" Jake asked.

Rafi asked and then translated again, "The young boys replace it with the other half of the toilet barrel and burn the contents every few days."

"Sounds efficient," I said and slapped Jake on the back. "It ain't the Phoenician, but it'll do," I laughed.

We followed the driver out of the building and into the street. He introduced us to a few more of the neighborhood people. Each one gave us the traditional Middle East greeting of hands on the shoulders followed by two cheek kisses.

"They seem pretty happy to host us," Jake said as he kissed more cheeks and smiled at everyone.

"It helps that we just delivered the most food they've seen in over a month," I said.

We walked past a storefront that had a sign with the green plus symbol of a pharmacy over the door. The windows were shattered and partially covered with blankets and plywood. A large white bed sheet flapped in the light breeze as it hung next to the door with a large red cross and red crescent symbols hand drawn onto it.

"What's this place?" Jake asked.

"It's the local medical clinic," Rafi said. He turned and asked a few questions of the driver and translated his answer. "It used to be a pharmacy, but when the pharmacist was killed by the security forces several months ago, the neighborhood people took it over. They use the store as an emergency room and his two apartments upstairs over the store where he used to live with his family as a small hospital."

"Do they have any doctors?"

"He said that they have one lady doctor, a male nurse, and a few old men and women volunteers."

"Why only old men and women?" Jake asked Rafi.

"All of the young men are dead or off fighting with the resistance groups. They do not want the young kids in there to see the wounded and dying, so only the older people are available in the neighborhood to help."

We looked around at the cots, neatly stacked blankets, and cardboard boxes of medical supplies.

"Where is the real hospital?" Jake's voice echoed from the tile that covered the entire room from floor to ceiling.

"It is several miles from here, but inaccessible because of the siege. They have to take care of themselves for now."

Rafi led us out of the largest room on the ground floor that served as the operating room and on to the sidewalk outside.

"What siege?"

"The government forces have cut off the power and water, and all supply shipments to this neighborhood," Rafi said, pointing to the power lines coiled up in the street and hanging from toppled power poles.

"Why?"

"Their neighborhood overlooks the main road that leads to and from Homs. The regime has been getting shot at from here. Not necessarily from the residents, but from ISIS and the FSA, and the regime is taking it out on them by besieging their neighborhood. That's why they can't leave or get any supplies or help."

"That's barbaric."

"That's why I chose this spot. It's characteristic of the bullshit these people have to endure," I said to Jake.

The driver shook Rafi's hand and spoke to him for a moment in a low murmur, his voice cracking as he spoke. The driver looked Rafi in the eyes at arm's length before he moved in to give him a hug. He moved around to each of us and shook our hands before he disappeared into the clinic, wiping the tears from his eyes.

"What did he say?" Jake asked.

"He said that he is very moved and optimistic that we were willing to risk our lives to come and tell their story to the world. He told me that he was confident that our stories would be even more effective than their small arms against the Assad regime. He is very happy we are here; every life in Al-Waer depends on us getting their story to the world."

* * *

After our neighborhood introduction, we went to Jake's room so I could show him what I looked for when I write a story. Similar to my room, a jumble of debris and destroyed furniture lined the walls of Jake's room as well, a far cry from the suite at the Phoenician indeed.

"I write constantly," I said as I sat on the ground leaning on my backpack with my iPad on my lap. "I put things down in small notebooks I carry or bigger notebooks in my backpack. I don't use everything I write or even file a story every day or even every other day. But when I get something with enough information to cobble together a meaningful, if not compelling story, I'll put it together, post it, and let the GRL know it's there for them to shop around.

"When I have a chance, I put everything on my iPad or laptop, whichever I happen to have. I save everything locally and then to two different e-mail addresses but only post to one. That way, as long as I have a cell network and a smart phone, I can file stories."

"What does the GRL do with your stories?"

"They're basically article brokers for freelance journalists. I let them know my stuff is there for them to use and they work to place it with their clients," I said as I brought up some files on my iPad.

I handed the iPad to Jake and pointed to a list of a few dozen stories I had saved from my last trip to Syria a few months before.

"Those are a sample of what I do."

Jake tapped the screen, opened one of the files, and scanned a few lines from one of the stories.

Jake handed my iPad back to me. "Who are their clients?"

"All the major news outlets and a bunch of smaller ones. I've sold stuff to everyone from the *New York Times* and *The Christian Science Monitor* to *Esquire* magazine. It's just all about getting a compelling story, getting the facts right, and then getting it out there."

"Sounds easy."

I looked at Jake. "It's not. It takes practice and you need to know the wants of the market. I may write a story hoping the *Times of London* will pick it up but it will get sold to *The Daily Mail.* I might write one with exactly the *Men's Journal* in mind but *Popular Science* will pick it up instead. It's okay to me as long as someone buys them, but after a while I had to stop obsessing who the audience may be and just keep writing. Sometimes I file stories and the GRL can't place them. Either the people I thought would be interested weren't or no one wanted a story on the topic I wrote at the time. The market is fickle and cyclical."

"I guess that aspect can be tough."

"It is tough unless you just keep writing articles and forget about them as soon as you edit and send them. If they sell, great, and if not, I'm already polishing the next one and the one after that. I just have to keep going, trust my instinct, and put down the best writing I can on stuff I'm interested in finding out about. That's it."

"I hear the writers on the set constantly complaining about writing. I guess it isn't that easy."

"Like I said. It takes practice. The hard part about being freelance is that it's just you. So, you do the video, make the contacts, hire fixers, chase stories you believe are important, and then put it all together to paint a picture of what's going on, or simply report what you find out. But you have to keep going, constantly moving like a shark on the hunt. That's why you see so many journalists globe-trotting to the next story. They're following leads and making interviews and writing stories. We never stop, especially freelancers. We have to keep going and write to earn our next meal."

I handed my iPad back to Jake.

"What's this for?"

"It's your turn to battle the blank page. Start typing about how we got from Lebanon to here."

"I don't think I can replicate your style."

I laughed. "Don't worry, just start typing how the story plays out in your head. I'll help you edit later. You can add freelance writer to your Twitter profile to better your image."

Jake shook his head, clearly not appreciative of my sarcasm, but he began tapping words out.

* * *

After about an hour, we had a workable story. I managed to get a strong enough cell signal on the roof of the building we were staying in to let Chuck know we made it to Al-Waer safely.

Joining the Besieged
Posted to GRL by Angus Conn
Al-Waer, Syria
Filed May 15, 2013

I stopped in a small town near the Syria-Lebanon border and met with a local contact who gave me what amounted to a shopping list for the people of Al-Waer. My fixer, my assistant, and I went to the local market to buy the specific food items and other common things that the besieged people of Al-Waer desperately needed. Things like flashlights, batteries, duct tape, bars of soap, toothpaste, toilet paper, plastic bags, aspirin, powdered milk, cigarettes, matches, sugar, flour, and coffee. Mundane things we all take for granted until you run out of them.

We met up with our contact late at night, weighed down with our own gear and one bulging duffel bag each filled with the things we bought at the market. I didn't know it at the time, but my fixer was told that he must also bring a few AK47s and ammunition if they were going to smuggle Americans across the border. The trip had to be worth it for the smugglers.

We shimmied down an open manhole into complete darkness and walked, hunched over, about a half mile through a long underground cement drainage system and came out on the other end in Syria where a truck awaited us for the next phase of our journey. Grateful but serious men met us with smiles and kisses. "Welcome to Syria," they said.

We bedded down in a nearby town in an abandoned farmhouse until just before daybreak when we were most likely to be able to slip through the regime roadblocks as the Syrian soldiers on night watch turned over their guard responsibilities with the soldiers of the day shift.

Our transporters communicated with a local group who sent a truck with a mounted machine gun to fire a few rounds at the regime roadblock to lure them away from the road while we passed unnoticed as they pursued them. That was the plan, anyway.

The armored vehicle guarding the road pursued our friends in the truck but also left a few soldiers to guard the road. They shot at us as we sped by, but they were unable to stop us. The armored vehicle was too far away to chase us and we melted into the next town and continued on to Al-Waer.

We delivered the supplies we brought to a grateful neighborhood that has endured a government siege for several months. The government has shut down the water and electricity, monitors the cellphones and other communications, and limits most of the vehicle traffic in and out of the Homs suburb. We were successfully smuggled in and are now the newest members of the besieged town of Al-Waer, a small ventricle in the heart of where the Syrian uprising began.

* * *

I saved the story to my computer so I could send it when we had either Internet capability or, if worse came to worst, I would type it out in several text messages to Chuck when cellphone coverage was available. The government forces could monitor the transmissions, but there was not much they could do about it once it was sent. They would be able to read my story, but they already knew what was going on in Al-Waer, so what did it really matter? The driver told me it was okay to send my story since they would not be smuggling anyone else in the same way we had come. He told me that the locals changed their smuggling tactics frequently and were flexible according to the movements of the regime. Jake's real-world education began with that first story we did together. But I was anxious to complete it as soon as possible.

Chapter 14

Al-Waer, Syria
May 15, 2013

After Jake and I finished writing the story, Rafi came and got us for dinner. I ran a couple handfuls of water through my hair, wet my face, and washed my hands from the small amount of water I had in my water bottle. We went downstairs and met the men in a large room that was set up with some of the same rugs that we saw in Tamir's room on the third floor. A dozen men from the local neighborhood block greeted each of us and sat us in a place of honor around Tamir.

The women came in with tea and small dishes of olives, humus, and flat bread to start. We all talked quietly and laughed. The mood was not festive, but relaxed. It didn't feel like there was a siege on, but it also didn't feel like a party. There was an understandable somberness within scratching distance of the surface of everyone's attitude in the room.

When the first course was finished, the women returned to clear the plates and brought in the main course of rice wrapped in grape leaves and a platter stacked high with grilled lamb and chicken on a bed of divinely spiced rice. One of the women, wearing a gray one-piece shador and headscarf, which only covered her head and accentuated her delicate round face and placid hazel eyes, set the platter of meat in front of Tamir and bowed slightly as she turned to go.

Tamir addressed her, "Amala, have you met our guests?"

She turned and looked at Tamir. "No," she said in Arabic.

"These are the men we have to thank for this food and for their bravery in helping to tell the story of our sacrifice."

She turned to us and smiled. "Thank you for being here. We are grateful you came," she said in English.

"We hope it will do some good. Where did you learn English?" I asked.

"In the United States. I went to live there when I was a little girl."

"She came back to us to help her family and neighbors. We are grateful she came to help us in our time of need. She is our only doctor. All the rest have fled or have been killed," Tamir said in Arabic.

Jake leaned over to me, "What did he say?"

"She's the doctor here at the clinic."

Jake stared at Amala as she spoke. "I am happy to be of service," she said and locked eyes with Jake for a few seconds.

She undoubtedly recognized him as a famous person. She turned to go and I caught her looking back one more time at Jake before she disappeared into the kitchen.

I looked at Jake and then nudged him, "Don't even think about it, my friend."

"What?"

"You know what. No charming the locals. Remember, you're my assistant here, not a movie star."

"I'm sure you won't let me forget it."

* * *

Once the main course was gone, the women returned to take the plates and deliver a few trays of coffee for the men. Amala handed Jake a coffee and smiled at him.

"Thank you. Can I talk with you later? Only Angus and Rafi speak English that I know of and I'm tired of talking with them," he said and offered his multi-million dollar smile.

"Of course. I'm not going anywhere," Amala said and retreated to the kitchen, but not before she looked back and smiled when she saw Jake staring at her.

* * *

It was custom in the Middle East for the women and men to eat separately and only after dinner would they gather together, but only if invited by the patriarch. Tonight was special. We were the guests and we were here to talk with the men about the uprising, about the government, and about war, so the women were not invited until later.

Rafi and I talked quietly with Tamir over our coffee. I made notes as we spoke and recorded his story as he told it. Tamir had lived in Al-Waer for most of his adult life. He had volunteered for the Syrian army when he was young and did two years as a truck driver and mechanic in several different military areas throughout Syria in the 1970s. He then came back and opened a garage and fixed cars for a few years with the expertise he learned in the army. He decided one day that he should go into business with his brother, who had been in the Syrian navy in Latakia in the west where the Mediterranean Sea lapped at Syria's shores.

Tamir and his brother saved up enough money to buy a few trucks. Tamir got them in running condition and his brother used his connections at the Latakia seaport to start a transport business that grew to supply all of Homs with imported goods and seafood.

Now, in retirement, he said he was heartbroken to see all that he and his family had worked for go to waste over political imbecility. That's exactly the word he used, "imbecility," because I had to ask Rafi twice what it meant. After his brief introduction of his life, I was eager to get his take on the recent uprising.

"What saddens you the most?" I asked Tamir.

Tamir shrugged. "All of it. This neighborhood used to be a peaceful slice of heaven. I knew every family that lived five blocks in every direction," Tamir said as Rafi translated for me. "We would walk to the park or the market with our children and grandchildren. I would buy them fruit juice and candy and watch them play in the park as the sun went down in the cool of the evening."

Tamir stared at the rug as he spoke and then looked up at me. I could see his eyes were glazed with tears. "We can't do that anymore and probably never will. The park is now a cemetery, filled with the bodies of some of those same children and their families."

"Who in your family did you lose?"

Tamir stared at the rug again for a moment and then wiped the tears that dropped onto his cheeks. "Everyone," he said. He then looked up and met my eyes. "My wife was killed in a barrel bomb attack only a few weeks ago and my two boys were killed by the regime a few months ago. Their wives and my grandchildren were killed when the building they were hiding in took a direct hit from regime artillery only a week after I lost my sons. I have no one. Just whoever is left in this neighborhood and my home. They must not die for nothing. We will fight. They will not die for nothing."

Tamir looked down again and breathed deeply for a few moments. I let him compose himself before I continued.

"Isn't there a cemetery near here?"

"It became full and we had to use the park. That is where we bury the dead now."

"How did the uprising come to this neighborhood?"

"I heard of the demonstrations. There had been demonstrations before. People want to be heard. They want something changed. But these demonstrations were calling for big changes and I knew from the beginning that much change was going to be impossible."

"Like what?" I asked.

"Like equal representation in parliament for all religious sects and the removal of al-Assad."

"Did you think that the government would have reacted in this way?"

"No," he said, shaking his head. "It took everyone by surprise to hear that people were being fired on by the *shabbiha* and government troops at demonstrations. I knew it couldn't be army troops but their corrupt officers. The generals and commanders who had much to lose if they disobeyed."

"Why did you think the army could not be to blame?"

"Because the army is made up of all kinds of people. There are all sects in the army. The shooting had to have come from the *shabbiha* and their influence on the leadership. They are the ones loyal to Assad. They are the ones who want to keep power. The boys of Syria are not murderers. They are pawns."

"How did the government begin to crack down here?"

"We saw the army come to the international road. It is the largest road that leads into Homs from the west. They came to our neighborhood and told us not to make trouble. They told the people there would be no trouble if they were respectful and did not have illegal demonstrations."

"Did people have demonstrations anyway?"

"Yes, they did because when the people applied to the local government offices for permits to organize a peaceful demonstration, their requests were denied. But they demonstrated anyway."

"What happened?"

"Demonstrations only happened a few times. The army just blocked the roads, contained the protestors, and didn't allow filming."

"No one was arrested?"

"No, they knew we were not a threat to anyone."

"When did it change?"

"It changed when the *shabbiha* arrived and witnessed an illegal demonstration and ordered the army to round up all of the people and take them away."

"Did the army do this?"

"Yes, they put them in trucks and took them out to the Ring Road to the west. Some of the soldiers refused to take the people away because they knew what was going to happen."

"What was happening?"

"They were taking them to prison and some who fought back were being executed. One soldier brought an entire truckload of people back to their neighborhood, hid the army truck, deserted from the army, and stayed in the neighborhood. The people hid him when the army and *shabbiha* came looking for him. They probably thought the demonstrators overpowered him and killed him, but he lives. I talked with him. He said he couldn't take people to jail to be tortured and killed who just wanted a voice in their government. The people had done nothing wrong except challenge the current state of power."

"How did the neighborhood get to be demolished?" I asked, pointing outside.

"When the *shabbiha* came back to collect the people who had escaped, they came back with a mind to teach the people who rebelled and anyone who helped them a lesson. They came to the neighborhood and smashed their stores and took the men for torture and the women for their own demented fun. When the people fought back, there was shooting. The *shabbiha* went away and then returned with the army. With tanks and artillery and airplanes and helicopters. They shot at everything and everyone."

"How did you defend yourself against that sort of attack?"

"Most of the people fled, but some stayed and linked up with other groups like the FSA and Jabhat al-Nusra to help defend themselves against the *shabbiha* and the army."

"So, you fight with them too?"

"Only in self-defense. We are defending our homes and businesses, not trying to overthrow the government. But if they come here and try to kill us, we will do everything in our power to keep what we have and protect our families."

I wrote as Tamir spoke, trying to take down as much of the conversation as I could to transcribe later while thinking of the next question to get at the root of the story here.

"Do you believe you can overcome the regime?"

"I just want to keep people from ending up in the park. There are too many there now."

I looked at the sadness in the old man's eyes. "You said before that the local park is now the cemetery? Is that right?"

He nodded his head slowly and tried to smile. "I try to busy myself with productive work, the work of helping to defend Al-Waer so I do not dwell on the senseless deaths."

"Why haven't you gone to the camps?"

"Why should I? This is my home. What could I do for my family or countrymen in a camp in Turkey or Lebanon or Jordan? I can do much more here to help stop the killings."

"I have heard about many children being hurt here. Is this true?"

"Anyone can be hurt here. It is up to the government how much pressure they want to put on us. Right now we have no water, no electricity, and no deliveries of food. They are trying to punish us for resisting and blocking their deliveries to their troop concentrations that travel along the highway. But we will not go. They will have to come and get us."

"Why are there still children here? What choice do they have? Shouldn't they go where it is safe until the violence is over?"

"It is almost as bad in the camps. There is little food and only tents for shelter. Disease is breaking out because there are too many people and too few resources to help them. I think that the people may have a better chance pulling together as a community, and as long as we don't become a target, we will get through it and order will be restored.

"Some of the people do not have any way to travel to the camps. The camps are not close and it costs money to go there or you have to barter for a ride. The rich hoard, the middle class make do, and the poor starve. But not here. I have gotten all of the families who have chosen to stay to combine all of our resources and we help each other. We have opened a clinic because people cannot get to the hospital. It is several miles away to the local hospital and there are roadblocks. We will help each other just as we always have. We will be poor together. I was poor for many years. It does not bother me to share what I have with my neighbors in hard times. And these are truly hard times."

"You are very generous, Tamir."

"It is my duty as a citizen and as a Muslim to treat strangers as family and here no one is a stranger except you," he said and pointed at Rafi, Jake, and me. "But even you are family when you are here. You will suffer with us and we are grateful for you to see what is happening and tell our story to the world. I trust you will tell of our kindness and our willingness to stop the violence. We are only here to defend ourselves. You must tell them."

I looked up from my notes and stared into Tamir's eyes as if we were sealing a contract between us.

"I will, Tamir."

Chapter 15

Al-Waer, Syria
May 15, 2013

I spoke with Rafi after dinner and he told me that Tamir knew of the museum director, Doctor Halabi, who wanted to meet with me. He told Rafi that he wanted to meet with me alone and that he would be in touch with Tamir with instructions for me to go with a driver the next day who would take me to him so we could discuss specifics.

"Do you think that's safe?" I asked.

"Angus, what else are you going to do? This is why we are here. Go get the story. I'll keep Jake out of trouble."

"Keep him away from Amala. I saw them eyeing each other at dinner."

"You can't get in the way of human nature, Angus. You know that."

"Just do what you can. We don't need any complications."

"I know. I'll watch him."

"You know the drill. If I'm not back from this meeting in twenty-four hours, you make arrangements to get Jake out of here and get a message to Chuck to send someone to find me if he can."

"I know. Don't worry. Tamir says that he knows Doctor Halabi personally, and he trusts him. That's really all we've got right now."

* * *

The neighborhood shook for about twenty minutes from government artillery fire right after midnight and again just before the call for morning prayers at sunrise. A man used a handheld loudspeaker in the street a few blocks away for the morning call to prayer. His shrill voice filled the streets and alleyways. It sounded like the pall of dust from the ground up dirt and sand that hung in the air around us from the artillery barrage was itself crying out to the people to pray for it. It was the most eerie call to prayer I had experienced in my many years in the Middle East.

Most of the people in the clinic ignored the call and kept working on the wounded. A few men prayed on the sidewalk outside the clinic. Some even chose to stop picking through the rubble to salvage anything useful and pray in the street. They leaned forward and kissed the ground that seemed to cry out to them. They had much to pray for.

I was told that the regime shells the neighborhood on random days, sometimes a few days in a row, and sometimes they take a break to let the people relax a bit before they shatter their nerves out of the blue again. The objective, I'm told, was to wear them down, so they would not fight back and just leave.

The regime remembers where the resistance came from and Al-Waer is paying the price with no electricity, no food, no water, and no re-supply of any kind except high explosives from the sky at all hours of the night. It is not difficult to understand why most here are not sympathetic to the government.

* * *

May 16, 2013

The next day, Rafi told me that Tamir instructed me to wait at a bus stop down the street for a driver to pick me up at 2:00 p.m. We still had a weak cell signal on the roof of our building, which I suspected was because the Assad regime wanted to monitor the transmissions. It took a while for the message to get out, but I was finally able to send my daily message to Chuck before I met with Doctor Halabi in case it was a trap.

I walked down the block to what used to be a functioning bus stop not too long ago and waited. As I looked around at the decimated buildings and blown-out storefronts, I knew it would be years before another bus would travel this route in peace. I leaned against the pole with the bus stop sign affixed above my head and smoked a cigarette, waiting. At least the blown-out buildings provided a little shade from the sun.

Two cigarettes later, a small white sedan with a taxi sign on the roof came around the corner two blocks away. The driver gunned the engine when he saw me waiting at the bus stop in the distance. The car came to an abrupt stop at the curb where I stood.

The driver leaned over to the passenger side. "Angus?" he said with a thick accent.

"*Nam.*" I said. *Yes.*

"In, in. I drive you."

I flicked my cigarette away and climbed in the passenger seat.

"*Shukran,*" I said. *Thank you.*

The driver just smiled. Despite my repeated attempts to ask him about how things were in Syria, he just shrugged and pointed out the window.

"It is bad," was all he said.

He drove me several blocks, dodging piles of debris and smashed and burned-out cars in the roadway to a storefront with the front door propped open by bricks. The taxi driver motioned for me to get out.

I got out of the cab and began taking out my wallet.

He waved his finger back and forth at me. "No, no, professor pay."

I smiled and handed him a pack of Marlboros. He smiled back and took the smokes.

"*Shukran,*" he said and tore off down the road and turned right at the first cross street.

The taxi's engine noise faded around the corner. The neighborhood he dropped me in seemed a little less demolished than others I had seen, but still looked deserted. It was eerily quiet. I looked in the darkened shop and heard a faint hissing sound from deeper inside the darkened building.

"Come in, please," a voice said from inside the abandoned shop.

"Doctor Halabi?"

"Yes, come in."

I walked slowly past the empty, most likely looted, shelves. Only trash and broken furniture remained. I picked my way around fallen bookshelves and rounded a corner to find Doctor Halabi leaning over a camp stove that was resting on a broken chair, brewing tea.

"Doctor Halabi?"

"Yes."

"*Salaam alaikum.*"

"*Alaikum salaam,*" he said, returning the traditional greeting.

He offered his hand and I shook it. "Don't worry, Mr. Conn. I know you speak Arabic well, but I think it may be better to converse in English."

"That sounds good to me. Where did you study English?"

"I earned a Master's degree in archeology at Cambridge some years ago," he said with a slight English accent as he offered me a dusty chair. "Please, sit."

"Thank you."

I sat across from him as he tended to the water over the stove that was making the hissing sound I heard when I walked in.

"Do you like tea?"

"Very much."

"Good. I've been saving it for just such an occasion. We have much to discuss. I'm afraid I can't offer you any sugar; it and lots of other things have been gone for quite some time."

"That's okay, I understand."

"Were you able to verify the authenticity of the statuette I had delivered to you on your previous visit?"

"Yes. A contact I have at the Met in New York was very impressed."

I didn't have the heart to tell him that I still had it as a good luck charm here in Syria.

"Good."

"But he seemed to think that it may be difficult to move anything from Syria."

Doctor Halabi looked up from dunking his tea bag and smiled. "Yes, it will be very difficult indeed."

"No, I mean, he thinks that even when the artifacts are out of the country, there may be no buyers interested in paying for stolen relics from Syria."

I saw his expression change from tranquil to furious in an instant. "Don't you think I know that? I have people in Lebanon waiting for what I have. Their cooperation and payment is assured."

"Okay, I don't dispute that. I'm just telling you what my expert has told me."

"Expert?" he said indignantly. "Who can be an expert in something they have never experienced? Not even I am an expert in what is going on here. I have never had the occasion to empty my entire museum and load it on trucks in the middle of the night for fear of being shot while doing so."

He calmed and handed me the tea he was steeping for me in a porcelain cup that had managed to escape the destruction all around it with only one tiny chip on the rim. He then poured a serving for himself into a slightly more damaged cup with cracks like spider webs showing on the outside.

"Where are the artifacts?"

"They're safe."

We sat in silence for a few moments and sipped our tea. It was so pleasant that I momentarily forgot where I was. The tea was hot, strong, and soothing. It had been a long time since I'd had a good cup of tea. I looked around and collected my thoughts.

"This buyer you have in Lebanon, he can't get into the country to help you get the artifacts out?"

Doctor Halabi looked at me over his cup, "This man is an international banker with contacts in Dubai who will fly the artifacts where they will be stored safely once he takes possession of them. However, neither he nor any of his people are willing to come to Syria to retrieve them."

"How many trucks?"

"I could only salvage one truck's worth. The rest was looted after I loaded what I could. I managed to salvage the most important pieces, but any loss is great. These things are not just our heritage as Arabs, but it is the history of civilization itself. It makes me sad that we cannot look beyond our petty self-generated importance, greed, and politics to see what is important to protect in life."

"And what is that?"

"Our history and our future. Our link to history sits in a single truck waiting for someone to escort it to safety and our future lies with the children who are being killed every day here. My contact has promised me that if he is able to deliver my artifacts to his contacts, he will ensure a steady stream of weapons and aid will come from the deal."

"Did he tell you who was financing that?"

"Saudis, Qataris, Kuwaitis. They all want a chance to show the Arab world that they help safeguard its heritage while people like Assad squander it with deals with Russians and Persians."

"Where do I come in?" I said, leading him on.

"I need you to be there because if these men know that someone is watching, they will follow through. But if they think that no one knows, they will take but never pay."

"So you want me to accompany the truck to Lebanon?"

"Yes. I want you to go there and I want you to tell them that if they do not do as we agreed, you will go to the international press with the story. They will do the right thing if they know someone is watching. That is why I needed you here, Mr. Conn."

"Why do you believe you can trust me?"

"You are here, aren't you? At this point you are all I've got. No one else has agreed to help. Is there any reason I shouldn't trust you?"

I felt bad lying to him, but there was no way I was going to trade artifacts for weapons and help pour gasoline on the inferno that was engulfing everyone in this country. I would deliver the artifacts in exchange for buses to take the children of Al-Waer out of this conflict, just as I had planned.

"No. This is just a very risky enterprise. I need to know where everyone stands. It'll be my pleasure to help in any way I can," I said and raised my teacup in a sort of toast.

Damn the story. This trip is for the kids.

Chapter 16

Al-Waer, Syria
May 16, 2013

"Where are you going?" Rafi asked.

"Doctor Halabi wants me to accompany the artifacts to the Lebanese border where we crossed into Syria. A contact of his will meet us there and we'll make the switch," I said.

"I think this is a bad idea. You don't know these people. What if the deal is compromised in any way?"

"I guess I'm willing to take that chance. These people are risking everything. I don't think they're going to be careless. I think they'll have what they promised us."

"That's a lot of faith."

"Well, I'm not asking you to go, Rafi."

"I'm going, right?" Jake asked.

"Do you want to go?"

"Yeah. I think going by yourself is a bad idea. And I'm here as your assistant. You need an assistant, right?"

I looked at Rafi, but he just shrugged at me. "Yeah, I do. You think you're up for it? You'll be a bit more protected here, though."

"Really? Getting shelled every night is more secure than going with you to the Lebanon border?"

"He has a point. Maybe you should stick close to him," Rafi said.

"Now you want me to go?" I asked Rafi indignantly.

"Angus, you're going to go anyway, so we all might as well deal with it."

"Rafi, this is the story I came here to get. It's shaping up. I have to do it."

"I know. You go on your own with Brando here and make sure to give me a message when you get there. You'll be able to send me a message to your draft e-mail."

"Thanks, Rafi."

"I would have a boring life without crazy family. It's a gift."

I laughed at his sarcasm. "Good attitude."

"So, what's next?" Jake asked.

"He's going to send a runner for us when the meeting's set. He told me it would be in the next day or so. He's anxious to get the artifacts out of the country, so he's not wasting any time. Have your shit packed and ready to roll—"

"In one minute or less, I know," Jake interrupted.

"It's good to see you can take direction, Brando. An asset in your chosen profession I would think."

"Screw you. I'll be ready, 'Iceman,'" Jake said in a mocking tone.

* * *

May 17, 2013

The runner came the next day in the form of a ten-year-old boy in dirty, ripped jeans and a filthy red T-shirt. Rafi found me interviewing a rebel fighter on the roof who was assigned to watch for and report any regime tank movements while trying not to get sniped. I was lying on my stomach, scribbling in my journal as the soldier and I spoke in Arabic.

Rafi crawled up to me from the rooftop doorway. "The runner is here. The doctor wants you and Jake at his shop just after sunset this evening," Rafi said.

"Okay, thanks, Rafi."

"Are you sure about this, Angus? You don't have to do this."

"You know I do."

"You don't have to go kill yourself over guilt."

"It's not about that anymore. This has to be done. Who else will do it?"

"No one else will do it because it's too dangerous."

"You know I have to, Rafi."

Rafi just shook his head. "Don't forget to e-mail Chuck. If you don't come back, I don't want to waste any time letting people know."

"Thanks, brother."

Rafi just shook his head and crawled back to the doorway.

Chapter 17

May 17, 2013

The same driver picked us up right at sunset. He took a different route to the doctor's shop than when I went with him a day earlier.

"Is the other way blocked?"

"Yes. A building collapsed yesterday after the regime shelled the neighborhood. It crushed a whole family," he said in Arabic. "The way is blocked. I must go around two more blocks to get there. But don't worry. It is out of range of the snipers."

Now that people know I'm here and speaking with Doctor Halabi, I wonder if Rafi's right. This may be a setup.

"What are you guys talking about?" Jake asked.

"He said a building collapsed and blocked the way, but this way will get us there safely."

"I'm sure safely is a relative term."

I smiled.

He's dead-on. Everything here is, indeed, relative.

A few minutes later we pulled up to the doctor's shop and we all got out. I handed the driver two packs of cigarettes and he smiled. Then we heard the incoming shells.

"Get inside," I said to Jake as I pushed him through the door. The driver hit the gas and chirped the tires as he sped off down the street.

The ground shook as several shells impacted a block away and covered us all with dust. We waited for a few seconds in case there was another barrage coming, but it remained quiet.

I heard a rustling in the backroom where the doctor and I shared tea the day before. "Doctor? Are you okay?"

"Yes," he said from around the corner. "Are you okay?"

"You okay?" I asked Jake.

"Yeah."

"We're okay," I yelled loud enough to be heard.

"Come in, I'll make some tea before the next barrage."

I looked at Jake. "You're right. Everything's relative."

* * *

I introduced Jake to Doctor Halabi and he thanked us for being there. We sat around the small room and sipped our tea, hoping for enough time to enjoy it.

"What is the plan for tonight?" I asked.

"We will walk to a nearby football field. Oh, sorry, you Americans call it soccer. My contact will pick us up and take us to the man who will drive the truck with the artifacts to Lebanon."

"Where is the truck?"

"It is hidden in a garage a short walk from the football field."

"Who is your driver?"

"He is a friend of one of my colleagues. I trust him with my life."

"But you don't know the driver?"

"No. I don't need to. I just need to trust my friend."

Jake and I looked at each other. I had a bad feeling but had to trust him or we couldn't move forward with my plan.

* * *

An hour later, Doctor Halabi, Jake, and I stood around in the dark at a dirt soccer field where the community's youth had gathered at one point to play. It was covered with trash and debris from nearby bombed-out buildings. It was a sad reminder that things had not been normal here in a long time. We waited in the dark for the doctor's driver to arrive.

"When did your friend say this man would arrive?"

"Don't worry, he'll be here," Doctor Halabi said.

A few minutes later we heard footsteps approaching from the dark street behind us.

"Who is there?" the doctor challenged the man in Arabic.

"*Salaam alaikum*, I am from Aleppo. Are you from the museum?" the man said in return as he appeared from the darkness.

"Yes, my friend. *Alaikum salaam*," Doctor Halabi said.

"Good, I am here to help you," the man said.

Doctor Halabi embraced the man and kissed him on both cheeks. "Who are these men?" the man asked, looking at us.

"These are my friends who will accompany you to Lebanon."

The stocky man in dirty brown desert camouflage pants and a black T-shirt, who would be our driver, looked at us and smiled. "*Allahu akbar*," the man said.

He shook our hands and embraced Jake and me with cheek kisses as well.

"You are not coming?" he asked Doctor Halabi.

"No, just these two will go with you," the doctor said and pointed to Jake and me.

"Okay, where is the truck?"

"It is not far, let's go."

We all followed Doctor Halabi, single file, down a rubble-ridden street to a garage door about a block away. The doctor took a key from his pocket and unlocked a padlock that secured the corrugated metal garage door, which rolled open with a loud rumble. The headlights on the front grill of a large, dusty flatbed truck stared at us from the dark garage. We shimmied past the truck and the scrap metal, tires, and engine parts that lined the walls.

"This is it," the doctor said. "The artifacts are packed in the back."

"Let's take a look," the driver said.

He took a flashlight from his pocket and made his way to the rear of the truck. We all followed as the driver climbed in the back and pulled up the tarp that hid the ancient contents. He flashed his light around and unwrapped a few blankets that protected the artifacts. He inspected the first few he saw, then replaced the blankets and hopped down from the truck.

"It looks good, my friend," he said to Doctor Halabi.

"I left a little bit of room for some barrels filled with scrap metal that we can put at the tailgate to hide the load in case you are stopped and inspected. You can say that you are taking the metal to a town in the west to trade for food and water."

"Good," the man said.

"We should load the barrels now. There are enough of us to form a line and fill the barrels with these piles of scrap metal I have collected over here," Doctor Halabi said, pointing to the dark corner of the garage.

The driver shined his flashlight behind him and illuminated several piles of rebar and pieces of metal from destroyed appliances and vehicles he had collected.

"This is good work. Doctor, you are truly a patriot for the Syrian people," he said. "*Allahu akbar.*"

"Should we get started?"

"No, let's see if the truck starts first," the driver said.

"It works. I parked it here only a few days ago."

"I want to make sure," the driver said as he walked around to the driver's side door, opened it and climbed in the cab.

"What's he doing?" Jake asked.

The man stopped cold at the sound of Jake's voice. "Americans?"

"Yes. These men are journalists who will come with you to document the trip and help arrange the transfer in Lebanon."

The driver sat for a moment and stared at the doctor and then smiled. "*Allahu akbar.* Do you have the keys?" he asked Doctor Halabi in Arabic.

Doctor Halabi handed him the keys and the driver put it in neutral and cranked the engine. It took a few times but the truck roared to life with a cloud of black smoke. He revved the engine for a few moments and then let the truck idle. He looked at the doctor and smiled a sinister smile as he laid on the horn and sent out three distinct signals into the night air.

"What are you doing?" Doctor Halabi cried.

He jumped up to the cab to stop him from honking the horn. The driver held the steering wheel and kicked the doctor in the chest, which sent him to the ground in a heap. The driver jumped down and pulled a small revolver from the cargo pocket in his pants and pointed it at my face.

"On the ground," he yelled in Arabic.

I put my hands up and got to my knees. "Get on the ground," I said in English so Jake could understand.

The driver pointed the gun at me, "Yes. Do as he says," he said to me in English as he smiled.

As Jake and I got to the ground several men, dressed in standard Syrian Army camouflage, poured into the garage from the darkness, toting AK-47s and shouting, "*Allahu akbar!*"

The soldiers cuffed each of us with zip ties and dragged us to the back of the garage. They lined us up in a row and closed the garage door.

The driver walked up to Doctor Halabi, knelt down, and pulled his head up by the hair so he could see him. "How did you think you were going to get away with trading our country's heritage for weapons to defeat us? You are a traitor and will pay dearly for this," he said and slammed the doctor's head into the concrete floor.

The driver got to his feet and began kicking Doctor Halabi in the head and torso. A few of the soldiers ran over and began pummeling his body relentlessly.

I yelled out in Arabic for them to stop.

The driver shouted to his men to stop and knelt down beside my head next. "You should be more concerned about your own life, American. I can assure you that the regime will not be kind to foreigners who try to impose godless American influence where it does not belong," he said in English.

The driver stood, called his soldiers over, and told them to put us in the back of the truck. Two soldiers took us one at a time and threw us on top of each other in the back of the truck.

After a few moments of writhing pain, the three of us managed to arrange ourselves in the bed of the truck so we could breathe and not suffocate one another as our bodies intertwined. We heard the driver issue orders to his men to follow him as he got in the truck and drove us out of the garage into the darkness with the soldiers following in a pickup truck close behind.

I managed to catch Jake's eyes in the glare from the truck's headlights. I could see he was scared and pissed at being wrong. I just shook my head and looked away. Who was right or wrong didn't matter at that moment. Just like that, we were prisoners of the regime.

Chapter 18

Six miles west of Homs, Syria
May 17, 2013

The truck bounced down dirt roads that led away from the city. I saw that the soldiers were following too close behind us to attempt an escape. The doctor was bleeding from his nose, mouth, and multiple lacerations on his face, and probably was suffering from internal bleeding as well. He winced in pain with every bump in the road. I couldn't bear to think of leaving him like this, even if he was responsible for getting us into this mess. My hands were bound but my mind was running itself ragged trying to figure every angle. I couldn't see us getting out of this situation easily. Then there were gunshots.

I put my head down below the steel tailgate of the truck to protect myself the best I could. Bullets pinged off the side of the truck. The noise was deafening as the soldiers in the truck behind us stopped and returned fire.

Our truck kept its pace down the dirt road and then picked up speed as the driver tried to get away from the unknown assailant's kill zone. We were tossed into the air as the truck launched over the constant potholes and ruts in the road.

I saw a bright flash out of the corner of my eye and knew what it was.

"Get down, RPG!"

We all hugged the floor of the truck and waited. The seconds seemed to slow down as we awaited our fate. The truck shuddered a half-second before the force of the explosion catapulted us into the air. I saw the burning cab of the truck from a surprising perspective about ten feet above and behind it. And then I began to fall. I saw the dark ground approaching below me right before I blacked out.

* * *

I woke to a steady ringing in my ears with a glorious view of the clear night sky and a random sprinkling of billions of stars staring down at me with an infinite variance of intensity. The stars should have soothed me, but they actually deepened my despair over our situation. While I was relieved to still be alive, I was taken by the thought that if the universe was so large, it made the suffering I've witnessed and my own struggles virtually insignificant next to the boundless mural of glittering radiance above me.

My depressing thoughts were interrupted by searing pain in my hips and legs as I realized I was lying in the bed of a small truck this time. It felt as though we were climbing a hill as the truck struggled against a slight incline. I looked around as best I could, as I didn't want to be noticed in case there was anyone in the back with me.

My right side was pressed against the side of the truck so I looked to my left and saw a blanket covering something. My hands were still bound behind my back so I couldn't reach out to feel for anything. I pushed up against the blanket beside me and it felt like a body. I pressed my arm up against it and it still felt warm. That was a good sign.

The government obviously decided not to honor Bill and his contacts' arrangements and wanted to teach us Westerners a lesson. But ISIS hijacking us and destroying the artifacts was something I hadn't forseen. There wasn't much I could do about my situation so I just stared at the stars for a few minutes. I finally closed my eyes and tried to ignore the pain in my legs and arms as the truck continued uphill.

Chapter 19

May 17, 2013
Unknown Location in northern Syria

I wasn't sleeping, just resting my eyes, when I heard the men in the truck shouting, "*Allahu akbar*," out the windows. They were answered by dozens of, "*Allahu akbars*," on both sides of the truck as we drove past. I could just see their heads racing past from my vantage point lying in the back of the bed. Some wore black headbands and some shrouded their entire head in black cloth with just a slit for the eyes.

The truck slowed to a stop and the men in front got out. The sky had lightened to a pale blue as the morning sun brightened the horizon in the east. I took note of where east was to orient myself.

Men on either side of the truck's bed, dressed in black balaclavas, black shirts, and ammunition vests, reached in and grabbed me, forcibly pulling me out of the truck. I cried in agony as my left hip felt injured but I didn't know how badly. I just knew it hurt, and my legs were asleep. The men stood me up and I immediately fell to the dusty ground.

They all laughed. I could hear a couple comments in Arabic on how weak the Westerners were. I thought I was doing okay for surviving an RPG attack only a few hours before. I didn't say anything because I didn't want anyone to know that I could understand a bit of Arabic. That would remain my secret as a captive.

Two black-clad soldiers pulled me up by my armpits and dragged me to a nearby cinder block building. They dropped me at the base of an external concrete stairwell that led a few flights to the top of the building. I watched as they pulled Jake, who might have been unconscious but alive, I couldn't tell for sure, and the doctor who was definitely unconscious.

Once we were all lined up at the base of the stairwell, they grabbed me first and pulled me up each flight of stairs. I tried to move my legs but they were still asleep from lack of circulation on the drive. They pulled me with much effort as the tops of my feet dragged over each step. I chuckled to myself. I could see that it was difficult for them, but I didn't care.

They sat me in the far corner of the room and left one guy as a guard while other men delivered their prisoners. There was one small window covered with a blanket that looked to be nailed to the cinder block wall. There was also a small door that led out to a balcony. Two large metal wardrobes placed side by side blocked the access to the door and the balcony beyond.

When all three of us were finally delivered to what seemed to be our prisoner's cell, the men left and I heard one of them instructing a guard to post himself at the bottom of the stairs near our floor and shoot us if we tried to escape.

I rolled over and lay on the side that wasn't injured and tried to ignore the pins and needles that were plaguing my legs. It hurt, but that was a good sign. Since my blood circulation was returning to my legs, I didn't seem to be permanently disabled. Only my left hip was bothering me and the zip ties had cut into my wrists, but that seemed fairly minor considering our recent ordeal.

After my eyes had adjusted to the near darkness in the room, I looked over at Jake. He was breathing steadily and didn't seem to be in any visible pain or have any bleeding wounds that I could see. I looked over at Doctor Halabi next and noticed he was wincing with his eyes closed, another good sign. He had come out of unconsciousness and was feeling pain.

"I'm sorry, Angus," Jake whispered to me as he looked into my eyes.

"What are you sorry for?"

"I shouldn't have made you take me into Syria or on this story. We all knew it was dangerous."

"Come on, Jake. It was my stupidity that gave in to you. I would have gone anyway. I can't blame you for this."

"Good. Can I blame you then?" he chuckled.

"If it makes you feel better." I smiled.

"I don't think anything will make me feel better right now. What do you think these guys are going to do with us?"

"Once they figure out who they have, I'm sure they will try to get some ransom," I said.

"What do you think they'll do to the doctor?"

"I don't know. Maybe they'll try to recover the artifacts."

"Do you think they were destroyed? After they blew up the truck, I don't know what happened," Jake said.

"The truck was blown over on its side by an RPG. It's probably still there on the side of the road. I don't know if they knew there were artifacts in it. They may still be there."

"These guys are ISIS, right?" Jake asked.

"Judging from their black clothes and the fact they attacked a regime convoy, I would say that's a safe bet. We could be in for a long stay with these guys," I said.

"Yeah, but we're getting some exclusive stuff here," Jake smiled.

"Yeah, no other journalists are dumb enough to get captured by ISIS just to get an exclusive story. Congratulations," I said.

"In some circles that's called dedication, isn't it?"

"Not in my circle."

Chapter 20

ISIS compound outside Al-Waer, Syria
May 17, 2013

I wasn't sure how long I had been asleep, probably not for long. It was difficult to sleep in the constant heat. Even at night. The heat enveloped us and made it feel like we were sitting in a sauna.

My consciousness was alerted by footsteps crunching the gravel outside on the way to the stairs to our door. My stomach was doing cartwheels and not in a good way. These guys were known for torture and even executing Westerners.

The man outside unlocked the padlock that kept the door secured and kicked it open. The door swung open violently and smashed up against the wall. The latch on the inside of the door hit so hard it made a divot in the cinder block wall. The man stood in the doorway wearing black from head to toe. He just stood there for a second, probably letting his eyes adjust to the relative darkness in the room. For all he knew, I could have been waiting to attack him when he came in. After this visit, I would seriously think about it.

He finally saw me sitting against the wall near the corner and came after me with crazy eyes full of rage. He wrapped his arm around my neck and dragged me halfway across the room. I tried to yell but could only grunt as his tight grip on my throat cut off my air. He threw me to the ground and my head bounced off the hard floor. I immediately saw stars and gulped for air as I tried to catch my breath.

My hands were still bound behind my back so there was no way for me to deflect his next assault. The man grabbed my shirt at my chest with his left hand and pulled my back up just off the ground and pummeled my face with his right fist. He threw jabs to my nose and cheek, a slight roundhouse to my left jaw, and followed up with a solid punch to the neck just to keep me guessing and coughing again. Then the kicks began.

He let me go and my head hit the floor again. My entire face was throbbing, and I was coughing up blood while trying to breathe, thanks to his punches to my neck. I rolled onto my side to try and get more air and felt his steel-toed boot impact my ribs. I cried out in pain and absorbed another kick to the stomach.

I wasn't sure how much more of this I could take. If he kept on, I would suffocate or die of internal bleeding. I felt like I could at least try to knock him off balance, but that would most likely not make me his favorite prisoner and would earn me more beatings later. I just steeled myself as best I could, took his kicks, and tried to ignore the pain. Lucky for me, he got tired and quit after one more kick.

"You filthy infidel, I'll teach you to come here and interfere with things that do not concern you," he yelled and then spit on me a few times before he turned his attention to Jake.

When the guy tried to pick Jake up and do what he did to me, Jake leaned up and head butted the guy hard enough to knock him down stunned. I guess Jake had seen too many movies, go figure. The guy's buddies must have seen it happen from the outside because in a second or two, there were two of them working Jake over.

"Just take the beating, Jake. Don't fight back," I said between coughs.

I only heard Jake grunt in reply as he dutifully took his beating.

* * *

I had managed to fall asleep despite my injuries, the hard concrete floor, random gunfire in the distance, and the incessant heat. I heard heavy footsteps that belonged to combat boots on the stairs that led up to the only door to the room we were in. I had to think for a second to figure out where I was and what had happened over the course of the last several hours. I actually thought a few of the things I conjured up from my memory could have been a dream, but then I felt the pain. The same pain that I had felt in what I thought was my dream. But it was all really happening. I was still being held captive by ISIS after they RPGed the regime truck we were riding in a few hours before.

I steeled my nerves for what I was sure to be another beat down, but two men ignored Jake and me and just came to take Doctor Halabi away. I felt like a shit for thinking it, but I was relieved that they turned their attention to Doctor Halabi instead of us. I'm not sure what they did with him; we never saw Doctor Halabi again.

My fears returned a few hours later when the door to our makeshift cell flew open and a line of dark figures filed into the room, their bodies silhouetted against the deep blue night sky outside. Two men grabbed Jake and me and didn't even give us a chance to stand. They yanked us by our bound hands face down with the tops of our shoes dragging across the floor behind us again. They pulled us down the stairs and across a small dirt courtyard to an open door on the first floor of the main building across from where they were holding us.

My escorts threw me down to the ground and walked out. Jake's guys just dropped him next to me and then filed out behind the first two. We were alone in another dark room with only the light shining from under a nearby door to an adjacent room.

"What do you think they're doing?" Jake whispered.

"I don't know. Sometimes they like to make propaganda videos or intimidate their prisoners. So, just be cool and don't piss them off. But fight for your life if you need to."

"What the hell does that mean?"

"It means I don't have all the fucking answers. Sometimes you have to go with the flow. Do whatever you need to do, but remember that you have to live with your actions, so try to think before you act," I said, a little annoyed.

I saw footsteps approaching the door where the light was coming from. It opened and a single figure stood in the doorway, his body dark against the lit up room behind him.

"Abdul Haqq will see you now," the man said in English. "Get to your feet and kneel before him."

Jake and I got to our feet, our hands still bound behind our backs. I walked up slowly to a man dressed in all black with a mask that covered his whole face except for his eyes. Those eyes scowled at me from behind his costume.

I knelt down a few feet in front of Abdul Haqq. Jake followed my lead and did the same. I looked around the room as far as I could without moving my head, recognizing a large lion statue and an armored rider atop a majestic horse with a flowing mane that flanked Abdul Haqq's chair. I recognized the rider from the back of the archeologist's truck before it was RPGed.

Abdul Haqq caught me looking, smiled, and rubbed the head of the horse rider that sat at eye-level next to him. "Do you recognize my new decorations?" he said in British-accented English.

"These are from Doctor Halabi's truck," I said.

"They were never his property to take," he said in a low and even tone. "They belong to Syrians and they belong in Syria. They definitely do not belong in the hands of Westerners who aim to trade them for weapons to kill Muslims."

"Are you Syrian? Where did you learn English?"

"Silence!" Abdul Haqq yelled. "You will only speak when you are spoken to. Is that understood?"

Jake and I both said nothing in reply.

The man who ordered us in the room was standing behind us. He came around and kicked me in the ribs and then did the same to Jake. We both fell to the floor, wheezing in pain.

"You both are pathetic. You have the audacity to come here and report lies about things you know nothing about and embroil yourselves in conspiracies that will kill people in my organization, Muslims, and you do not think we will find you and punish you for this. You are arrogant imbeciles."

Abdul Haqq flicked his wrist in a nonchalant gesture and said to his assistant, "Hit them again."

"With pleasure," his assistant said in English, but with an accent I couldn't place.

He kicked me again in the ribs. The pain nauseated me so badly I felt like I could have thrown up at any moment. I watched the man kick Jake in the stomach, but it didn't look like it fazed him as much.

We both coughed in pain and panted for a few seconds before Abdul Haqq continued. "These ancient decorations that we recovered from the truck stand as vivid reminders of what exactly my mission is in this country. It is to return to Syria what has always been for Syrians. To purge non-believers and Western forces alike from these ancient lands. To take back what is rightfully ours and give it to the believers of Allah, the one true God, and pledge our eternal efforts to fighting all who aim to oppose his will on Earth," he said, and then paused for a moment. "*Takbir*!" he cried.

"*Allahu akbar*!" the other man yelled.

"I can tell you one thing. You will both regret your decision to come to Syria to tell lies about our cause to the world. I will truly make you pay for this mistake. It will be up to your government or your news agency whether you leave here in one piece or not. Until word comes whether we will be compensated for your arrogance, I will be a gracious host and use your abilities as journalists to show the world the truth. You will be my guest journalists until it is decided whether you will live through this experience or not. Now, get out of my sight before I change my mind about showing you undeserved mercy."

I looked at Jake. He just stared at a spot on the rug a few inches in front of him. I didn't move.

"Abdul Aziz, get these infidels out of my sight before I execute them right now."

"Yes, Abdul Haqq."

The other man grabbed my bound arm and pulled me hard across the room to the closed door. He returned to where Jake lay and pulled him almost gently across the room next to me. He opened the door and ordered the same four men who dragged us in to return us to our holding room in the building next door.

Chapter 21

May 18, 2013

I couldn't tell how long it had been since Jake and I were first introduced to Abdul Haqq, the leader of this local ISIS unit, but I saw daylight pouring through the crack under the metal door that held us in our small prison room. I looked over and saw Jake lying on his side. I could see him breathing and was envious that he was sleeping.

I tried to roll over and go to sleep myself, but couldn't. My ribs hurt and the circulation in my legs was still not fully recovered. I felt pins and needles whenever I moved either one of them. I tried to relax and think of what Rafi and Chuck were doing right now to help us get out of this mess. By now, Chuck should have seen that I hadn't checked in via any means, e-mail, phone call, anything. In that instance, he would mobilize anyone in the area he could contact to try and get information on our whereabouts. He would have already begun communicating with the U.S. Embassy in Beirut and other journalists who could possibly verify information and standby to help any way they could.

A few minutes later, I heard the dreaded footsteps come up the stairs outside. The metal door swung open and Abdul Aziz, the short, stocky assistant to Abdul Haqq, closed the door behind him and walked right past me.

He sat down a foot or two in front of Jake. "Wake up, my friend," he said to Jake.

Jake stirred and sat up with a grimace on his face from similar pains that I too felt from our earlier beatings. Jake finally rested against the wall but didn't look him in the eye. He stared down at the floor in front of him.

The man smiled and reached forward to lift Jake's bowed head under his chin with his fingers. Jake looked at the man's smiling face with a blank expression.

"I am Abdul Aziz and I know who you are," the man said in his accented English. "You're from Hollywood, yeah?"

The way he said Hollywood and the way he ended it with a "yeah" gave him away as an Aussie or a Kiwi. My guess was Aussie.

"No. I am just his assistant."

"No. I will show you that you are lying. I have proof," he said and smiled.

He pulled a thin DVD case from his cargo pocket. It was a bootleg copy of a Hollywood movie that was easy to get from street vendors all over the Middle East. This one was *Ghost Hunt*, one of Jake's recent movies.

Abdul Aziz handed the DVD case to Jake and pointed to a picture of someone on the front. "This is George Clooney and this is you, my friend. I know it. I have seen this movie many times."

It was ironic to see Jake using all of his acting talent to deny that he was actually a movie star. Not something that was easy for him. At this point in his career, he would normally be very happy to be recognized by people on the street. But at this moment, being recognized was not good for anyone, most of all him.

"No. That is not me."

The man began to look a bit angry and then took a deep breath to suppress his frustration. "I know it is you. You are Jake Westin. I have seen all of your movies. You have done four movies. Each one better than the last."

I wanted to get a little heat off Jake, so I tried my best. "Your English is excellent. Where did you study?" I said to Abdul Aziz.

He shot me a look. "I am from Sydney. We have come from everywhere, committed to defend our faith from your corruptible ways that have permeated our world."

"Are there other Westerners here?"

"Shut up, liar. You and your colleagues lie to the western world about us and our faith for a living. I will not speak to you. I am speaking to Jake. When I speak to you, I will use my fist," he said and held up his fingerless-gloved hand.

"This is you, correct?" he said to Jake.

"No."

Abdul Aziz smiled and shook his head. "I know it is you. You don't have to be afraid. I will not tell Abdul Haqq. He will only try to ransom you for more money. More money would be good for us, but if he did not get it, he would kill you. And then I would not be able to see any of your future films. So do not worry. This will be our secret."

The movie lover dug into his vest pocket and pulled out an iPhone.

He looked over at me. "You see, we have technology, too. We use your inventions to further our cause. We use the Internet and social media to good effect. This is your curse. The West does things in an arrogant, self-righteous, and condescending manner and you do not even realize that what you create will one day defeat you. We will use everything to keep you from poisoning our culture."

The irony of his words almost made me laugh. I suppressed it because I didn't feel like taunting him into beating me, but watching him lecture me on how our society and way of life were a detriment to his own in one moment and then, in the next, accost his favorite Hollywood movie star like a giddy teenager, was a telling contradiction that was going to make it into print if I lived through this ordeal.

He showed Jake his iPhone, positioned himself next to Jake, and held the phone up in front of them. "Come, look up. I will take a picture. What do you call it? A 'selfie'? It is an honor to have you as a prisoner, Jake."

Jake stared into the phone's camera with an expressionless look that could have won him an Oscar. I knew he was thinking the same thing.

Abdul Aziz snapped a few pictures and looked at them and smiled. He got up and pocketed the DVD case and his phone. "Thank you, Jake. It is a pleasure to meet you," he said and walked out.

A few minutes later, once I heard Abdul Aziz had walked away and knew no one was listening, I whispered, "Good job, Jake. Don't ever admit who you are. It could be bad for all of us."

"I know," he said. "Don't be the story, right?" he said and lay down on the concrete floor with his back to me.

* * *

Later that evening, a soldier came in with a portion of flat bread and a small bottle of water for Jake and me. We each devoured the bread and sucked down the water.

About an hour later, Abdul Aziz came in and dropped a pack of cigarettes and a lighter in Jake's lap. "These are for you, my friend."

"I don't smoke," he lied.

"Now may be a good time to start," Abdul Aziz smiled. "Come, you must go outside and get some fresh air. Don't worry, Abdul Haqq is not here. He went to ambush another regime convoy. It will just be you and me. I want you to tell me about Hollywood."

Abdul Aziz offered Jake his hand and helped him to his feet. They walked out together. I looked at Jake as he left the room, but he avoided my eyes.

* * *

Jake returned thirty minutes later and sat down in the corner as far away as he could get from me.

"What did you tell him?"

"I told him a few things I knew about Hollywood but never admitted anything."

I shook my head. "You need to be careful, Jake. You can't confide anything in him. It will come back to bite us all."

"What the fuck do you know? We're all in this mess because of you," he said and lay down facing the wall.

"You're the one who insisted on coming here, Jake. Remember that."

Chapter 22

May 19, 2013

Abdul Aziz came to our cell the next day and, this time, centered himself on me instead of Jake.

"You two will come with me. Abdul Haqq wants to show you what happens to non-believers in the new Islamic State."

Two of the ISIS fighters put a blindfold over our heads before they led us to what I perceived to be the back of a van. It made me laugh to think that they actually thought we may be able to recognize landmarks among what amounted to a dusty moonscape littered with clumps of smashed and burned-out apartment buildings.

The driver was constantly making violent turns and even made a few U-turns along the way. I wasn't sure whether it was because the roads were blocked from debris, if they happened upon regime soldiers, or if they were just enjoying throwing us around the back, but the drive lasted an arduous twenty minutes before we stopped and they took off our blindfolds.

When my blindfold came off, Abdul Aziz stood in front of me and handed me my digital video camera.

"You will document our triumph," he said.

Abdul Aziz turned to go up a flight of stairs in front of us. Jake and I followed him slowly up each section of stairs. My limbs ached from being lethargic in captivity and sleeping on the concrete floor, not to mention the cuts and bruises we'd accumulated from being beaten and thrown around the back of our truck as it was RPGed.

We arrived at a doorway that led to the roof. Abdul Aziz stopped there and allowed us to catch up.

"When we go onto the roof, you will duck down so you will not be seen. If you make any attempt to be seen, we will shoot you in the head. Is that understood?"

We both nodded yes.

Abdul Aziz smiled. "Good. Do not worry. This will be fun."

* * *

I couldn't believe what I was looking at. An ISIS fighter sat in an old wooden office chair mounted to a steel frame that was connected directly to the back of a large parabolic satellite TV dish. It was also mounted on a swivel so it could turn and follow targets but keep the shooter in the chair hidden behind the dish. They had drilled holes large enough for the barrel and scope of a sniper rifle to peer through the dish and engage targets without being seen. The only hazard I could see was the flash of the muzzle or dust rising up from the shockwave of the bullet as it left the gun. As rudimentary as it looked, it was also an example of how innovatively devious and ultimately dangerous these people were.

Abdul Aziz slapped his hand on the base of the contraption. "This is one of our most effective secret weapons."

"This satellite dish hiding a sniper is your most effective secret weapon? I'm not sure that's going to be enough to take down Western non-believers and the Assad regime."

Abdul Aziz's smile faded. "I said it was just one of our most effective weapons. You may laugh your condescending laugh, but we have hundreds and hundreds of these things on rooftops throughout the country. One or two shooters are an annoyance but thousands of them will sustain our dominance. One of these may make you a believer one day," he said as he slapped it again, "right before it sends you to hell."

I didn't say anything in return. There was nothing to say. My words would have just made things worse. I shouldn't have said anything in the first place.

"Where do you want me to film?"

Abdul Aziz pointed to a hole a bit larger than the two drilled for the sniper to the right of where he sat and just about at a six-foot eye level. There was a flat platform mounted to the back of the satellite dish that was attached to hold a video camera.

"You will place your camera on the platform, line up the lens to view through the hole and then you can let it run. It will record everything our brave warrior sees from his chair."

I moved over to the platform and placed my camera on it. I lined up the lens to the hole they had drilled and started it rolling.

I looked over at Abdul Aziz and smiled. "I guess you guys thought of everything."

"We are not as stupid as you think, Mr. Conn."

"I never said you were stupid. I just don't think you're going to win."

* * *

"Abdul Aziz, I have a target," the sniper said in Arabic from behind the satellite dish.

"*Allahu akbar*," Abdul Aziz said. "Come, you will watch how effective we can be."

Abdul Aziz, Jake, and I all crawled over to the edge of the rooftop and slowly raised our heads above the low wall. I saw two regime tanks approaching through a dusty field in the distance. Both tank commanders had their hatches up and were standing in the open turret with the top half of their bodies exposed. There was an armored plate that protected them from direct fire from the front but nothing from the sides or overhead.

If the tanks turned toward our position, the sniper would not pass up such a juicy target. I watched as the tank crossed what used to be a dirt soccer field and rolled over the fence on the other side. The driver turned to his right to continue down the street in our direction. I silently cursed the driver and tank commander for being so stupid, but there was no way to know every hazard. They would likely pay with their lives for their carelessness.

The sniper let out a laugh. "Abdul Aziz, they are turning toward us," he said, keeping his eye on the scope of his Russian-made Dragunov sniper rifle.

"*Allahu akbar*. Shoot the second tank commander first so the lead will not notice and then shoot the lead commander," Abdul Aziz said in Arabic to his soldier.

I watched intently at the scene below. I hoped these two men, regime or not, would be spared. It is tough to watch men die. Even when you know some may deserve it. I had witnessed many deaths in my time reporting the news and every one affects you. Some more than others, but the images are held in your brain forever.

I didn't want to remember these two men's deaths, but I'm a journalist, so I couldn't look away. If there was nothing I could do, at least I could document it and show it as an example of what's going on here. There has to be some good that comes out of all of this bad.

The lead tank commander was wearing a bright green bandana around his neck. I didn't know if it was of religious origin or not, but a deep green is the color of Islam. These were Syrian regime tanks. The governing elites were Alawites. I wasn't sure why one of their tank commanders would be wearing an Islamic green bandana, but there were Sunnis and Shi'a in the army as well.

I watched the tank in trail as the crack of the sniper's first round hit the tank commander in the face. I saw a cloud of red mist explode from his head and he fell out of sight into the open hatch of his tank. I shifted my eyes to the lead tank commander, the one with the green bandana. I knew he was next. The far tank hadn't sent a radio message that their commander had been hit yet, because the lead tank just kept going. He was getting closer and closer to his inevitable death.

Just as the sniper shot a second time, the lead tank commander swiveled in his cupola to look to his rear. He must have just gotten word of his comrade's death. Sparks shot up from the armored plate in front of the lead tank commander as the sniper's shot impacted it. I saw him clutch his neck and disappear inside the tank and shut the hatch. I smiled.

Lucky fella.

* * *

It only took about ten seconds for both tanks to swivel their turrets in our direction and begin firing both their machine guns and their cannons at our building. I didn't think they could see any real targets, but they knew the general direction of where the sniper's rounds originated. They weren't taking any more chances. They were hosing down the place. The building shook beneath our feet as multiple tank rounds impacted the building on floors below us.

Abdul Aziz grabbed his AK-47 and got up to a crouch. "Stay here. I will come and get you and we will all go together. But first, I must fight."

He took off running in a crouch to the far side of the building and took up positions just below the low roof wall with a few of his fellow ISIS fighters. They stood two at a time and unloaded their magazines on the tanks below. When the first two had shot their magazines empty, they crouched down to reload as another two stood to keep a constant rate of fire on the tanks. They were very disciplined in their fighting skill, but not very effective since small arms against tanks were virtually useless. I was happy to watch them waste their ammunition and scream, "*Allahu akbar*," in what amounted to nothing but a morale-building exercise.

The tank's fire had gotten a bit more accurate after Abdul Aziz and his men opened fire from the roof. The tank's machine gun rounds were impacting the low wall where they hid. A few seconds later, the ISIS secret weapon and the sniper hiding behind it took dozens of direct hits. I looked back and saw the sniper fall to the ground with several bright red splotches on his black tunic. He wasn't moving. Several more machine gun rounds knocked the satellite dish to the ground.

I looked at Jake. He had his head between his knees and his fingers in his ears. It would only be a matter of time before we would be victims of this attack as well.

I nudged Jake. "Come here. Help me."

"Help with what?"

"We're gonna send this thing over the side."

"What?"

"Just follow my lead and help me get this satellite dish."

I looked over at Abdul Aziz. He was fully engaged with firing at the tanks below.

"Let's go, now!" I yelled and crept over to the satellite dish a few feet away. "Get on that side and help me pick it up."

"Why?"

"Just do it."

I grabbed my video camera from its place on the satellite dish and placed it on the ground. It was intact. We both grabbed a side and picked up the dish. It was lighter than I expected and we easily lifted it up and pushed it over the low wall. It disappeared over the side of the building. The noise from the gunfire was so loud that we didn't hear it hit the ground below. I grabbed my camera and we both ducked back down as if nothing had happened.

"Why the hell did we just do that?"

"It will be found by the tankers and then they'll know about the ISIS secret weapon."

"I thought you weren't supposed to be the story, Angus."

"Yeah, yeah. Screw these guys."

Abdul Aziz returned to our position about a minute later once he and his men were out of ammunition. He had his men carry the dead sniper off the roof and down the stairs. I could see in his eyes that he was pumped up on adrenaline. That was probably why he didn't notice that his secret weapon was gone.

"Come, we are done here. We need to go before they call for reinforcements."

We gladly followed Abdul Aziz down the stairs and away from the kill zone on the roof.

* * *

Abdul Aziz didn't bother blindfolding us for the return trip to their base. The driver drove even faster and more violently on the way back. All of the men were jubilant despite the fact that one of their own was dead and still bleeding in the back of the van. A few of them praised him for his sacrifice and spoke of how grateful they were to serve among martyrs like him.

Jake and I were escorted back to our cell on the second floor and Abdul Aziz took my camera.

"I am glad you retrieved your camera. Now we have proof for Adbul Haqq of our brother's martyrdom. What happened to the satellite dish?"

"The tanks destroyed it with machine gun fire," I lied.

I held my breath and hoped he hadn't seen us throw it off the building.

He nodded his head. "That is okay. We have many more of those tools and many more men willing to die for Allah. Now you see our dedication. Do you think we will lose now?"

I didn't say anything. I fought the urge to reply.

Abdul Aziz smiled. "You will see, Mr. Conn, there is no way we can lose. It is only after much sacrifice that we will be triumphant over the dead bodies of the infidels. It will take time, but as you have seen, we have many who are willingly filling the ranks to establish an Islamic State."

Chapter 23

May 20, 2013

The day after we witnessed the ISIS attack on the regime tanks, an ISIS escort took Jake and me on an errand to get water. It was a task they accomplished twice a day. They kept the dangerous chore for the youngest and lowest ranking in their organization. They were told that they could prove their bravery and dedication by carrying five-gallon plastic buckets and jerry cans full of water a few blocks past regime sniper positions to the nearest community well, recently made operational by local engineers at ISIS gunpoint.

Our escort raced across the side streets first where he knew the regime sniper's crosshairs looked for ISIS fighters dressed in black. The idea was to catch them by surprise by being the first one across the street and then we would follow, taking the bullet once the snipers had been alerted instead of him.

The trip to the well was less hazardous when the buckets and jerry cans were empty and we were more agile than the trip back when they were full. More than enough people had been picked off by regime snipers at the cross streets carrying water back that it became a deadly chore for new ISIS recruits eager to prove themselves, prisoners from other sects or, in our case, journalists and Hollywood movie stars.

We were lucky, not one shot was fired at us on the way to the well. The snipers must have had something else to do. Jake and I carried a jerry can in each hand to fill and return for drinking, cooking, medical use, and the last priority, bathing and washing clothes.

The well consisted of a metal hand pump attached to a spout, which was mounted on a water pipe that stood atop a pedestal of circular masonry with the middle filled with concrete to hold the water pipe in place. The well was surrounded by a circular patio of cracked and crumbled stone pavers. Three dead olive trees, their trunks riddled with bullet and shrapnel damage, their branches splintered and hanging limp, stood around the well, giving it a look of a defunct oasis.

We began filling our containers with water as soon as we arrived at the well. I wanted this dangerous chore done as soon as possible. Our ISIS escort pushed me and unnecessarily told me in Arabic, along with some pantomiming, to fill the water jugs. He liked to push Jake and me just to see us squirm in pain from our wounds. I felt like an injured cat in the hands of a demented toddler who was fascinated by watching pain in another living thing's face. The escort pushed Jake one too many times and Jake turned around on him and bumped him in the chest so hard the guy fell down.

"What the fuck, man!" Jake yelled.

Jake made the mistake of laughing for a second as he watched the guy fall backwards to the ground. The man jumped to his feet, his surprised face turned to fury as he began pummeling Jake's face with his fists. Jake hit him with a plastic jerry can and I moved over to try to get in between them. I took one solid punch on the cheek but Jake took at least four in the face before the man quit. He yelled at Jake in Arabic as Jake fell to his knees.

In an instant, we heard the whistle of incoming mortar rounds. The regime must have known we were at the well. I helped Jake to his feet and we ran across the small courtyard and dove behind a lone tree that was surprisingly intact despite the local heavy combat.

I peeked around the tree as my journalist instincts were rapid firing impulses to my brain to record as much as I could see. When you're in combat, you only remember a fraction of what actually transpires. There have been countless times that I would review video footage and only remember snippets of the actual action that happened right in front of my face. For this reason, it is imperative that I always have a video camera on me to see exactly what my over-stimulated brain discarded in its most basic survival mode of either hiding from or fighting its way out of danger.

I saw the three figures clad in a brown and green camouflage pattern pants, brown T-shirts, and sand-colored tactical load bearing vests. They each carried an AK-47 and surrounded our escort. The shells were falling on buildings and the pavement only a few dozen yards from the well. Each impact shook the ground and rained gravel and bits of concrete onto us. The three men walked deliberately but did not run.

I was impressed by their confidence in the face of grave danger. No doubt a by-product of relentless exposure to such dangerous situations. One of the men had a thick dark brown beard and mustache and wore a sweat-stained, faded black baseball cap with a well-formed bill and the distinctive black stallion on a yellow shield logo of Ferrari on the front.

Two of the armed men pulled our escort up by the hair and drug him across the street and behind the burned-out hulk of a car. The man with the Ferrari cap headed right for us. He trotted over to the tree and knelt beside me. Another mortar round went off a half block away in the direction the men had come. He didn't even flinch. He just casually looked down and let the bits of dirt and concrete bounce off the bill of his hat before he looked at me again.

"Are you Angus Conn, the journalist?" he said in perfect English.

"Yeah."

"Hi, I'm Gary. I am your brother-in-law's Plan B. You and John fucking Wayne over here need to follow me right now."

With that message, he stood and moved at a half run across the street to the well. He turned and saw that we weren't following him as he had just told us.

"Come on, right fucking now!" he yelled and then aimed his AK-47 at us to let us know he wasn't going to let us off the hook.

I turned to Jake, "I guess we're following our new friend Gary."

Jake looked at me. "Are you sure?"

I looked at Gary pointing his rifle at us and then back at Jake. "Pretty fucking sure," I said.

Artillery rounds shook the ground as I got to my feet and ran toward Gary. I looked behind me and Jake was right on my heels.

Gary led us at a half run to a building a few doors down from the corner in the direction he had appeared with his men. I noticed bars on the windows and a half shot out sign that read, "Police," in Arabic. He led us through the blasted out entrance and into the darkened building. We followed him down a corridor to the end and then down two flights of stairs to a half open thick metal door. He disappeared inside the completely black interior.

I looked at Jake's face, barely illuminated from the ambient sunlight in the stairwell. I shrugged and followed Gary inside.

Gary turned on a flashlight and scanned the small space with the bright beam. There was concrete rubble and torn up bits of office furniture strewn about the space. Empty rifle racks lined three of the four walls and a waist-high metal table dominated the middle of the room. Gary kicked a metal bucket in my direction and shined his flashlight on a plastic chair in the corner.

"Hey, Brad Pitt, sit over there in the corner. Angus, you take the bucket." Then he hopped up on the table and rested his rifle across his lap.

"And I'll take the table. Make yourself comfortable. Their barrages usually last about five minutes."

"Where are we?" Jake asked.

"Well it ain't the fucking Beverly Wilshire, kid, but it'll keep those mortars from blemishing that moneymaker of yours."

"It used to be a police station," I said.

"That's right. Very observant of you, Angus."

"Do you two know each other?" Jake asked.

"No," I said.

"But everyone who's ever watched the news knows who you are," Gary said.

"Yeah, great, but who are you?" I asked.

"I told you. I'm Gary, and that's all you need to know. Now it's my turn to ask questions. I know why you're here, Angus. This is where the scoop is, but why in the hell did you drag this succulent piece of Hollywood ransom bait over here?"

"On-the-job training," I said simply.

"Holy shit, man. Do you have any idea what an uproar you've caused?"

"What do you mean?" Jake asked.

"You've got all sides falling all over themselves trying to get their greasy little hands on the next George Clooney here."

"What?" Jake said as he tried to process what it all meant.

"That's why they're mortaring us right now. This is the beginning of an assault to come and get him from ISIS."

"What?" Jake said again.

"Yeah, I was afraid of that," I said.

* * *

We sat tight for a few minutes as the barrage slowly died down. We all looked around and noticed the silence.

"Now what?" I asked Gary.

"Now, my men will clear a way for the three of you to get back to the ISIS compound."

"The three of us?"

"Yeah, your escort, you, and DiCaprio here."

"Why would you send the escort back? Or any of us?"

"We're going to have the escort deliver a message that there is no way the U.S. is going to pay a ransom for your sorry asses."

"How do you know that?"

"That's the message your friend Rafi told us. He couldn't get anyone to bite back in the real world and my group doesn't have the resources to keep you guys right now. I barely have enough food and water for my guys."

"Who are your guys?"

"I'm technically with the FSA."

"The Free Syrian Army?" Jake asked Gary.

Gary looked at Jake. "Wow, kid, I'm impressed."

"We can't go back in there, Gary," I said.

"Well, we can't bring on two more mouths to feed unless you can fight. If you can't do your part, then you're just deadweight to us. But don't worry, I'm working on a way to bust you out. Just sit tight. Let them feed you. We're watching them and we'll come get you when we're ready. Now come on, we gotta move."

Don't worry, huh? That's a fucking laugh, I thought.

* * *

Gary's men had our bloodied ISIS escort bound at the wrists and led him down the street as they cleared each cross street ahead of us. We ran with Gary to the end of the block and sat in a row against the wall where the block of neighborhood buildings ended. There was an open field just across the last street in front of us. Gary took a small set of binoculars out of his tactical vest, scanned the field, and then slowly looked around the corner. I was waiting for a shot to ring out and take his head off.

It never happened. He came back and kneeled next to me as he put away his binoculars. "Okay, from here across that field is all ISIS-held territory. If you guys run across that field and over that small rise, you'll see the ISIS compound. If you're with your escort here, they will probably not shoot you. So stay with him."

"Probably, huh? That's reassuring," Jake said.

Gary smiled. "That's all the reassurance you've got right now. You guys need to trust me. We'll come to get you. Just make it back to them and make sure this guy sends our message. It won't be long, maybe a day or two and we'll be ready for you."

I looked down and tried to think of other alternatives. "Fuck."

"Yep. It's a pisser, ain't it? Maybe next time you'll think twice about coming to Syria to get that big story."

Gary didn't give me a chance to respond. He moved over to our ISIS escort, took out a knife, and cut the zip ties that bound his hands. He whispered to him in Arabic and then gave him a light slap on the cheek. The man nodded but just sat there.

Gary stood up and pointed his rifle at the man's head. "*Emshi*," he said in Arabic. *Go away.*

Our escort got up reluctantly and walked slowly to the end of the street.

"Okay, follow him, guys. We'll be in touch," Gary said without taking the rifle off the ISIS fighter.

Jake and I got up and lined up behind our escort. I heard Gary yell, "*Emshi*," again from behind us and our escort took off running. We followed as closely as we could and didn't stop until we reached the ISIS compound about a quarter mile away, right where Gary said it would be.

Chapter 24

May 23, 2013

We spent three nights in our cell wondering what Abdul Haqq would do with us. They didn't feed us. They only brought us water. We even had to relieve ourselves in the corners and breathe our own stink. It was clear to me that, despite the fact that we came back after being taken by Gary and our escort was not killed, they seemed to be done with us. I think they thought we were somehow spying for Gary's FSA force. I felt it was only a matter of time before we'd be killed. I hoped it would be soon. I knew of colleagues who had been taken as early as 2011 and were still believed to be alive and imprisoned, their captors waiting for just the right moment to use their bargaining chip or make their statement.

The morning light of the sixth day of our captivity came through the door to our cell as Abdul Haqq burst in with Abdul Aziz close behind. He stood over us and spoke in Arabic too fast for me to understand. He didn't look happy.

Abdul Aziz spoke up. "The United States government is unwilling to pay a ransom for you, liar," he said to me. "It looks like you are of no use to anyone. But there is good news. I convinced Abdul Haqq to play a little game. Come with us."

The soldiers pulled Jake and me to our feet and escorted us out of our cell and down the stairs to a pickup truck painted in the light brown of Assad's army's colors. They sat us on the lowered back tailgate side by side. A dozen of the ISIS fighters, dressed in black with covered heads and faces, stood around in a semi-circle behind Abdul Haqq. It looked like a black-clad hangman convention. It would have been funny had it not been so serious for us. Most of them carried AK-47s, one had a Russian-made PKM machine gun, and a few rested the distinctive and ubiquitous RPGs on their shoulders.

They were smoking and laughing as they stared at us and listened to Abdul Haqq speak. He paced a few steps back and forth, staring at the ground as he spoke to us in Arabic while Abdul Aziz translated. Abdul Haqq spoke

English but wanted his men to hear of our decided fate more for propaganda purposes than anything else.

"Abdul Haqq has decided to use you as target practice. You will get in this truck and drive down the hill toward the city down there," he said and pointed to Al-Waer that lay just at the foot of the hill we were on.

Abdul Haqq kept talking and Abdul Aziz translated periodically as he spoke. "You should consider yourselves lucky. He wanted to cut off your heads and put the video on YouTube. But I convinced him that this arrangement would be better for the morale of our men."

Abdul Aziz looked at Abdul Haqq and continued to relay his words. "We will chain you to this truck that we confiscated from the Assad regime. We cannot use it because we do not have a way to show that it is ours and not the Syrian army. No paint, no markings, we would get shot at by anyone but the regime. Since we cannot use it, we were going to destroy it. This is just an entertaining way to get rid of you and the truck all at once."

Abdul Aziz pointed to his men. "As you can see, the men are excited to show off their marksmanship. Abdul Haqq has faith in our capabilities, but me, I give you about a thirty percent chance of survival. We are good, but there is always a chance you could survive. This is good for you. There was no chance that you would have survived the alternative."

Abdul Haqq stopped and noticed that Abdul Aziz was not exactly translating his every word. He stepped up to Abdul Aziz, grabbed him by the collar, and slapped him hard across the face. Abdul Aziz took the slap like a man, put his head down, and explained in Arabic that he was doing his best but it was difficult to translate exactly.

Abdul Haqq looked at him for a second and turned away and gave a few orders to his men to put us in the truck. Two men slung their rifles, pulled me off the tailgate, and pushed me into the driver's seat. One of the men locked a padlock to the end of a thick chain and hooked the open padlock under my zip-tied hands. He then locked one end of the chain to the seat mount on the floor of the truck with another padlock. If I had a knife, I would have been able to eventually cut myself free, but they took my knife.

Two other men shoved Jake into the passenger seat and secured him with chains and padlocks in a similar way. They slammed our doors and laughed. They were giddy with excitement. Ready to take out their aggression on any Westerner.

Abdul Aziz appeared outside Jake's window holding an RPG over his shoulder. "*Inshalla*, I will see you in more Hollywood movies, my friend," he said and laughed.

I watched as the soldiers moved away from our truck and took up positions they figured would give them the best vantage point to shoot at us. Some were near the building and others were on the roof with RPGs and machine guns at the ready.

I looked over at Jake. I could tell he was scared. My adrenaline pumped and gave everything a bright sheen in my eyes. I had to try and calm myself to stay focused. I reached for the gearshift with my right hand and was unable to reach it. I tried a few times but the chain was too short.

"Jake, look at me," I said. "We're gonna get out of this."

"How do you figure that?"

"I can't reach the gear shift. Can you?"

He reached for it with his left hand and could barely reach it.

I pressed the clutch in, "Try to put it in first," I said.

Jake pushed the gearshift all the way to the left and up. "It works. The truck's in first," he said.

"Okay, now pull it down to second and then up to third."

Jake managed to hit each gear.

"Okay, now fourth."

He pulled the shifter down into fourth. "Do you really think we're gonna get to fourth?"

"I don't know. But we've got to try. Put it back in first and keep your hand on it," I said.

Jake reached over to the max length of the chain and put it in first.

"Okay, I'm going to call out gears. When I do, that means the clutch is in and you hit the next gear."

Abdul Aziz appeared in Jake's window again and smiled. "Yes, teamwork. That is good. This will be a good exercise. I wish you good luck. You will need it, my friends," he said.

Abdul Aziz held up a rock the size of a baseball and showed it to us. "When I hit your door with this rock, you are free to go," he said and trotted away to a safe distance.

I looked through Jake's window at Abdul Aziz as he wound up his pitch and threw the rock. It hit Jake's door with a thump. I revved the engine and popped the clutch. I heard ISIS rifles erupt all around us and heard bullets begin tearing into the truck. I looked down and saw that I had stalled.

* * *

"Goddammit!" I yelled and ducked below the dash to protect my head. The windshield cracked from bullets and the back window exploded tiny shards of glass all over us. "Get your head down!" I yelled at Jake as I started the truck. I revved the engine and eased the clutch out slower this time. We began to move as more bullets tore into the hood.

I couldn't hear anything above the gunfire and just concentrated on the tachometer. It got to six thousand RPM and I yelled out, "Second gear," as I pushed in the clutch. Jake pulled the gearshift down to second and I released the clutch. The truck was picking up speed as I wound out second gear. We hit a few potholes that bounced us around the cab.

Jake screamed. I looked over and saw blood streaming down his left arm. "Stay down," I yelled.

I looked up briefly so I could keep us on the dirt road. I saw an ISIS soldier pop up from behind a burned-out hulk of a car to our right and begin firing his rifle at us. I instinctively turned the steering wheel to the right at the last second before we passed him and heard him scream as his body flew over the hood. The fighter left his blood on Jake's side of the windshield.

I looked back inside at the tachometer and pushed down on the gas. We hit six thousand RPM again and I yelled out, "Third gear," but Jake was slumped over in the seat. The truck slowed a bit and an RPG flew from behind us and exploded in front of the truck, right where we should have been if we had accelerated into third gear.

Dirt and dust consumed the cab and it was impossible to see where I was going. I tried to reach over and put the truck into third gear but couldn't reach. We were just coasting down the hill and slowing quickly. I saw Jake convulse and then scream as he regained consciousness.

"Jake, third gear, third gear! Fight through the pain or we're gonna die, third gear!"

Jake pushed the gearshift up into third and I released the clutch. The truck bogged down and shook on the verge of stalling.

"Come on, you son of a bitch," I grunted.

We slowly picked up more speed and I looked out as the dust cleared and I found the dirt road again. I kept up our speed and recoiled at another explosion close to Jake's side of the truck from another RPG.

I kept driving. I turned the steering wheel erratically in both directions to try and confuse their aim. Bullets kept impacting the truck but we were still moving. I looked down at the tachometer and kept turning the steering wheel back and forth. The tachometer approached six thousand RPM and I looked over at Jake. He had passed out again.

I looked out the cracked windshield and saw the blown-out apartment buildings in the distance ahead of us. I could just make out a few figures on the roof of one of them, probably watching the spectacle of our imminent death. I kept working the steering wheel at random intervals. Our bodies bounced violently around the cab from my erratic driving and the speed we were traveling down the rocky dirt road.

The truck was screaming as fast as it would go in third gear. I scanned the tachometer again and in was in the red. I looked up to see a succession of bright flashes followed by thin smoke trails from the roof of the apartment building ahead of us.

They had people waiting for us. We're fucking dead.

I cringed as the three RPG contrails approached us from the apartment building roof but streaked way off target, high over the truck. I heard three distinct explosions behind us. I hazarded a look out my side window and saw that the building we had been held in had disappeared behind a huge cloud of smoke.

I didn't hear any more rifle fire after the trio of RPGs flew over the top of us. I kept driving side to side and then noticed the silence. I looked at the tachometer and it was at zero. They shot out the truck's engine. We were coasting and losing speed fast.

The truck hit a large rock and bottomed out hard. I fought to control the steering wheel with my chained hands. Then I felt a searing hot explosion. All I saw was red and yellow fire as it swept through the cab and singed my face and arms. I looked out the windshield when the fire died down and the world was spinning outside. We were tumbling. The truck was rolling down the hill. Then I blacked out.

Chapter 25

Al-Waer, Syria
May 24, 2013

I woke and stared at the many cracks in the ceiling. Everything hurt a little bit, but my right leg and my right arm hurt the most. I tried to lift my head but my shoulder and neck muscles screamed out in pain and became the immediate runner-up for the most painful parts of my body.

I pushed through the pain and was able to get myself up onto my left elbow and look around. I was on a dirty mattress that rested directly on the floor. The only window had cardboard duct taped over it so it was impossible to pin down what time it was from the ambient light outside. It was daytime but it could have been anytime between breakfast and dinner. The door to the room was propped open and there was a slight warm breeze coming in from the hallway. Everything was quiet. I wondered if I was still in Syria. In the whole time I'd been here on this trip, it had rarely been quiet.

Truthfully, I was surprised that I wasn't dead. There was no way I was dead. The pain that I felt and an exact replica of the shithole that Syria had become would never have passed as heaven in anyone's religion. I wondered where Jake was and if he made it through our crash. I didn't want to lie back down because I knew it would hurt and then I thought that it would hurt again when I eventually wanted to get up again. I decided to face my pain and forced myself to just try and stand.

I eased myself up to a sitting position and tried to move a little bit of everything. It worked okay for a minute until I tried my right leg and arm. They hurt like hell. My neck was also sore. I knew when the truck rolled that it was going to hurt us. I guess I should have felt lucky to be alive but not so lucky to feel so much pain. I reached over and felt that I had miraculously held on to my little statuette. He was proving his worth as my good luck charm.

I immediately fell over when I set only a little bit of weight on my right leg as I tried to stand. I fell to the ground and involuntarily pushed out a grunt when my body hit. I heard footsteps coming up the stairs right to my door. I looked up and saw black combat boots near my face.

"Well it's about time you're awake. I haven't gotten that much sleep since I was a fuckin' newborn. Come on, let's get you back on your bed," Gary said.

He reached down to help me up. I winced in excruciating pain as he locked his meaty hands into my armpits and hoisted me onto my bed.

"Oh, come on, it doesn't hurt that bad. Our doc says you only had a dislocated shoulder and maybe a broken arm and leg."

"Maybe?"

"Yeah, well, fuck, we don't have an X-ray machine out here, so his guess is as good as yours. Does it feel broken?"

"It doesn't feel unbroken."

"Well, your shoulder is better now. He had to reset it. You were unconscious, so that was probably good. It took him a couple tries."

"No wonder I felt like my arm got run over by a truck."

"It kind of did. We pulled you out from under that truck you were driving, if you want to call it that. You were partially thrown out the cab window when it rolled. The chains kept you mostly in, but the cab came to rest right on your upper arm and shoulder. If you hadn't been chained in, it probably would have cut you in half."

"How did you guys find us?"

"I told you when we found you at the well that we've been watching you. We haven't stopped. When those idiots were playing games with you, one of my guys knew what they were doing. He'd seen it happen before. We had a few guys on the roof to counterattack right when they began shooting at you. We tried to get their heads down and draw their fire. I wasted three perfectly good RPG rounds on you two idiots."

"I know. I saw you guys fire them. What happened to the ISIS guys?"

"We exploded your home away from home where they'd been keeping you two, but I didn't want to waste any more of my firepower, so they still have a little country house on the hill. We suspected they were there for some time but the day they decided to do target practice on you guys was the first time we could actually confirm their presence. So, it was a nice turn of events for us. They may re-occupy that base again, but they're gone for now and we think we took out Abdul Haqq, the CO of this local ISIS chapter with one of the blasts. My comms guy picked up some chatter about him being a martyr."

"He interrogated us a bit while we were there."

"We suspect his XO is now running things but we don't know much about him."

"Jake does."

"Did he interrogate you guys?"

"A little. But he mostly wanted to talk with Jake. He recognized him as a movie star."

Gary pointed at me. "I told you that shit would happen."

"I know. I'm not sure what they talked about, but Jake shared a few cigarettes with him and had a couple private conversations."

"I'll have to ask him about that."

"Did he make it?"

"Who?"

"Jake. Is he alive?"

"Yeah. We pulled him out of the truck before you. He was laying on top of you bleeding out pretty good. He took a round in the upper bicep, but it went clean through the muscle. He bled a lot but he should recover just fine."

"Good. That would have been a rough way to go."

"Yeah, but it would have made a good story, am I right?"

"You are fucked up Gary."

"Come on, you know you'll be tellin' this one in the bar for fuckin' years and no one will believe you."

"You're probably right."

"Shit, I know I'm right. It happens to me all the time. No one believes the true shit."

* * *

Gary helped me into the room where they had Jake resting. He was on his own filthy mattress and sleeping when we came in.

I sat down next to him. "Hey, Brando. How you feeling?"

He rolled over and looked at me. "Since every bad guy in Syria knows I'm here can we cut the stupid call signs?"

I smiled. "Yeah, I guess so."

Jake finally smiled. "It's good to see you."

"Yeah, you too. I thought it was lookin' bad there for a minute."

"What? This doesn't happen to you foreign correspondents all the time, Iceman?" Jake asked sarcastically.

My chuckle made me wince in pain. "Not usually. You're really getting your money's worth on this trip."

"That's one way to look at it, I guess."

"How's your arm?"

"It hurts."

"Yeah, me too. They think my leg and arm may be broken but they don't know."

"We'll have to have Amala look at it," Jake said.

"That'll be good if we can get back there."

"Gary didn't tell you?"

I looked over at Gary. "Tell me what?"

"He's gonna take us back to the old neighborhood."

"I thought this was a perfect opportunity to join forces with your militia guys. We deliver their beloved Western journalist and movie star for an agreement to join forces and kick these ISIS guys outta their neighborhood," Gary said.

"You're always looking for the angle, huh?" I asked to Gary.

"It's my job, Angus. What do you care? It's better for everyone if we can join forces. The more firepower and legitimate self-interest to keep these squatters from ruining their country, the better. Besides, it'll make a good story. Just don't mention me."

"Ruining their country? That's a laugh," Jake said.

"Actually, ISIS has its sights on taking over and making Syria an Islamic State. Not a good idea for the locals and not healthy either. If they're successful in any way, they'll draw the fire of every democratic nation who cares even a little bit about counter-terrorism."

"The locals are always caught in the middle," I said.

"Well, they have an opportunity to fight back and we can help with that."

"What makes your guys any better?"

"My guys want to get rid of Assad, keep the squatters out, and rebuild their lives. My guys are Syrians who just want to have a better arrangement, minus Assad. ISIS is not a better arrangement for them. Oh, and we happen to have the backing of some pretty heavy-hitters."

"Who's that?"

"Saudi Arabia, Qatar, UAE, Turkey."

"When they deliver," I said.

"Yeah, they've been spotty lately, but they're the only ones who've ponied up lately. Honestly, my guys will take any help they can get as long as they believe they'll come out with their country to themselves in the end. ISIS isn't offering that, so the FSA needs to make sure they aren't successful. After the shooting stops, the politics will take care of itself."

"You think this is a good arrangement?"

"It's better than going it alone. I think you've seen that firsthand."

I looked at the floor for a second. "When do we go?'

Gary smiled. "Tonight."

Chapter 26

May 24, 2013
Evening

Jake and I had no hope of walking the several blocks of contested real estate between the shot out building Gary and his men were using as their base and our old neighborhood. So he arranged for an old delivery van that his guys managed to get running after they cannibalized a few parts from the burned-out truck they pulled us from the day before.

Gary helped me down the stairs of the building we were staying in to the truck.

"How many contested cross streets?"

"Just a few. I found two sections of steel plate you and Jake can hold in front of your head when we get going. It won't protect your whole body, but it should do the trick for your head and chest."

"That's reassuring," I said.

"Well, you could be covering Hollywood gossip columns, but that shit don't sell as well, does it?"

"No guts no glory," I said, trying to play along.

"Fuckin' A, brother."

* * *

Gary and two of his men helped us into the small van. Gary got in the driver's seat, one of his men got in the passenger seat up front, and the other rode in the back with us.

"Don't you guys have night vision goggles?"

"We used to. We ran out of batteries about a month ago. It's okay though. All the firing that I think is coming our way will only wash them out and make it hard to see. Keeping our night vision is better."

"I have a fresh set of batteries in my pack back in our neighborhood. If you can get us there, they're yours," I said.

"That's a deal," Gary said. "Okay everybody, here we go."

The two fighters were ready to return fire if we were fired upon as they drove us the few blocks to our neighborhood in the besieged Al-Waer suburb of Homs. Gary started out slow for the first block that was familiar to him and then pre-empted his next action with some instructions.

"Okay, boys, it's gonna get a bit dicey here. I suggest you think small and hide behind those metal plates," Gary said.

Gary wound out first gear as he got the van up to speed. He had just slammed it into second gear when we began taking fire in the middle of the first cross street. They were waiting for us. Every window on the right side exploded from rifle fire. Shards of broken glass rained on us like hail. The inside of the van got exponentially louder when Gary's men began returning fire. Bullets, glass, and hot shards of metal were flying around the inside of the van. Hot shell casings were flying through the air from Gary's men returning fire.

I clenched my teeth and held the steel plate Gary had given me as close to my head and chest as possible, just as he instructed. I peeked around my makeshift armor and saw Jake was doing the same thing.

I began laughing. The moment was ludicrous, one of the most surreal experiences of my life. But my mind's eye was watching it as if I was editing a bit of footage I had already shot. I was looking at our situation as if I knew we had already made it. But that was not guaranteed and I was trying to suppress the thought that anything could still happen on the way to our safe haven only a few blocks away. And it did.

A burst of machine gun fire zeroed in right on my steel plate and punched it into my chest. The plate felt like Thor was pounding away on it with his sledgehammer at three or four rounds a second. The sudden impacts surprised me so much I nearly dropped the plate; an action I knew would be instantly fatal. I held on to the plate with a grip like a vice and yelled at the top of my lungs.

Gary must have heard me because he shouted back at us as he threw the van into third and kept going, "You alright back there?"

"Yeah," I managed to yell as soon as the shooting stopped.

I hazarded a look from behind my steel plate and noticed we were in the middle of the next block. We made it through the first cross street.

Only one more to go.

"Okay, one more, you guys ready?"

"No," Jake yelled.

"Good, me neither. Let's get this shit over with," Gary said.

He hit the gas, wound out third gear, and dropped into fourth. This time we must have been going faster than the snipers had anticipated because they only managed to hit the very back of the van as we sped across the last cross street.

Gary yelled as he kept the engine working at full speed, "More target practice, bitches! You don't know shit about windage."

We roared into the next block and took a left at the next street. We were relatively safe for the rest of the short drive into our familiar neighborhood.

The van roared around a corner and onto the street we had spent most of our short time at Al-Waer. I didn't recognize anything flying past in a dark blur.

Gary stopped the van out in front of the medical clinic and I dropped my heavy steel plate onto the floor. Gary killed the engine and turned to look at us in the back as he opened his door to get out, "Fuckin' A, gents. How is that for door-to-door service?"

"I think I'm gonna throw up," Jake said, still clutching his steel plate.

I slowly got to my feet as Gary pulled the van's sliding door open to let me out. I hunched over and climbed out onto wobbly feet. Adrenaline still ran through my body. A few red-filtered flashlights bounced around and I thought I was hallucinating as I caught a glimpse of Bobbie. I could just make out her shoulder-length brown hair, sweet smile, and slim figure in the dim light from the clinic as I climbed out of the van.

She rushed up to me and I collapsed into her arms. "What the hell are you doing here?" I asked.

"I was going to ask you the same thing," she said.

"I couldn't get the artifacts. My bargaining chip is gone. I don't know what I'm going to do to save the kids."

"I know, Gary told me. We'll figure something out. There's got to be a way to make this work."

"I don't know how," I said.

"It's okay. I've got you now. Let's get you fixed up."

Chapter 27

May 24, 2013
Evening

Bobbie had Jake and I sit down in plastic chairs in the dark street near the clinic. One of the neighborhood kids appeared out of the darkness and gave Jake and I each a bottle of water, a truly kind gesture as water was the most valuable commodity next to life itself in Al-Waer. Jake and I gulped down our water as Gary turned the van around and drove slowly past us. He leaned out the window as he crept by in the van, "I'll be right back. I gotta make another delivery before those snipers learn how to shoot."

"Jesus, Gary, be careful," I said.

"Hell, if I was careful, I would have joined the damn Coast Guard. I'll be right back," he said.

Gary jammed the van into gear and disappeared around the corner at the end of the block. We sat for a few seconds in the dark silence and guzzled our water. Bobbie returned a few moments later with Amala close behind, carrying fresh bandages and two bags of saline.

She handed the medical supplies to Bobbie, knelt at Jake's feet, and gave him a sweet smile.

"I'm glad you're back," she said to Jake.

"I'm glad to be back."

Amala got up, flicked on a red-filtered flashlight, and immediately went to work. Just like that, she dropped into work mode and began cutting Jake's bloody bandage the FSA guys had given him off his bicep. She redressed the wound with fresh gauze and medical tape. Bobbie assisted Amala as she stuck us both with an IV and hung our saline bags on a rolling clothes rack behind us, hooking the bags to a couple of clothes hangers.

"Here, take this and keep drinking water. You both are dehydrated," Amala said and handed Jake and me a pair of pills each.

"What is this?" I asked.

"It's acetaminophen."

"Gee, thanks," I said and swallowed the pills.

"Sorry, it's all we have."

"I know."

We all turned our attention to the corner as we heard more machine gun fire in the distance.

Gary came screaming around the corner in the van and screeched to a halt in front of the clinic. He jumped out of the driver's seat, threw open the sliding door, and helped one of his men who had been wounded at one of the cross streets inside the clinic.

Gary came back out a few moments later and walked up to Jake and I as we sat with our IVs in our arms.

He put his hat back on his head and wiped the sweat from his face. "Well, that beats a damn nine-to-five job any day," he said.

"Damn, Gary, you're crazy."

"Yeah, usually that's a liability. But today, I think it's paying dividends. You guys all right?" he said as he readjusted his hat.

"Yeah, I think so."

"Well, welcome home, gents."

"Thanks. Thanks for everything," I said sincerely.

"My pleasure."

"How did you know you could bring us back here without our neighborhood guys getting spooked and blasting you?"

"You can thank your little lady, Bobbie, here. She sent me a message and told me we were cleared to get our asses over here and drop you guys off any time we wanted. We made a deal with the patriarch, Tamir, that we could hang out together and pool our resources against our ISIS buddies."

I looked over at Bobbie. "How did you know what was going on with us?"

"Chuck e-mailed me that he hadn't heard from you in a few days and I made a few calls. I found out Gary was here and I was able to get ahold of him and found out he had you two."

"How the hell were you able to do that?"

Bobbie looked at Gary and Gary winked at Bobbie. "I gotta go check on my guys," he said and went back into the clinic.

"We've worked together before. I knew he was somewhere around here and I still had the info on how to get ahold of him. And it just so happened he knew exactly where you were."

"Thanks, Bobbie. You saved our lives." I said.

"I'm sure you'd have done the same for me."

Chapter 28

May 26, 2013

I was grateful to spend some time with Bobbie and recuperate for about half a day before my journalistic instincts kicked in. I felt like I was missing something. Like I should be out getting stories.

The remaining people of Al-Waer took my soiled clothes, washed them, and hung them up to dry. I was given water, a few figs, and a piece of stale bread, whatever they could spare from their own plates as I recuperated from my ordeal. I managed to find a building across the street from the clinic that had a relatively clear cell signal so I could send Chuck my daily status e-mail and file stories. I also used the roof to charge my cell phone and iPad with my photovoltaic charging cells. Getting my equipment back online and writing a few stories got me a bit antsy to get back on the horse, even before my wounds had healed.

I rummaged through my pack and found the hiding place where I kept the gold statuette. I had debated whether to bring it with me on the artifacts delivery trip. I was glad I didn't. I thought it would spread more good luck here for the people in Al-Waer and be relatively safe from thieves until I returned, and if I didn't, at least it would be where it belonged.

Turns out, this little guy had lots of luck for everyone. I wonder when it'll run out.

I studied his ancient face from all angles for a few minutes and then put him back in his hiding place. His good luck seemed to be working at least a little bit and we surely needed all the luck we could get.

Bobbie went with a few of the local boys to document the water situation and why it was so difficult to get water in the besieged areas. I told her to be careful and also asked her to find out if there was any way to rustle up any local support for my philanthropic goal of getting these local kids out of the war zone. She just smiled, told me not to worry, and to rest up.

Amala said my arm and leg were not broken but the muscles and tendons near my left hip were badly bruised. She told me that I needed to stay off my leg as much as possible for a few days and to also limit my arm motion. She had no splints to help immobilize my arm so it was up to me to take it easy.

I had to do something while I sat around, so I decided to give Jake a little on-the-job training by interviewing Gary, even though I knew I probably couldn't use much of his stuff directly because of the necessity to protect his identity. But I was legitimately interested in his stake in this game and Jake could use the experience if he truly wanted to get the feel for my job.

Gary agreed to talk with us as long as no one else was present.

He came in and handed Jake and I a used plastic water bottle with a brownish liquid in it.

"What's this?" I asked.

"It's good for you. Drink it."

"I don't drink alcohol."

"It's not alcohol. It's water."

I looked at the bottle again and saw floating pieces of something in the bottle. "What are those?" I said and pointed to the small brown flakes floating in it.

"I put an iodine pill in it to purify it," he said as he lit up a cigar.

I looked at Jake, shrugged, and drank some with clenched eyes and a sour look on my face.

"You can go get some of your own with Bobbie and the snipers if you want," he said and smiled.

"No, this is good. Thanks," Jake said and took a swig.

"You know you can't use any of what we talk about, right?"

"I know. I just wanted Jake to practice his interviewing skill a bit and find out a little about what drives you as a participant in this thing for deep background."

Gary smiled. "Deep background, huh?"

"Come on, you're gonna need to trust me on this one," I smiled.

"I'm only doing this because it's you. You can't call it a favor because you already owe me too many damn favors. But I guess I can answer some questions to give you a bit more understanding."

"That's all we're after. I won't quote you on anything."

"Damn right, you won't. You know I'll come find you if you do."

"Okay, I know you can't give me that much detail, due to the nature of your job, but give me what you can."

"You ask and I'll either tell you or I won't."

I looked over at Jake. "Okay, go ahead."

Jake looked at a folded piece of paper in his hands where he had written down a list of questions for Gary. "When did you get to Syria?"

He just shook his head.

"Where are you from in the States?"

Another head shake.

"What is your purpose here in Syria?"

Another head shake, this time with a smile.

"Damn, Gary, what the hell can I ask?" Jake asked.

"Look, brother, professionally, journalists and I are like oil and water. I'll give you a little about who I'm working with here and what our goals are. Good?"

"Okay, who are you working with?" Jake said, a bit frustrated.

"I'm working with the Free Syrian Army, the FSA, to make them more effective against the Assad regime."

"Do you believe the FSA will be successful in Syria?"

"I'm obviously betting my life on it."

"Right, dumb question. Can you give me your opinion on what's really behind this conflict?"

"Russia, Iran, and China are backing the Assad regime against Saudi Arabia, Qatar, Israel, Turkey, and the United States for a major foothold in the Levant."

"Why does each of the players care?"

"Saudi Arabia and Qatar care because it's a Sunni fight against the Iranian-backed Shi'a Muslims. Assad is happy to have Iranian help against Western-backed Sunni governments even though he doesn't much care for the Sunni or Shi'a sects of Islam. But if the Saudis and Qataris help depose Assad, the U.S. and Israel will allow them to help finance the rebuild of a government friendly to Sunni Arabs. Russia and China just want a country they can rely on to counter U.S. and Israeli influence, so they keep Assad flush with weapons and resupply."

"So, you see this as a proxy war with Russia, China, and Iran against Israel, the U.S., and her allies?"

"Absolutely."

"Do you think it's worth all the civilian lives it's costing?"

"Of course not. That's why we're here. If we can get the FSA to get their shit together and overthrow the Assad regime, the suffering would be virtually eliminated."

"Do you think the overall population cares about the big politics involved?"

"No. They never do. The populace is the innocent bystanders in the conflict, just like hundreds of similar conflicts before it."

"Based on what you just told me, why do you think the UN, the EU, or NATO can't get together on helping Syria? What's the difference between why they helped in Libya but not in Syria?"

"There's a lot of difference, actually," he said as he took a long drag off his cigar. He blew a thin wisp of sweet smoke from his lips as he thought of his answer.

"I can think of three reasons right off the top of my head. One, the UN Security Counsel won't do anything because Russia and China will veto any movements to oust Assad. They have too much to lose in business and military interests to let that happen. Two, the EU and even NATO won't do anything without the U.S. leading the charge. Three, we won't do anything because we'll be damned if we're going to send American sons and daughters into a third Middle Eastern war. Many Americans can forgive Afghanistan in the wake of 9/11, but not many are forgiving of charging into Iraq. Ousting Assad because he used WMDs sounds like Iraq in 2003 all over again."

When I give an interview, I try my best to be expressionless and let the interviewee speak, but I caught myself shaking my head as I listened to Jake ask questions and Gary give his answers.

Gary looked at me, "Don't get me wrong, Bucko. I think that if we put the right resources behind the right people over here, we'd be waltzing Assad around by his willy and giving the finger to Russia, China, and Iran. But those sorts of comments are exactly what got me shipped out here in the first place."

"What do you mean?"

"My suck ass boss tells me, 'That's an interesting observation. Why don't you head out there and recruit us the right kind of people to make that happen.' And twenty-four hours later, I'm gettin' shot at just like everyone else around here. The difference is that I believe what I said. I'm a people person and a pretty good shot, so I made some quick friends. We started kicking some Assad ass on the way to putting together my vision of what the world should look like around here."

"So, are you optimistic about the outlook?"

"If I wasn't, I'd probably be better off putting a round in my own head and calling it a day, don't you think? Sometimes a positive attitude is all you got. In this case, we have some talented fire-pissers who feel strongly about their cause. With the right backing, who knows?"

"What do you think of ISIS?"

"I think they should stay the hell out of it. They're opportunists that see this as a way to expand their influence and power base in an area where there's a vacuum of legitimate power. Fortunately, there are lots of people here who see through it and are ready to back their opinions with bullets in order to ensure that the people that succeed Assad won't be worse."

"Do you think there's hope for this region?"

"With a bit more firepower on the correct side, I think there's a chance. If that firepower doesn't come, I think we stand a good chance to fight this thing out in the streets of other Middle Eastern countries and eventually Europe or America."

"Do you think there would be any way to get these children out of this mess?"

"What do you mean?" Gary asked.

I smiled and chimed in. "I have secrets of my own, Gary. I had Doctor Halabi's contacts ready to drive trucks and buses in to get the children out of here in trade for his artifacts. Doctor Halabi lost his whole family in this civil war. He wanted to trade what he had for weapons to depose the regime. But I made a few calls and got his backers to convince their contacts in the Assad government that it would make better press to trade Syria's past for its future, its artifacts for its children. But without the artifacts, there's no way to finance the transportation and the bribes to get the trucks in here to get them."

"How many trucks?"

"I had about forty lined up. The intermediaries were ready to cut a deal with the government to allow the trucks in and out with a Syrian government escort. But now, it looks like the government changed their mind. That's why Jake and I were taken with the artifacts by the government. It was just dumb luck we were ambushed by ISIS."

"Do you think those contacts would still be willing to come in here and get the children?"

"They can't without regime support or they would be blocked at the border. And then there's the matter of money."

"How much were they charging?"

"I wasn't privy to all of the monetary dealings, but I know it was in the millions."

"Excuse me? I'm doing an interview here," Jake said.

"Sorry," I said. "Go on."

"No, wait a minute," Gary said, still talking to me. "What about your Hollywood kid here?" Gary said, pointing at Jake. "Think he would front some cash?"

"I'm charging him half a million dollars to come here with me, so I have that to play with. I'm not sure if he'd be interested in emptying his bank account for the cause right now," I said and looked over at Jake. "But it doesn't much matter if we can't get the Syrian government to allow us out at the border."

"Sorry, man, sounds like you're screwed," Gary said.

"No, the kids are," I said.

"Same as they ever were."

* * *

Lost and Found
Posted to GRL by Angus Conn
Al-Waer, Syria
Filed May 26, 2013

I was following a local story about a Syrian archeologist who was trying to trade the entire contents of his museum, where he was the head curator, for ammunition and anti-tank and anti-aircraft missiles to help depose the Assad regime. My assistant and I were unlucky enough to be captured by Assad's undercover agents there to broker the deal. We were all captured, loaded into a government truck, and were to be escorted to an unknown destination.

The reason the destination is unknown was because the government convoy we were in was ambushed by ISIS fighters. We were subsequently taken by the ISIS fighters and held hostage for several days. The local ISIS leader sent word to my fixer that we were captured and wanted ransom for us. As we were held with minimal food and water, we were interrogated and tortured, not for our information, but for the amusement and morale boost of the ISIS fighters to take out aggression on a Westerner.

The ISIS fighters brought us along to document their fight with the regime and I managed to videotape a sniper engagement between the ISIS group who held us and two regime tanks. ISIS managed to kill one regime tank commander, but was forced from their positions after the tank returned fire and killed the ISIS sniper.

A few days later, I received word from my fixer via several intermediary runners that no ransom was to be paid for my assistant and me. The ISIS leader then chained us to a captured regime truck and made us drive through a gauntlet of machine gun and RPG fire as sick entertainment and a morale boost for his men.

The FSA, staunch enemies of ISIS, had been closely monitoring their actions and came to our rescue by returning fire. This gave us just enough advantage to crash the truck I drove behind FSA-controlled boundaries, where my assistant and I were extracted.

The war between rival gangs, such as ISIS, al-Nusra, and the FSA, along with normal citizens defending their homes and businesses, and the Assad regime, has turned this country into not only a war zone, but also somewhat of a free-fire zone.

The international community must recognize that the only losers in this fight are the innocent civilians caught in the middle. I witness daily atrocities against women and children as a result of random acts of violence to secure geo-political advantage for their respective interests. More must be done to stop the killing of innocents and to mediate a truce before this uncivil war breaches the confines of Syria and spreads further throughout the region.

Chapter 29

May 27, 2013

Since our rescue from the ISIS compound, I'd been able to hobble around and get some strength back in my sore limbs. I used this time to gather small bits of culture and human interest stories as we shared these people's suffering. They still had no electricity, food, or essentials. Every few days, people would arrive with a carload of things they managed to smuggle from nearby communities that were not under siege. But on the whole, the regime was keeping the noose quite tight on Al-Waer.

One thing that always seemed to get through the siege was cigarettes. No water, food, or basic supplies, but someone always seemed to be able to barter for cigarettes. If bellies couldn't be full, at least you could soothe your nerves with a smoke. I could see the logic clearly. Why worry about starving to death or dying of cancer when the next few hours could bring your death?

One afternoon, I found Jake sitting with Bobbie and some of the local kids. I sat down with them, handed out a few pieces of candy to each of the three who were there, and we talked a little. They didn't want to speak about big issues, as most kids don't, but one of the kids shared more about his situation than we could have ever gotten from a formal interview.

A little boy, about ten years old, named Shawqi had taken a liking to Jake and was having Bobbie translate for him. She spoke better Arabic than I.

Shawqi looked at Jake and said in Arabic, "You are my big brother from Hollywood."

Bobbie smiled and told Jake, "He said you are his brother from Hollywood."

"You should be honored. He told me I was his big brother from Beirut the last time I was here," I said.

Jake smiled, a little embarrassed. "Come on, kid, I don't need to be your big brother. Don't you have other brothers and sisters?"

I knew the answer, but I wanted Jake to hear it from him. Bobbie told Shawqi what Jake said.

Shawqi frowned and shook his head.

I told Shawqi, "Tell him where your brothers are."

Jake didn't need the translation. Shawqi pointed to the sky and said in English, "With Allah."

Jake, ever the actor, ruffled the kid's hair. "Okay, then, I'll be your big brother from Hollywood," he said and gave him a red carpet smile.

Shawqi brought us all right back into the uncomfortable silence as he buried his head in Jake's shoulder and hugged him.

Bobbie had to get up and leave. I could hear her sniffle as she walked away down the street, wiping her eyes.

We've all seen too much.

* * *

I wandered into the clinic to see how Amala was doing and to find out when would be a good time for her and I to sit down and talk. I wanted to find out more about her story and what brought her here from being a doctor in the States. I suspected I knew the answers, but my job was to get the answers in people's own words.

I walked in and noticed that the place had been cleaned up since the chaos of a few days ago when Jake and I were rescued by Gary and dropped off there for treatment. The medical supplies had been neatly put away and organized. The floor had been mopped of all the blood and dirt. There were even two army cots set up with pillows and sheets for future patients, which I learned could happen anytime in Al-Waer.

I found Amala in the back room doing her best to clean a few of the medical instruments they were lucky to have. There was no way to boil hot water consistently to sterilize anything, so she did her best with a small amount of rubbing alcohol and even looted booze from abandoned Christian houses.

"Hello, Amala, how are you?"

She looked up from scrubbing her instruments in the sink. "Hello, Angus, I am doing well today. How are you feeling?"

"I'm feeling better. I can get around okay today. I think I just need to ease into being more active."

"Yes, but don't push it. You need to take time and heal."

"I wanted to find out when we could get together so I could interview you. I'd like to find out your perspective on being here."

"Okay," she said and continued cleaning. "I think maybe when I'm done here we can sit down for a few minutes. I should be done in about ten minutes? Is that okay?"

"Sure, do you need any help?"

"No, I just need to dry these and put them away. It's probably easier if I do it since I know where everything should go," she said and smiled.

"Okay, I'll be outside. You can come and get me when you're ready."

I went outside and lit a cigarette. I sat on the sidewalk and jotted down a few things in my notebook as I smoked. A light breeze was coming down the street and my shaded area actually felt peaceful for the first time in a long time. That was about to change.

* * *

I heard the entourage coming before I saw them. There were several young boys who ran from around the corner far down the street. They ran just in front of the main party of two adult men carrying someone in a blanket between them. The boys ran before the cross streets to draw sniper fire, if there was to be any, before the men got there with the wounded person.

Each cross street had no shots fired until the last one, the one closest to the clinic. One single shot rang out just after the men had crossed. The snipers must have been dozing in the afternoon and were not so alert.

As the group got closer, I got to my feet and began to understand their haste. The two adults carried a young girl who couldn't have been more than six or seven years old. She was bloodied from her neck to her waist. One arm was missing from the elbow and the other was badly mangled. One of the boys ran by with the evidence of what had happened.

He was carrying a small gray cylinder with a canvas loop at the end of it. It looked like a child's toy, but I recognized it as a submunition from a Russian-made cluster bomb the Syrian regime was known to have in their weapon stockpiles. When cluster bombs are dropped from attack aircraft, they release hundreds of small submunitions that range in size from golf ball to grapefruit. This particular one looked like a fat metal dart with a canvas flap on the end that helped stabilize it in flight.

The problem was that most of the cluster bombs in Syria were manufactured by the former Soviet Union in the 1960s and 1970s. When they were recently pulled out of decades of storage and deployed by the Assad regime, many of the munitions never exploded. They just fell to the ground until someone stepped on them or a child picked them up, thinking it was a toy. Many of them had caused instant death and maiming across the contested country.

This poor little girl was being carried by a man with tears streaming down his face, yelling for everyone to get out of the way. The little girl's tiny brown curls bounced on her head as the man ran her toward the clinic. I thought twice of snapping a few pictures of the scene. I reluctantly vetoed my journalistic instinct and opened the door of the clinic for them instead.

I pulled one of the boys who had been running with the group aside and asked what happened. I could barely understand his Arabic because he was crying so much.

"My sister, she found a little bomb. It looked like a toy. She tied the end to a bit of string and was swinging it around then it went off."

I wrapped him in a hug and held his face against my chest. He threw his arms around me and sobbed. I wiped the tears from his dirty cheeks.

"It'll be okay," I lied.

I went inside and watched from the entrance as the men laid her small body on a high table near the back window where the daylight was best for assessing trauma patients during the day. Amala leaned over her, checked her vital signs, and directed her two assistants to get her a bucket of water to wipe away the blood. I crept into the room and guiltily snapped a few pictures on my iPhone from afar but didn't want to get too close and interfere.

One of the men saw me taking pictures, grabbed my arm, and took me right up to the girl, shouting to me in Arabic, "Take pictures, they need to see what they're doing to our children!"

I took a few more pictures as he watched and then he broke down and began wailing at the side of the table.

Amala shouted to clear the room, except for her assistants, and kept working to save the little girl.

Jake came running. "What's going on?"

"This little girl came in here wounded from a cluster bomb. It looks pretty bad. I don't know how she's doing."

Jake took a few steps toward the operating room, watched Amala for a few seconds, and looked at the lifeless little girl, with mangled arms and torso on the table. I saw Amala look up at Jake for only a moment and shook her head almost imperceptibly before she looked away and kept working.

"Come on, let's get a few statements from the kids who were there," I said to Jake and pulled him outside.

* * *

Jake and I came back to the clinic about two hours later to see how Amala was doing and if she needed any help. There was no one in the operating room where Amala had worked on the little girl for over an hour. There were clean sheets on the high operating table near the window and the floor had been freshly mopped.

I heard a faint cry in another room. I followed the sound to a door that led to the adjacent room where the cots were set up in the patient holding area. The door was only open a crack, but I saw some movement and opened it a little more to see who was in there. Amala hunched over a small body wrapped in a white sheet. I could only guess it was the little girl she couldn't save. Amala rested her head on the little girl's chest as she cried over her little body.

The door squeaked as I opened it and Amala stood erect and walked quickly into a back room as she wiped her eyes.

"Amala, are you okay?"

"I'm fine, thank you," she said from the other room. "I just need a minute."

I looked at the little girl's body and saw Amala had just written her name on the white medical tape that bound the sheet over her lifeless little body. The name in black felt-tipped marker read, "Amani." It means "wishes" in Arabic.

"Okay," I said and walked out.

"Is she okay?" Jake asked.

"She's fine. Just give her a minute."

Jake just stood there and contemplated going in anyway.

"Jake, give her a minute. She needs to deal with this on her own. We all do sometimes," I said and pulled him out the door with me.

* * *

Jake retreated to my writing spot at the end of the street. He sat on the sidewalk and leaned his back against the wall, probably to be available when Amala decided to emerge. He needed his space too, so I went looking for Bobbie.

Everyone needs a confidant at some point in this business and Bobbie and I had been that for each other at various points when our careers had intersected in the past. I could sense that, recently, I needed her more than she needed me. I was envious of her mental strength. Mine had eroded over time. I needed a colleague to help me sort out my thoughts.

I interrupted a few boys who were laughing and kicking a tin can, as if it were a soccer ball, around the rubble in the street and asked if they'd seen Bobbie. One of them told me she was in an alley with the old ladies sewing. I watched the boys continue their game and was amazed at how they could smile or laugh at all.

A half block up from the tin can soccer practice, I found Bobbie seated on a wooden dresser with all the drawers missing that had been flipped on its side. She was smiling and chatting softly in Arabic with three older local women who all wore black shadors and black headscarves. They each had a piece of clothing in their hands and worked a needle and thread, repairing rips and tears.

As soon as I rounded the corner, they all stopped talking and looked at me.

"Oh, hi, Angus. Want to help us?" Bobbie asked.

I smiled. "Sorry, no thanks. I wanted to see if I could talk with you for a few minutes."

"Sure," she said as she got up and placed a little flower print dress on the dresser.

She excused herself in Arabic to the ladies and followed me around the corner onto the sidewalk. I walked a dozen feet from the alley and sat down on the sidewalk where I leaned back against a relatively intact cinder block wall.

I pointed to the wall space next to me. "Have a seat."

"Okay," she said and sat down beside me, leaving a foot between us. "What's up? Is everything okay?"

"That depends on what your definition of 'okay' is," I said as I looked over at her and smiled. "No, I'm fine. I just never got to thank you for referring Jake to me."

Bobbie smiled and began fidgeting with the rocks and rubble near where she sat. "I know it doesn't seem like such a favor but I figured it probably wouldn't hurt having some monetary backing for your plan for these kids. But I didn't think you'd bring him all the way here."

"I didn't plan to. He actually paid Rafi to smuggle him in the trunk of his car when we were on our way to the border. I told him he couldn't go and thought I'd gotten rid of him. Once I found out he was hiding in the trunk, it was too late to turn back or I was going to lose the opportunity to meet with our guides who got us here. So I made the very bad decision of bringing him with us. But what else could I do? I wasn't going to throw away all the coordination I'd worked on to get here."

"How did you get across the border?"

"Through a drainage culvert near Qasr that emptied out into Syria on the other side. How'd you get here?"

"I went through Jordan. I was at a refugee camp near the Jordan-Syria border when I got a message from Chuck. He said he hadn't heard from you and told me you had gone back to Al-Waer. I got in touch with Gary and he helped me link up with an FSA contact he knew near where I was and that he would bring me here to help get you back if we could."

"Did you have any problems?"

"There were a couple tense moments at a highway checkpoint just north of Damascus. But the FSA guy bribed a few people that were Sunnis like him and they let us through. We were lucky," Bobbie said.

"We've all been pretty lucky considering the circumstances. I hope it holds out."

"The people here have been cut off for a long time. I'm not sure how long they can last in this situation. No food, no basic supplies, little water or medical help and lots of different groups trying to kill them off. This is as bad as anything I've ever reported on."

"Yep. Me too. I just want to get these kids out of here," I said.

"I've been meaning to ask you, what made you stop reporting and start crusading for kids?" Bobbie asked.

"I haven't stopped reporting. But the last time I was here, it just hit me. I'm tired of yelling from the mountaintops about all the horrors that are going on over here. No one seemed to be listening. I wanted to make a difference for the people I was seeing in front of me. These people. But my reporting didn't seem to be doing the trick. I needed to give some real help. Then I was introduced to Doctor Halabi and I figured that trading his stuff for some food, water, medical supplies, and trucks to get these kids out of here would work. And here we are, all in this mess together. Sorry to drag you into it with me."

"You know me. No place I'd rather be," Bobbie said.

"I know. Me too. But haven't you thought of hanging it up at least for a while and focus on a different way to effect change?"

"I don't know. Maybe."

"I think you could still be effective without all the risk," I suggested.

"Yeah, maybe you're right. But it's in my blood, you know? I've gotten a taste for it and there's nothing like it. Plus I'm pretty good at it. I feel very underutilized if I'm not doing this sort of thing somewhere," Bobbie said.

"I know exactly what you mean. I've been doing it practically my entire adult life. I just got fed up with how little my contribution seemed to be yielding."

"Without crazy people like us, how would anyone know the truth? I think all of our contributions are worth something or we wouldn't do this," Bobbie said.

"I guess I'm at the point in my career where I need a bit more direct input to effect a positive outcome. I was serious before when I asked if you wanted to do something else."

Bobbie picked up a rock in front of her and threw it into the street as she digested my words. "I know."

"If I get these kids out of here, I want to set up a foundation to keep the help coming for them from donors and sponsors. I guess that's why I gave in and took Jake. He threatened to withdraw his money. His payment would allow me to start something like that," I said.

"I figured that was part of the calculus."

I turned and looked into her eyes. "Would you be interested in doing something like that with me?"

"You mean I wouldn't need to chase you around war zones to rescue you from your own bad decisions anymore?" she said and smiled.

"That would be one perk, I guess," I said and smiled back. "Another would be not quite as much competition to get the stories. We could actually be the story for a change. A positive, human interest story."

"That may be worth considering," Bobbie said, smiling sweetly.

"Aren't you tired of proving and re-proving yourself?" I asked.

"I don't think I need to prove myself anymore. Being a woman in this business isn't so out of the ordinary anymore and also has its advantages. Not so much here. It's a bit of a liability in a war zone in the Middle East, but I think I'm holding my own, don't you?"

"You're definitely doing that. But wouldn't it be nice to step off the treadmill for a while and take a breather?" I asked.

"Is that really what you're going to do?"

"I have to," I said as I looked into her eyes.

"Well, if you do that, I would probably have to quit because there wouldn't be anyone worth competing with anymore," she said and smiled.

I maneuvered to sit in front of her so I could look her in the eyes again. "I want you and I to work together to make a difference directly. Will you do that with me, at least for a little while?"

"If we get out of here, I'll seriously consider it."

"That's it? That's all the commitment you've got?"

Bobbie gave an incredulous expression with her mouth open as if she couldn't believe what I just said. "I just ran across Syria to get your sorry ass out of a big fucking jam. I think that counts for colleague commitment in spades."

"I'm talking about personal commitment, too."

"Well, let's take it one crisis at a time. Let's make it out of here with those kids first and I'll consider your offer if it still stands," she said as she got up and smiled at me before she disappeared around the corner.

Chapter 30

May 29, 2013

The whole neighborhood had turned out to bury Amani, the little girl that Amala had taped up in a sheet, after sunset. It was too dangerous in the daytime. There was a community park three blocks from the clinic right in the heart of the neighborhood. The older ones told me that they used to walk their children there after school or stop there on the way to or from the local market. Now, it was the only place they could bury anyone. The local cemetery was over three miles away and it was full.

The park's eastern side was exposed to a government security forces observation point. Anyone from the middle of the park to the eastern side had a high probability of being shot at by snipers. Recently, it had been noticed that the government forces' marksmanship had been improving. One neighborhood kid was wounded by gunfire when he strayed a bit too close to the center of the park to retrieve his soccer ball near dusk.

The neighborhood procession began with about fifty people next door to the clinic. The little girl's picture was propped up on top of the wooden casket that held her young body. One man in the neighborhood volunteered to drive the thirty miles to pick up her casket. He wasn't a mortician. He happened to own a pickup truck and was willing to make the trip through dangerous streets to get what he knew people would pay for.

He told me he would usually go with an empty truck and return with four child-sized wooden caskets polished to a high gloss with ornate carrying handles. He said no one wanted to bury family in a plain wooden box. The soldiers at the roadblocks always inspected the caskets for smuggled contraband but would always let him through. He said they would always confer amongst themselves and then finally decide that it was right to let him through so the families could bury their dead. Sometimes the right things happen, just not enough of the time.

He only charged the survivors a bit more than he paid for the caskets. If the surviving family members cannot pay, he respectfully accepts all manner of equivalent bartered supplies as substitute for cash payment. He told me that he usually makes one run per week, but this week alone, he had made three trips, all for child caskets.

Everyone was dressed in black. There were no lights, just a full moon that threw dark shadows and illuminated the ground with silvery light. These people had done this so many times the process had become sadly routine.

As a precaution, an old man would drive a black delivery truck ahead of the procession and stop in the middle of each of the three cross street intersections for the short time it took the people to cross the street as interference to help block incoming rifle fire from the government security forces. All three cross streets from the clinic to the park were in clear view of government snipers.

There were too many people to traverse the circuitous route through the holes busted through interior walls on the inside of the buildings, which was the way most people got around on any given block to keep safe from sniper fire. But the procession had to get to the park three blocks away. They knew there would be risk, but their commemoration would be part funeral, part protest. They were ready for anything.

During the day, everyone had to sprint across those streets to keep from being picked off. The black truck actually took two bullets at the last cross street. One went clean through the cargo area and the other shattered the glass on the passenger side, lodging itself in the driver's seat right behind the old man's shoulder.

Later, the old man told me that he had been shot at plenty of times and he considered it a privilege to run interference for the funeral processions. He had lived a long life and didn't want any of the younger people getting shot doing it. He had gladly volunteered as a way to do his part for the community.

We arrived at a park the size of a soccer field with scraggly olive trees that lined the perimeter. Some had been knocked down by artillery which created a large gap. I wondered if regime snipers would eventually use those gaps to target Al-Waer residents.

They set the little girl's casket next to a hole in the ground adjacent to the pile of fresh dirt that would cover her little casket. She was being laid to rest near her father and older brother. The park used to have grass, but there had been no water to sustain the people of Al-Waer, let alone the local grass, for a long time. Every piece of vegetation was as brown as the dirt and sand of the desert that surrounded Al-Waer, slowly reclaiming the once green oasis of the neighborhood park.

The dead were laid to rest in rows as they were killed. You could walk the several rows, twenty plots in each row, and see from the dates on the makeshift headstones, made from nearby building rubble, and read who was killed in chronological order. It was a tangible history of the human toll the civil war had on this particular community. Her father was buried a few rows east of her and her brother only one row east at a plot near the middle.

People chanted and sang. It seemed like everyone was wailing and crying; the sad and heartbreaking din of survivors left behind to weather the hell of their painful existence. It was easy to see that the western half of the park only had enough capacity for about a hundred more plots before they would have to find another place to bury their dead.

The little girl's mother moved to the casket, kissed her daughter's picture, and hugged the casket for a few minutes. Her wailing was drowned out by the crowd's incessant chanting of defiant phrases that denounced Assad and the government forces.

Jake and I stood in the back of the throng as a group of men lowered the girl's casket into the hole and began covering it with dirt. I looked over at Jake for a second. Tears were streaming down his face.

I gotta find a way to get these kids outta here.

Chapter 31

May 30, 2013

I was sitting at a spot on the sidewalk, just up the street from the clinic near the end of the first block. I was smoking some smuggled cigarettes and writing in my journal when I saw Jake and Shawqi sitting together outside the clinic on a couple of overturned buckets. Jake had earbuds in his ears. The white headphone cords that hung down were connected to a small iPod in his hand. I heard the faint sound of "Have You Ever Seen the Rain" from *Creedence Clearwater Revival* filling the air.

The boy tugged on Jake's arm and pantomimed that he wanted to hear it too. Jake smiled and took an earbud from his right ear and put it in Shawqi's left ear. As soon as Shawqi heard the music he couldn't stop smiling. Jake played the air guitar with his hands at all the solo guitar spots. Shawqi laughed and began copying him.

Jake chose another song, "Paint it Black," from the *Rolling Stones.* I immediately had a little more respect for Jake after hearing his obvious love for classic rock. I got my camera and shot a few stills and then moved to the video camera to capture the sound as well. It was good to see some laughter after seeing so much pain.

Shawqi kept saying, "Rain, rain," asking Jake to play the *Creedence* song again and again.

* * *

A few hours later, I was sitting on the stairwell inside the clinic, trying to put down words for another story while I waited for my electronics to charge in the sunlight on the roof. I was grateful to have the photovoltaic cells with different adaptors to charge my equipment for exactly these types of circumstances.

I could see into the small courtyard in the center of the building. Amala was there alone, smoking and staring at the ground. I didn't want to disturb her for an interview now. I knew she didn't have much time to herself and didn't want to disturb that.

I went back to concentrate on my writing when I heard a door open to the courtyard and Jake appeared. He grabbed an empty plastic bucket and set it down next to her.

"Can I join you?"

She puffed on the cigarette and slowly exhaled the smoke. "Sure. Do you want a cigarette?"

I felt a little sleazy, since they didn't know I was there and I could hear their whole conversation, but I also wanted to witness their interaction, so I stayed put and listened.

"I usually don't smoke, but under the circumstances, why not?" Jake said.

"Of all people, I should know better, but it's the only way I can relax here," Amala said as she pulled a white stick from the pack and lit it for him with her lighter.

They sat in silence, staring off, lost in their own thoughts for a few seconds.

Jake finally broke the silence. "How can you see this every day and not lose it?"

"What makes you think I don't lose it?"

"You're always in control of yourself when everything is chaotic and others are losing it around you."

"I'm trained for it. I worked in Detroit for my residency. I saw a lot of trauma patients come through the doors of the ER at all hours."

"So you got used to it?"

"I got used to adults being stupid and cruel to each other. But I've never been able to get used to seeing the children suffer. I have a hard time with that."

"Me too. I keep seeing that little girl's adorable, pudgy face and her curly brown hair. She was so beautiful and peaceful lying on the table. She looked like she was sleeping. I have to think of her that way. It was too much to see her taped up under a sheet. It seemed so final. I didn't want to believe it." Jake took another puff and blew out his smoke. "It really pissed me off. It made me want to kill."

"It's hard for me, too. I cry in the bathroom at night when the shells are falling in the distance so no one can hear me. I cry for them, all the little ones who I know are scared at night, the ones who have lost parents and family. I cry for the already dead and those who will be dead soon."

One of the men burst in from the kitchen around the corner. "Doctor, we need you," he said in Arabic.

Amala tamped out her cigarette and got to her feet. She stopped at the door and turned to Jake. "You're welcome to join me anytime," she said before disappearing around the corner.

Chapter 32

Al-Waer Park Cemetery
May 31, 2013

A few days after Amani's funeral, Jake and I agreed to accompany the little girl's mother, Shadi, to the park so she could set some wildflowers at her grave. It was a few hours before dusk, but not much fire had been coming from the snipers that day. We hustled across the three cross streets with no shots fired.

Once in the park, Jake and I hung back and smoked a few cigarettes to give Shadi some privacy with the memories of her little daughter. I watched as she knelt beside the small fresh pile of dirt where the neighborhood had laid Amani to rest.

"This place is just surreal," Jake said.

"I don't think very many people have any idea just how bad things are here."

"It sure doesn't get much attention at home."

As we talked, I took a few shots of Shadi with my point-and-shoot Nikon and its zoom lens. She knelt at the little girl's grave and kissed her picture that hung on the piece of concrete rubble that now served as her headstone. I only took a few shots. I couldn't help but feel as if I was intruding on her private moment as I recorded the images of her pain.

"It's weird. Half the time I feel like an asshole foreigner ogling at these people's suffering. Like a sleazy ambulance chaser looking for the next story to post."

"But if you weren't here to do it, people wouldn't know what's actually going on."

I put the camera in my pocket and looked at Jake. "That's the justification I've been using for years. But the truth is, I can't shake the excitement. I need to be where there's something to report or I feel useless. Yes, this is horrible, and I'm here to record it, but there's no place I'd rather be. No place that scratches the itch."

"Your motives are like the negative exposure of Amala's. She can't leave and neither can you."

"Yeah, except she actually cleans up the mess and I just shoot pictures of it."

A shot cut the relative silence and shocked my system like jumper cables to my heart. We both flinched and I hit the deck. I looked up to see Jake crouching, but still standing, looking around for where the shot came from.

"Get the fuck down, Jake!" I yelled.

He looked at me with glazed eyes, like he couldn't understand my words, but flung his body down next to me a second later. We looked at each other for a moment.

"You okay?" I asked.

"I think so. What the fuck was that?"

"It was a sniper shot."

We both looked in the direction of Shadi at the same time. She was lying facedown on her daughter's grave and not moving. I got up and ran toward her.

"Come on! Help me!" I yelled over my shoulder at Jake as I ran.

I reached Shadi and saw that the black shador she wore was soaked with blood from her right shoulder to her waist. She was moaning. The shot had hit her, shattered the picture of her daughter, and cut the headstone in half. The remaining chunk of stone and the flowers she had just arranged were splattered with her blood and tiny pieces of muscle, fat, and bone.

"Grab her arm and let's go," I said as I took the lady's right arm.

Jake took her left arm and we positioned her onto her back. Another shot rang out and hit the dirt at Jake's feet.

"Goddammit!" Jake cried.

"Pull, Jake, pull!" I yelled.

Another shot hit the adjacent headstone and peppered us with pieces of concrete shrapnel. We pulled with all of our strength and dragged that poor lady, moaning and semi-conscious behind the base of a tree that blocked us from the sniper's view.

Jake let her arm go and crumpled to the ground next to her. "I thought they couldn't get us over here," Jake said, wheezing.

"Me too. I guess they found a position that covers the whole park."

"What do we do?"

"We gotta get her outta here."

Shadi had slipped into unconsciousness but was still breathing. Blood was pooling in the dirt around her right side.

I got to my feet but was careful to keep behind the tree.

I grabbed her arm. "Come on. We go on three."

Jake got up to a crouching position and grabbed her left arm. I looked at Jake and could see in his eyes that he was struggling to put himself in a different place in his mind.

"Hey, look at me," I said.

We locked eyes.

"Stay with me now. I need you to concentrate on me, not the shots. Nothing you can do about it anyway."

"Got it."

"Okay, on three."

I took three deep breaths as if I was going on a deep free dive to the bottom of the ocean. "One, two, three…"

We both strained against Shadi's weight and pulled like a team of spooked horses. We made it to the edge of the park, only stopping once to catch our breath.

"Okay," I said in between breaths, "we've got three blocks. We pull her all the way to the clinic and stop every half block and at each cross street before we cross."

"Okay," Jake said, breathing heavily.

The first block drained our strength. I was light-headed from the adrenaline and the exertion. I was breathing as if I'd just run a mile at a full sprint. We stopped short of the first cross street. I looked at the sidewalk where we had just dragged her body. There was a jagged trail of her blood that showed our path along the ground.

"If we don't get her to the clinic ASAP, she's gonna bleed to death."

"Okay," was all Jake could say between his rapid breathing.

"You ready?"

"Yeah."

"We have to be fast. I don't know if they have a bead on this cross street or not," I said.

"Okay."

"On three again," I said and took three more preparatory breaths. "One, two, three…"

We pulled again as hard as we could. As soon as we were halfway across the street, I heard the quick succession of machine gun fire. They'd been waiting for us.

* * *

I pulled as hard as I could as I walked backwards toward the street. I looked up at Jake's contorted face as he carried Shadi's legs and grimaced. I had just stepped off the curb and into the street when a string of bullets impacted the street from my right to my left. I felt chunks of pavement fly up and hit my arms and face. I saw a bullet impact the woman's leg.

Jake and I dropped her and we both fell to the ground. Jake scrambled back to safety behind the building. I put my back to the incoming fire, stood, and grabbed Shadi's arms and continued to pull alone. Bullets were whizzing past my face and impacting the ground at my feet.

If I'm going to die here, it'll be while I'm helping this lady.

I kept pulling. I saw Jake hesitate for a moment as he saw me continue to pull. I would have given him a signal to stay there but I was concentrating too hard on my task. Shadi's body got hung up on the opposite curb and I fell down trying to get her over it. A bullet ricocheted off the sidewalk next to me and tore through my pants without hitting my skin on its way up to the sky. I felt the burn of the bullet but didn't see any blood or feel any pain. I staggered to my feet to try and get the lady over the curb.

I heard a truck's engine behind me and turned to see a black van coming my way from the clinic. The driver turned in my direction and positioned the van on the curb between the machine gun and me. Rounds were slamming into the van and coming out the other side. Two men got out of the back and pulled Shadi's unconscious body into the truck. Jake ran across the street as the van drew all the fire.

He took me by the hand and helped me to my feet. We both ran to the other side of the street and watched the men load her into the van. One of the men screamed in pain as he was shot through the door of the van. He held his bleeding arm, hopped in, and closed the door. The second man slammed the back door of the van and banged on the side as a signal to the driver before he ran across to join Jake and me. The driver backed the van up, did a U-turn beyond the machine gun's line of fire, and took off toward the clinic.

The man who hung back was breathing hard and looked at us both. "Are you okay?" he said in Arabic.

"*Nam*," I said. *Yes.*

"Okay, I go," he said and jogged down the street toward the clinic.

* * *

<u>No Respect in Syria</u>
Posted to GRL by Angus Conn
Al-Waer, Syria
Filed on May 31, 2013

A few days ago, I attended a funeral for a seven-year-old girl who had been killed while she unknowingly played with a cluster bomb submunition. The whole neighborhood turned out for the funeral procession. They had a driver draw rifle fire from regime snipers at the cross streets while the funeral attendees ran across the street, using the truck as cover. They laid the little girl to rest in a park that is now being used as a cemetery after the local cemetery had filled up.

A few days later, I agreed to accompany the girl's mother, Shadi, to her daughter's grave so she could lay flowers there and grieve. Shadi was shot in the shoulder by regime snipers as she wept at her child's fresh grave. My colleague and I ended up pulling her unconscious body to the clinic three blocks away. She was bleeding profusely and needed more care than my first aid skills could provide.

We dragged her two blocks before we came under fire from a machine gun at the last cross street. Shadi was shot one more time in the leg as the machine gun crew fired incessantly, working to get the correct range locked in.

Men in the same van that the people of Al-Waer use for the funeral processions came and parked between the machine gun and us. Two local men loaded her into the van. One of the two was shot in the arm for his effort. They delivered Shadi to the local clinic where she later died of her wounds. The neighborhood will lay Shadi to rest tomorrow in a plot right next to her daughter, a heartbreaking reminder that there is little respect for the dead and none for the living.

Chapter 33

June 1, 2013

"Can you get your hands cut off for touching a Muslim woman?"

"Why? Who did you touch?"

Jake looked at the ground and puffed on his cigarette. "Amala cries at night in the upstairs bathroom at the clinic."

"I know. I've heard her."

"She invited me to cry with her yesterday."

"Did you?"

"Like a little baby. I needed some sort of release, you know? The shit here is crazy. Seeing the helpless little kids come in here with no arms or no legs or their guts hanging out. Little babies torn apart from shrapnel or crushed under building rubble, you gotta cry."

"What else happened?"

Jake looked over at me. "What do you mean?"

I gave him a *you know what I'm talking about* look.

"It's not like that. She just hugged me. We both needed it."

"Nothing else happened?"

"We ended up kissing a little, but she said she felt guilty for feeling any pleasure when there wasn't enough to go around here."

I took a draw on my smoke. "Well, don't get caught doing anything with her. I'm sure you've noticed that the men here would come out of the woodwork to be her surrogate big brother if they find you banging her. Westerners desecrating their women could get both of us killed."

"I know."

I took another drag and blew the smoke in Jake's direction. "This ain't like home. She's not one of your groupies."

"I know."

I tamped out my cigarette and got up. "Good, let's see if we can help these guys get some water."

* * *

Jake and I were finally able to get a quiet moment to talk with Amala. We huddled in a back corner of the clinic with medical supplies stacked up against all four walls. Jake sat next to me holding the video camera steady on her peaceful, oval face. I figured she would be a bit more open with me if Jake was there.

"Where are you from?"

"I was born in Homs, but my family moved to the U.S. in the mid-eighties."

"How old were you?"

"I was seven."

"Where did you live in the states?"

"My father got a job in Detroit, Michigan, but after a few years we moved to Chicago."

"Where did you go to college?"

"I always wanted to be a doctor, so I did both my undergraduate studies and medical school at Northwestern and then residency in Chicago."

"When did you think of coming back to Syria?"

"I had been back a few times in high school and twice during college to visit family, but didn't think of coming back for any period of time until the protests turned violent in 2011."

"Did you come on your own?"

"I came once with *Doctors Without Borders*, but when Assad expelled them to Turkey and Jordan, I decided to come back on my own."

"How did you get here?"

"I came as you did. I was smuggled in with a few journalists. Once I got to Al-Waer, I stayed."

"What was your reaction when you saw your old neighborhood?"

"I was devastated. Not just from the destruction of the property, but also the absence of so many people I once knew. Friends, family, acquaintances, they were just gone. The more I asked about them, the more I didn't want to hear the answers."

"What do you mean?"

She looked at her feet for a second before she lifted her head and answered, "I wasn't worried for the people that left for the refugee camps in Turkey, Jordan, and Lebanon. I was worried for the people who had disappeared suddenly. One day they were here with no intention of leaving and then the next they were just gone. Some were known to have been killed and others were missing and feared dead."

Jake searched her eyes, "Were some of them family?"

"Yes," Amala said, looking back at Jake and not at the camera.

"Were you close with any of them?"

"I knew some from when I had visited. But they were family, so that's always difficult."

"Have you been anywhere else to offer help?"

"I went to Jordan and Turkey to try and coordinate the delivery of medical supplies and other aid, especially in the winter. Blankets are always needed in the winter because so many people bury their dead in blankets and then have none to keep warm. But I have only left Syria a few times. The last time was about six months ago. I could only get one truck full of supplies smuggled in from Turkey. I was detained at an ISIS checkpoint for several hours. I heard the guards talking of executing us for supplying medical aid to anyone but their group. We escaped when they began taking fire from government troops and fled."

"The government didn't stop you?"

"They were too busy chasing the ISIS fighters and didn't notice we had a load of medical supplies. We were lucky. Had they known, we would have been in a worse situation than with the ISIS fighters."

"What do you think the government would have done to you?"

"They would have taken us and probably tried us as traitors of the government."

"Do you see yourself as a traitor?"

Amala shifted in her chair but finally looked at Jake with a steely determination. "No. I'm a doctor. It's my oath to care for everyone. Syrian or not, government or not."

"Do you feel you are a target here?"

"No more a target than everyone else."

"Of all the things you've seen, what bothers you the most?"

Amala stared to her right out the window as she considered the question. "Seeing helpless people's lives shattered over unnecessary political posturing, especially the children."

"How many children have you seen hurt?"

She refocused her determined gaze back at Jake but was clearly speaking to the future audience of the taped interview, "I treat children every day. Some I can save, some I cannot. Even the ones whose lives I save are really not saved. They will have lifelong physical and mental disabilities. Many have lost their parents. There are a lot of orphans now. I feel bad sometimes when I save some of these children because I feel that I've prolonged their misery in this place." She looked at the ground again and looked up a few seconds later with tears welling in her serene brown eyes. "It's just so sad."

Jake smiled at her as an attempt to soothe her pain, "How do you deal with it all every day?"

She returned his smile with a tilt of her head and an imagined hug. "I cry when I'm alone," she said and stared at Jake for a few seconds. She lowered her head and readjusted in her seat before she looked up again. "I have to. But I can't leave. I have to be here to help them. There are just not enough people to help them. This is where I am meant to be. This is what I was trained to do. I have to stay," she said, her chin quivering as she fought back tears.

Chapter 34

June 2, 2013

As usual, I came out of the clinic to sit on the sidewalk and jot a few things down in my journal when I saw Jake and four young neighborhood kids with AK-47s. They were surrounding Jake in a circle as he showed them a few things about how to get a more stable firing position while standing and techniques on how to reload their magazines faster. I stood and watched at a distance before Jake noticed I was there.

Jake looked over at me.

"Can I talk to you?" I said.

"Sure," Jake said and handed the AK-47 off to his young Syrian student.

We walked a few steps away from the group. "What the fuck are you doing?" I said in a low voice, trying to be discreet.

"What?"

"Why are you teaching them shooting stances and combat reloading?"

"I learned some good stuff from special forces trainers at the actor weapons training school I went to for one of my movies."

"You're not here to teach them how to handle their weapons better. You're here to see what I do and get the essence of the job I do and try not to get yourself killed."

"I'm not going to pick up a weapon and go into battle, but you said yourself that they could use some training. You can see them as well as I can. They suck at handling weapons. They suck at shooting weapons. With just a minimum amount of training, they might be able to aim a bit better, and reload a bit better. It would give them at least a little better odds in a fire fight."

"You're not here for that, Jake. If anyone sees you with a weapon, even if you're just showing them how to reload, that makes you a combatant and an even larger target than you already are. It'll get you killed. You can't witness their story or retell it if you're training them or dead."

"What about you? You say you don't want to be the story but you take unnecessary risks. Like when you had us throw that sniper chair off the roof. We would have gotten killed if they caught us doing that."

"Some things are judgment calls, Jake. You learn that with experience."

"So I just stand back and watch them get slaughtered?"

"No, you film them and write about them. The camera and the pen are your weapons and ignorance is your enemy."

"What-the-fuck-ever. You should take some notes from your own lectures."

* * *

June 3, 2013

I woke up early the next day and went downstairs for a smoke to help invigorate me. Usually, it's coffee, but with limited coffee and rationed water, cigarettes became the equivalent of my morning coffee. Everyone was still asleep except one sentry sitting outside also having a smoke. We talked about simple things…the simple things I could think of with my intermediate Arabic. He seemed content not to talk much. We both enjoyed the eerie quiet after a full night of artillery near enough to us to keep most of the neighborhood awake.

After three smokes, I climbed the stairs to my room. I peered into Jake's room and saw he was still sleeping. But I also saw something else. Shawqi had nuzzled up to him sometime during the night, probably during the artillery barrage. They were both breathing long, heavy breaths of deep sleep. The boy had wrapped Jake's arm around him and was clutching it as if Jake were a relative.

I always had my camera on me because life has a way of taking you by surprise and it's my job to be ready to capture an instant of violence or tenderness. I knew I shouldn't take any identifiable pictures of Jake, so I made sure I was at an angle where Jake's face wouldn't be seen. I snapped a picture of the pair as they slept in each other's arms. The act of compassion made me smile. These types of moments were rare on this trip.

Chapter 35

June 4, 2013

I crawled low and dragged my camera bag across the terracotta tile that covered the floor of the roof. The roof access door was about thirty feet from a three-foot wall that ringed the entire roof area. My knees hurt as I crawled over the rocky rubble left from hundreds of bullet holes and shrapnel damage all over the building. I got down onto my belly and shimmied the last few feet so as not to expose my head above the roof's parapet. I turned over on my back and looked up at the stars as I let my vision adjust to the darkness of the desert night.

Gary and two other FSA fighters were already there. They whispered with Gary in Arabic for a few moments. Once my vision had adjusted to the point I could function, I prepped my camera and began filming Gary with my camera's night vision mode. He didn't mind because the night vision mode couldn't make out his facial features enough to identify him. I focused my attention on the scene through the camera's viewfinder and watched Gary's gray and green image take out a night vision device from his backpack. He had taken me up on my offer of batteries and had cleaned me out for all of his gadgets. He attached a long lens to the end of the optics on the night vision device that had a distinct Y-shape at the top.

He strapped the device to his head like a ball cap and slowly lifted the Y-shaped lens over the edge of the building while his head was safely below the low concrete wall. I shot video as he scanned the area below and the building across from us.

The building we were interested in was functioning as a bakery. Food was scarce because of the siege and this building had become a strategically important target. It looked much like every other building in the neighborhood, made of plaster, concrete, and tile, all decorated with thousands of pockmarks from bullets and random projectiles. Lucky for the community, this particular building was fairly intact. But ISIS had recently taken it over from the community and was making bread for its soldiers.

Gary touched my arm without moving his head, gave me a thumbs-up, and then pointed to the building we were watching. That was his signal to let me know it was safe for me to film over the side with the camera. There were no ISIS soldiers outside or he would have given me a thumbs-down.

I slowly got to my knees and lifted the camera over the edge and kept filming. The building's lights spilled out the windows below and made the light glow bright green in the tiny screen. I zoomed in on the door we were trying to get a look at and then panned left and right to get a detailed view of everything I could so we could examine the footage later for Gary and his men to plan their raid.

I taped a few minutes of footage and got back down below the safety of the low wall and trained my camera on Gary. He had taken his night vision goggles off, gave me a big smile, and flipped off my camera.

"You'd better black out my face on that thing before you sell it to your media pals or I'll have my flag-waving right-wing family members hunt you down and string you up by your balls Mussolini-style when the enemy figures out it's little old me that's been kicking their asses all over the globe," Gary said.

I took the hint and switched off the camera.

* * *

Twenty minutes later, Gary, two of his men, Jake, and I were on the ground floor of the same building where we had just been on the roof. The windows had been covered with rugs and pieces of cardboard boxes to keep any light from the camp stove and the few flashlights we used from giving away our position inside the dark building. We were sitting around the small stove brewing coffee and talking quietly.

After Gary reviewed my footage of the building next door, he passed the camera around and had both of his men look at the footage. Gary drew what he had observed about the building next door as a diagram on a piece of cardboard. He pointed to the doors and windows and talked through each phase of the coming assault with his men as we all sipped coffee.

Gary looked at me, "Okay. Where is this kid with the information we need?"

I looked at Jake. "Go get Shawqi."

A few minutes later, Jake returned with his little buddy in tow. Gary looked up from studying the video again and smiled.

"This is our little spy?"

"Yep," Jake said.

Gary motioned for the boy to sit next to him, handed him the camera, and had him watch the section of video I shot earlier. The boy smiled from ear to ear as he watched it. He had probably never seen a video camera before, let alone one that could record in the dark.

The video ended and Gary asked him several questions in Arabic.

"When did you first see the men come?"

"Yesterday."

"How many men?" Gary asked.

"Four. Always four."

"In a truck?"

"Yes."

"Where is the truck?"

"Inside the building," Shawqi said.

"When did they leave?"

"Right before sunrise."

I was thankful Gary spoke slowly so I could keep up with the Arabic. I listened intently to the rest of their conversation.

"Why were you awake?" Gary asked.

"I heard shooting and couldn't go back to sleep. And then I smelled bread baking. I wanted to see where it was coming from."

"Did they all leave together?"

"Yes. In the same truck. The back was filled with fresh bread wrapped in blankets."

"How do you know?"

"I could smell it and they were eating it. One of them pulled some from under one of the blankets and ate it as he got into the truck. He shared it with his friends. They were laughing."

"When did they arrive?" Gary asked.

"The same time. Sunset."

Gary looked at me and smiled. He pulled four hard candies out of his cargo pocket and gave them to Shawqi.

His big smile returned, "Thank you," Shawqi said.

Gary mussed the kid's hair. "Take these until we can have bread."

* * *

Gary sent three of his men to bed and one to the roof to watch for any movement. He told them to share the observation duties through the night and that they all would meet for coffee an hour before sunrise. They would need to be in position for the raid by thirty minutes before sunrise. They all agreed and filed out of the room.

"Why are we trying to steal people's bread?" Jake asked.

"It's not just anyone's bread. It's ISIS' bread. They set up little bakeries and cook a bunch of bread and distribute it to the people they need help from or want to recruit. It's a political message. They're showing that they care for the people better than the government to try and win their support. It's a classic strategy that worked well for Hamas in Gaza and Hezbollah in southern Lebanon," Gary said.

"And apparently still does," I said.

"Not without the bread," Gary laughed.

"What are you going to do with the bread?" I asked.

"Are you shittin' me? We're gonna eat it. Ain't you hungry? We'll distribute it here amongst the people who need it in this neighborhood."

"What about the people ISIS were going to give it to?" Jake asked.

"They're gonna be shit outta luck. Right now we need to curb ISIS' influence and the bread is influence. The bonus is everyone here can benefit from it. What's the matter? You don't like being Robin Hood?" Gary asked.

"But we're not stealing from the rich to give to the poor, we're stealing from the hungry to give to a different set of hungry people," Jake said.

Gary looked at me. "Are you fucking kidding me with this guy?"

I just shrugged.

"Hey, man. If you don't want to eat the bread I steal for you, you can fucking go hungry. But this mission is a go and I gotta get a little shut-eye before I eliminate four bad guys and take their shopping cart," Gary said and got up and left.

"It's either them or us, man," I said.

"This whole place is fucked up," Jake said.

* * *

June 5, 2013

We all met back in the small coffee room an hour before sunrise. Everyone had bleary eyes and varying afflictions of "bed head" except Gary. He had his dirty Ferrari baseball cap with his graying black hair jutting from underneath it, just covering his ears. He was kneeling down, making a fresh brew of coffee for everyone.

"Do we have enough water for that?" Jake asked.

"This is mission essential coffee, my man," Gary said.

I readied my video camera and made sure I had enough battery and computer storage for the video. I was going to be filming the raid from the roof with Jake. We each drank our coffees and fiddled with our gear until Gary looked at his watch and announced that it was time to go.

"I'll be on the roof for the show," I said.

"Good," he said to me, and then turned to one of his men and spoke to him in Arabic. "Remember, if you see a smoke grenade outside the building, one or both of us are down. You need to come in and get us."

The man grunted a positive reply and they all filed out.

Gary looked back at me. "We'll be right back. How do you like your toast?"

"With butter and jam," I said.

"Yeah, well, one damn thing at a time," he said and laughed as he walked into the darkness.

* * *

I looked to the east and saw the sky getting brighter with every minute. I looked at Jake. He was on his back snoozing as we waited next to the low roof wall. His pants and shirt were filthy and stained with his own blood. Neither of us had washed in days. Not even whore baths.

I was sure he was regretting every minute of his time here. I could identify with his fervor to be here in the beginning. Sometimes we need to see things for ourselves and then later wonder why when we experience the truth.

I peeked over the side and saw Gary and his FSA second-in-command advancing toward the building against the far wall of an adjacent building. They were each on opposite sides of the small parking area, covering each other with their weapons up and ready, in a tactical crouch as they crept closer to the target.

"Okay, here they go," I said as I began to record the action below.

Jake stirred but didn't get up.

I nudged him. "You gonna watch this?"

"I guess so," he said as he sat up and slowly raised his head over the side.

Gary gave a hand signal to his man and they made their way in a low crouch, weapons on their shoulders, to a personnel door next to a large metal rolling garage door for vehicles at the end of the building. I could see Gary try the handle of the smaller personnel door. It was unlocked. He pulled a flash-bang grenade from his pocket. Gary gave a count with three distinct head nods, pulled the pin, opened the door, and threw it hard on the floor and then shut it. I could see Gary and his man turn their heads away so they wouldn't be affected by the blast.

The flash of the grenade lit up the outside through the windows and a muffled explosion reverberated through the neighborhood. Gary opened the door and followed his man inside. I heard frantic screams in Arabic and a quick succession of gunshots followed by another set of shots a few seconds after the first. My camera continued to roll, recording the sights and sounds.

A succession of short bursts of gunfire riddled the early morning, followed by muffled, anguished screams. Silence returned for only a few seconds before the door of the bakery flew open. A smoke grenade the size of a soup can came flying out into the parking lot spewing a shaft of bright flame that transformed after a few seconds into thick dark smoke.

I knew what that smoke grenade meant.

"Holy shit. One of them is hurt," I whispered.

Gary's two men came running from around the corner and went one after the other into the ISIS bakery, just as they had been briefed. A few seconds later, there was a long spurt of rifle fire followed by a truck engine starting and then the driver revving the engine.

I flinched when the truck exploded through the garage door flinging the mangled door into a metal heap off to the side. The truck sped through the small parking lot and smashed into the building right in front of it. The driver got out and turned to fire his weapon behind him in the direction of the gaping hole where the demolished garage used to be.

The driver's weapon was out of ammunition and he dropped to one knee to replace his empty magazine. Before he could stand, he was thrown to his back by a torrent of bullets. I looked over at the building and three men emerged, two carrying the third between them. The wounded man had his arms draped over the other men's shoulders as he limped toward the truck.

The other two helped him into the back of the truck and I recognized Gary's confident stride emerge from the building as he walked straight up to the fighter near the truck. He picked up the man's rifle and tossed it into the back of the truck. He pointed his own rifle at the man's chest, shot him twice, and then adjusted his aim carefully at the man's head and shot him again. He leaned down, undid the man's ammunition vest, and threw it in the back of the truck as well, and then climbed in the driver's seat of the truck. The engine caught after the third try and disappeared around the corner, carrying all four men of Gary's assault team away from the scene.

I panned my camera around the destruction in the parking lot. The building was smoking through the windows and the garage opening was agape where the door had been destroyed. A dead ISIS fighter lay still where Gary had executed him only a few moments before. I turned off my camera, sat with my back against the roof wall, and blew out a deep breath.

I looked over at Jake.

"Why did you make me watch that?" he said.

"This is war, Jake. It ain't pretty."

"There's no way I'm eating that bread," Jake said.

* * *

An hour later, the FSA man who had been shot in the raid had his leg bandaged and was sitting in a chair with two large, round pieces of flat bread on his lap. He was laughing and recounting his story for the half dozen people who stood around him.

Outside, there was a line of smiling neighborhood people half a block long, waiting to get their share of the stolen bread as Gary's men distributed it from the bed of the captured pickup truck.

Chapter 36

June 5, 2013

After a short rest from being up all night on the bakery raid, I had convinced Jake to come with me to my usual spot at the end of the first corner to smoke and work out a few stories. The area I chose had a bit of a breeze and commanded a complete view from the medical clinic on one side of the block to the remnants of the park-turned-cemetery a few blocks in the opposite direction.

Sometimes, I would sit and stare at the blown-up and burned-out storefronts and the signs that advertised what they used to offer to the neighborhood: barber shop, electronics, books, clothes, hardware. Now only a ghost of these indications of the neighborhood's former normalcy remained. Each one had glass shattered on the sidewalk or a sheet of plywood or a blanket affixed to cover where the front window used to be. Some had burned and some had been looted long ago for the useful things by the living dead of Al-Waer.

Most of the time, when I sat in my spot, I had to focus on one object in the distance and stare at it, thinking of the story I was trying to write or I would get depressed. In the spot I chose, I had cleared out the debris and broken glass for a place to sit and began accumulating cigarette butts in a tin can next to me. There were dozens in there and there would probably be many more by the time I left.

We sat and I wrote while he stared down the street toward the cemetery park in the distance.

"Can I ask you a personal question?"

"Sure," I said, but kept writing in my journal.

"Why don't you drink?"

"What?"

"It seems like this sort of profession would make you need a drink, at least every now and then."

"I used to drink."

"Oh, sorry. Was it difficult to quit?"

"Not really," I said and finally put down my pen. "I used to drink socially like all the rest of my colleagues. You really couldn't be a full-blown drunk because you need to be in charge of your faculties when you're chasing stories or writing articles. But the downtimes in between the work is what gets you. The freelancers are more susceptible than network journalists. Freelancers tend to have more downtime. As soon as you have a lull in the action, you have time to take stock of things and reflect on what you've seen. Good and bad, but mostly bad."

"I have friends that take it a bit too far too. It's easy to do in Hollywood. I try to discipline myself, but it's difficult when everyone around you is doing it."

"I know what you mean."

"Did you ever work with a network?"

"Yeah, for several years in the nineties. I didn't like it because they had all the decision-making power. They had the money and told you where to go. I liked being off on my own with my own agenda. I felt like I could smell a story brewing before any network people could. And once I went freelance, I was usually right. Have you noticed, there's no network people here with us?"

"Too dangerous, right?"

"Yep. They would never put their people in this position. See how lucky you are to be getting the experience no one else gets?" I said and nudged Jake.

"Yeah, how fortunate we are to be here," he said sarcastically and smiled. "After you became successful with your freelance work, did anyone offer to fund you and do things how you wanted?"

"Actually, a few did. But I was used to being on my own and enjoyed beating their network guys to the next story. As long as they'd pay me for my work, I was happy to go it alone. But I had to drink to get through what I was seeing and reporting. The natural disasters, human trauma, social decline, it was killing my positive outlook of the world."

"So how did you give it up, cold turkey?"

"Pretty much. I'd only been working for a few years on my own as a freelancer. But getting original and compelling stories people wanted to read required me to travel. I had just gotten married and my first wife, Pam, said she understood what I needed to do and was cool with the travel, but when we got pregnant, things changed a bit. My situation changed, but I didn't. After our son, Ethan, was born, Pam wanted me to take more local stories so I could stay near the family, but it seemed to me that all the stuff that was selling was somewhere else.

"I appeased her for a while, but very few of my stories were selling and I resented her for it. There was a lot of downtime and I was drinking quite a bit. I used to hide the fact that I was drinking steadily throughout the day. I just needed a little to get me through the frustration. We'd had a big fight about me having booze in the house. She thought that if it wasn't at my fingertips, I wouldn't drink as much. That was nonsense. I just ended up lying to her and telling her I was out on a story when I was really in my car or at the park getting my daily dose to calm my anxiety."

"You couldn't just talk through it with her?"

I smiled. "That seems like the logical thing to do, but relationships are funny. I was stubborn. I didn't think we needed to talk about it. I felt I should just be able to do whatever the hell I wanted to do. Looking back, I know I was just being selfish. There was a solution there, but neither one of us really wanted to find it. We were both stubborn."

"What got you to give it up?"

"I killed my son."

"What? How did you do that?" Jake asked, taken by surprise.

I just stared at the ground and continued. "He was sleeping in his car seat in the backseat. I stopped at a liquor store to get a couple pints to hide around the house. I knew it was only going to take a minute to grab what I needed and get back to the car, so I left the windows cracked and even waited for the last customer to leave the store so I could be the only car in the parking area and be right in front so I could still see him. I also didn't want anyone else to see me leave him in the car and call child protective services. So, I waited for the last car to leave, parked in front, and ran in real quick."

I took another long drag on my cigarette, blew out the smoke, and continued to stare at the ground before I went on. "I see him right now. As if it only happened a few moments ago. I was at the checkout counter with my two bottles of vodka and a bottle of scotch. I looked through the front door of the liquor store to see if he was still asleep. He looked so peaceful sitting there strapped into his kid seat. Right then, he opened his eyes and looked around for a second, looking for me. The angle was just right so I could see him in the backseat from where I stood at the register. I saw his eyes find mine. He gave me a big smile from his car seat. He was so happy to see me standing there, only a few dozen feet away. I could see it in his eyes that he was relieved I hadn't left him."

"So, what happened?" Jake asked.

"Some guy passed out at the wheel about a half block up the street. He crossed the oncoming lanes of traffic, hit the curb in front of the liquor store and his truck went partially airborne and T-boned my car right at Ethan's door. They calculated that he was doing about fifty miles per hour. I never saw Ethan's smile fade."

I took a long drag on my cigarette, exhaled, and rubbed my eyes before I looked up at Jake. "He never saw it coming. He was never afraid. I can only hope he didn't feel any pain. He left my life forever just like that. I was right there and couldn't do a goddamned thing."

"That's not your fault, Angus."

"That's a nice thing to say," I said and took another drag before I continued, "but I was buying booze on the sly. Neither of us should have been in that spot at that time. Had I not stopped to feed my addiction, he'd still be alive. How could it not be my fault? There was no way I could take a drink after that. Every time I see a drink, I see Ethan's smile."

Jake and I were getting good at basking in uncomfortable silences. We both just sat and smoked for a few moments.

"Is that why you chase and report on misery, so you can justify your own?"

"Maybe. The things I see as a journalist tend to pound home the rationalization that, even though it breaks my heart, my son can't see and experience this world for himself. I know he's not missing much."

"How did your wife react?"

"When Pam found out that I left him in a liquor store parking lot to buy booze, it was over. We've never spoken since. I couldn't blame her. But I haven't had a drop since."

"Fuck, man. I had no idea."

"I know. It's okay. It's something I have to live with. I never had the balls to take my own life, but I figured if fate needed to take my boy from me in a freak accident, maybe fate would put me out of my damn misery if I could present myself as a large enough target. I went to the most dangerous places chasing stories and, if I got killed, so much the better.

"As it happened, I was chasing a story in Beirut when Hezbollah kidnapped an Israeli soldier on the northern border of Lebanon in 2006 and incited the full wrath of Israel in retaliation. I covered the fighting, met my second wife, Lilya, and her brother Rafi, and was awarded a Pulitzer Prize for my reporting."

"Not really what you were expecting to happen, huh?"

"I expected to die any day. You never know what's gonna happen. It's like you're rolling down the road with the sun in your eyes. You can't see clearly, but you know you have to keep going or you'll never get anywhere. So you make the best decisions you can and just bide your time until the sun gets higher and your vision gets clearer. That can only happen with time. Until then, we just keep on doing the best we can as we look into the sun."

"What happened to your second wife?"

"She died of breast cancer only a couple years ago. I guess I wasn't meant to have anyone around me for too long."

Chapter 37

June 5, 2013

Amala and Jake came up to me and looked as though they had some sort of plan.

I smiled. "What are you two up to?"

"Come with me. You need to see this," Amala said.

We walked one block over so we would not be in direct sight of the snipers and turned down a side street for a block. We stepped over splintered furniture and the soiled and bloody clothes discarded over the rebar embedded in demolished concrete buildings all around us. Shattered glass shimmered on the ground and decorated the mounds of rubble that were once the walls that encapsulated people's normal lives not too long ago.

"Where are you taking us?" I asked Amala.

"It's a garage just ahead," she said as she moved a mother's smashed high chair out of our narrow path.

We saw her disappear through a hole that had been blasted in the side of a wall just large enough for us to crouch through. As my eyes adjusted to the darkness inside, I could see we were in a former automobile repair shop large enough for only two vehicles. A truck with large tires was partially hidden with rugs and sheets that were stained black from dried blood. It sat next to a white truck with scores of white empty cardboard boxes stacked in front of it. I could see that the white truck had dozens of bullet holes in the door and a large red crescent painted on it.

Amala began moving boxes near the back of the truck, "A few women came to get me when this truck was ambushed by a regime tank not far from here. The soldiers in the tank killed the driver and his passenger with their machine guns and then pursued the armored vehicles that were escorting it."

Jake and I helped her clear more boxes out of the way until the tailgate was accessible. She pulled the chains holding the tailgate locked on one side and motioned for me to do the same on the other side. I pulled the pin and we let the tailgate down slowly.

"We must try not to make noise. No one knows this truck is here and I don't want anyone else to know about it."

"Why?"

"Climb inside and look beyond the boxes toward the front and you will see."

Jake and I looked at each other and then climbed in the back of the truck. I moved three rows of stacked boxes toward the back of the truck and instantly knew why this needed to be a secret.

"What are those?" Jake asked.

"Missiles," I said.

"Wow. Missiles for what?"

I read the white writing on the olive green containers. "They're heat-seeking anti-aircraft missiles," I said.

"Holy shit. How many?"

I pulled out my iPhone and tapped the flashlight feature on to see all the way to the cab of the truck and took a quick mental count, "Looks like twenty four cases total. If the stenciling on the boxes are correct, there are twelve anti-aircraft missiles and twelve anti-tank missiles."

I took out my knife and cut the thin wire security bindings off the latches. I sliced through the printed security seals that ran over the seams of the box and pulled it open. I shined my light inside. A long green missile tube with a brown pistol grip was neatly strapped to an internal metal frame bolted to the inside of the case to keep the missile from moving while in transit.

"Gary's gonna shit when he finds out about these," Jake said.

I looked at Jake. "There's no way he can ever know these are here. We have to destroy these things."

I snapped a few photos of both the anti-tank and anti-aircraft missiles for proof before we replaced the boxes in the bed and hid the truck just as we had found it.

We headed back to the clinic the same way we had come, careful to keep out of the sights of the snipers.

* * *

"How do you know about these?" I asked Amala as we walked back to the clinic.

"The women called me to help treat the driver and his passenger but there was nothing I could do for them. They were hit with too many bullets. The women said there were medical supplies in the truck so we went to get them. When we began to unload them to take them to the clinic, we found the missiles hidden behind them. I had one of the boys drive the truck to his uncle's garage and we hid it there."

"Where is the kid?"

Amala looked back at me as we walked, "He is dead."

"And the kid's uncle?"

"He is dead, too. He was killed a few months ago. The rest of his family fled to the refugee camps in Turkey soon after."

"So, no one knows about this truck except you?"

"And now you two."

"Why don't we hand them over to Gary so he can make sure they get to the right people?"

"There are no right people to operate one of those things," Amala said.

"But they could help stop the regime," Jake said.

"They will stop nothing. It will only make things worse no matter which side uses them. Angus is right. They must be destroyed."

Chapter 38

June 5, 2013

Jake and I sat with a quiet man in the medical clinic named Nagib, who had been working with Amala. He was dressed in the pale blue color of hospital scrubs and had a meticulously trimmed beard and kind, but tired, dark brown eyes. Amala had mentioned that he had fled from a Syrian government hospital to Al-Waer and I wanted to ask him why.

I warmed him up with a few basic questions like where he was from: Homs. Where he went to school: Homs and then emergency medical technician school in Damascus.

"Doctor Amala told us you came here from a large government hospital in Damascus. Is that true?" I said and Amala translated for me.

"*Nam*," he said. *Yes.*

"Why did you leave and come here?"

"I was working as a nurse in the hospital for a few months before the demonstrations began. I didn't like the hours of an ambulance driver. I had to be up all night and always ready to run out the door. The nurse job was much more stable and better for me. One day a number of people were rushed into the hospital with wounds during a public demonstration. They had broken arms, broken fingers, their heads were bleeding from being beaten, and a few even had gunshot wounds."

"One man I was assigned to help had a gunshot wound to his leg. The bullet had gone straight through, so it was fairly simple. I just needed to clean and dress it. When I was finished, a Lieutenant Colonel from the army came in looking for wounded demonstrators."

"This is the Syrian Army?"

"Yes, Syrian Army."

"Not *shabbiha*?"

"No, not the secret security forces, not the *shabbiha*. He was dressed in the uniform of a Syrian Army officer, a Lieutenant Colonel," Amala said as she continued to translate for us. "He was told that the man I had just taken care of had been shot. So he walked over to him to speak with him. He asked the man who had shot him and the man told him that the *shabbiha* shot him. The Colonel kept shaking his head and telling the man, 'No, you were shot by armed gangs, by rebels,' but the man kept saying that was not true, that he was shot by the *shabbiha.*

"The Colonel got angry and raised his voice to the man and told him that he would go on national TV and say he was shot by armed gangs at the demonstration. The man refused and the Colonel pulled his pistol from his holster and shot the man in the head right there in his hospital bed and walked out."

"When was this?" I asked him.

"October 2011."

"What did you do?"

"I told my supervisor that I couldn't work for the state if they were going to kill people whose only crime was telling the truth. I decided to come back to Homs and help the demonstrators any way I could."

"What do you think the biggest threat is right now?"

"Indiscriminate killing of civilians."

"What do you mean?"

He pointed to the ceiling, "Barrel bombs."

I nodded but Jake asked, "What are barrel bombs?"

"Will you explain the barrel bombs for us?"

"The regime wants to intimidate and instill fear where they do not have the influence on the ground. Where the army finds resistance and the people fight back against their homes being ripped apart and their businesses destroyed. Young men are taken to prison and sometimes their women are taken and raped and even killed. When the people will not tolerate this, they fight back. They kill soldiers and *shabbiha* who do these crimes. Then the government will fly over with helicopters and push barrels filled with explosives onto a neighborhood to kill whoever it falls on."

"And who does it kill?"

"Usually any rebel gangs are in the countryside and not in the neighborhoods. The barrel bombs kill mostly unarmed civilians, women, and children with no place to go or no money to take them anywhere to escape the violence."

"Do you see a lot of children in your clinic?"

"Yes, women, children, elderly. The young men are off fighting with the government or one of the rival groups. The victims are the ones who stay in their homes, hoping for peace."

Chapter 39

June 6, 2013

I had the bug again. I needed to capture some more action. I still hadn't found a way out of Al-Waer or found any suitable transportation to take anyone with me if I had. I figured, since I was stuck in Al-Waer until I could figure that out, I might as well go out and see what there was to see.

Gary offered to show me how his FSA guys were coming together to bother Assad's army. We sat on the roof of a bombed-out building just below the three-foot wall that ringed almost every roof in the neighborhood. We heard an eerie wail singing the noon call to prayer in the distance. Gary said that the army always moved its tanks around after the noon call to prayer and if we were "lucky" his guys could lure a few into a trap. I wanted to know more about how Gary was instructing the FSA fighters as we waited.

"There are three difficult things you have to get just right to kill tanks," Gary said. "The first is getting in position. These damn things are maneuverable and the tankers can just about go wherever they want. Except in a city. If you can drive them to a point where you have someone waiting for them, that's what you need to do."

"How do you do that?"

"There are a few ways. One is lots of observation. If they've been local for a bit, you may be able to predict where they will be. Another more dangerous way is to draw their fire. But you don't want to piss them off too much because they can just call in artillery or air strikes on you. However, if you give them a bit of incentive, just a little juicy morsel to chase, you can lead them into a trap."

"Don't they know that?"

"Yeah, some of them do. But when you deal with human nature, you have a pretty good chance that one of these guys will fall for the bait and chase your rabbit. Spielberg showed it pretty well in *Saving Private Ryan.* He was just highlighting what armies have known since the tank came along. Hell, they used to do it to horse-mounted infantry since the time of Genghis Khan. The principle's the same.

"Human nature is fairly constant across history. It's the real disciplined ones you have to watch out for. That's why Rommel and Patton were so good at what they did. They were smart, had discipline, and didn't let emotion get in their way. They saw the problem, knew the risks, evaluated the hazards, and then made a decision to either press the attack or fall back to fight another day."

"Have you seen many Rommels out here?"

Gary looked at me and smiled. "Not by a long shot. Chances are, if you present a favorable target, these guys get excited and will chase. As long as we can keep them interested and don't give them a chance to think about what we're doing to them, they get all in a lather and want blood. They all want to kick ass to prove that they're badasses. That's exactly what we want. So, we get the rabbit to shoot at them, the rabbit leads them to a street we control, and a few guys shoot small arms at them from either side, just enough to piss them off. Then, the rabbit ducks down a street where we have two anti-tank rockets positioned to take them out. If we're lucky, they bring their buddy to cover them. Then we wait until they're both in the crosshairs and let them both have it.

"A great tactic is to block off the end of the street so the lead tank can't just roll through the kill zone and get away. He has to stop and back up. Then, you shoot the second tank first and the lead tank can't back up because his dead buddy is blocking his exit. Then you have time to take careful aim and knock them both out."

"Has this worked for you before?"

"Yeah, we did it once a few weeks ago and it worked great. The air force bombed the shit out of the neighborhood we chose to ambush, so you have to be careful where you set up because you know there's gonna be some collateral damage coming your way."

"Okay, getting in position, then what?"

"The next thing is making sure the position you've chosen is manned with men who know how to shoot. If you are limited with the number of shots you have, you'd better make the ones you have count. That means hitting them on the first shot. There may not be time for any second shots."

"How many do we have for today?"

"We only have two shots, one on each side of the street. If we lure two tanks, that means the guy can't freeze. He's got to hit his target the first time. We have a few RPGs, but they're not as good and we don't want to waste them because some fucker can't take out a tank with an anti-tank rocket."

"Okay, making the shots count, that's pretty obvious. What's the last thing?"

"Getting the hell outta Dodge once you've shot. Whether you hit or not, you have to move. But if you miss, you gotta be faster than if you destroy them because they'll be gunnin' for you and they always call their friends. They usually get pretty pissed when you take out their tanks."

"How much training have you done with your men on this?"

"It really only took one screwed up attack to make everyone believers."

"What happened?"

"I had a crew that shot, missed, and then tried to engage from the same position with several RPGs. They kept missing and then when the tanks finally got a bead on their position and began shooting back accurately, too much time had gone by and their air force buddies showed up and turned most of the surrounding neighborhood, including their building, to dust. Those fighters got themselves and about a hundred civilians killed."

"How could you let that happen?"

"I wasn't there. They acted on their own. After that incident, they tried out my tactics and we've never looked back."

"How many tanks have you gotten?"

"I think we're up to eight or nine. It's not as easy as it sounds. The circumstances need to unfold exactly right to get a good kill. And the stars really need to line up to get two. Like I said before, the regime isn't stupid. They learn from their mistakes. But some of these guys have been on their own for a while and haven't gotten a chance to get debriefed by their superiors on what to look for. So, if we piss off the right idiot out there, we still have a shot at pulling it off. And besides that, it really keeps them on their toes, which tends to wear them down. You can't be on high alert all the time. But we try to keep them guessing."

"Where did you learn all of this? Were you in the army?"

Gary laughed. "No. But I get to talk to a lot of experts on a lot of things. And four out of five tank killing experts have taught me that we have a winning solution with good planning and solid execution. It won't work every time, but if our tank killing average was a batting average, my boys would be in the hall of fame."

Chapter 40

June 6, 2013

I was sitting with Jake on the top step of the stairwell that led to the roof of the building we occupied. It was Gary's chosen spot to station one of his two tank killing teams. The other team was on the roof of the building across the street. There was a gentle breeze coming from the west that made the hot air feel like a lukewarm hair dryer was blowing on you. For the most part, the air was fresh from the desert beyond the city limits. I was grateful to not have any smoke or rotting flesh wafting in.

We drank as much water as we could, but had to be somewhat conservative as we weren't sure exactly when we would be able to refill the few plastic water bottles we had with us. Along with the artillery attacks, barrel bombs, and snipers, the need for water was a constant concern. Food was a once per day luxury that could be satiated with cigarettes or some sort of physical action that kept it locked away in your brain as a fond memory, but your thirst was a nagging that could keep you awake at night with swollen hands and amber urine from a constant case of mild dehydration.

I jotted down what I remembered from Gary's earlier conversation about the tank killing tactics when he came around the corner in a walking crouch.

"Come on. My boys are about to set the bait," he said.

Gary hustled off toward the edge of the roof, still crouching so as not to be seen from the street below or other buildings. I got up, put away my pad and pen, and did my best imitation of his crouch to where he waited. I sat down with my back against the wall and took out my iPhone for a few pics.

Gary looked over at me, "You'd better get that fucking thing outta my face or it's going over the side. You can take pictures of my guys but none of me. And if you send anything out, I wanna see them first and ensure you black out their faces. The regime will come find these men and their families, you have to remember that."

"Okay, none of you and I'll black out their faces. No problem."

Gary's two-way radio crackled to life with a garbled transmission in Arabic. He lifted the speaker to his ear and closed his eyes to concentrate on hearing the message. It came to life again with only a few words.

He put the radio to his lips. "Okay, *emshi, emshi,*" he said in Arabic. *Go, go.*

"What's happening?" Jake asked.

"They are positioning themselves to get in front of two tanks. They're going to try to have the tanks chase them."

"How are they going to do that?"

"They drive by and shoot at the tanks and then the tanks chase them."

"That seems dangerous."

"I'm not sure if you noticed, but everything here is dangerous. We might as well take out a few tanks. We just have to be smart about it."

"Will the guys tell you when they're being chased?" I asked.

"No. We'll know. Just wait."

Not a minute went by before I understood what Gary meant. The concrete floor beneath us shook as if the whole area got hit by a small earthquake. I looked over at Gary and he smiled.

"They're shooting at our boys. It's gonna get louder."

A few seconds later, another blast ripped through the air but it was closer, and then another even closer. Gary got on the radio and spoke into it quickly, then raised it to his ear to wait for the response.

"Are you calling the other crew?"

"Yes. They're ready. They have a better angle. They'll see the tanks approach before we will. They'll tell us when they're coming."

"Is it safe for me to look over the edge?"

Gary laughed. "It is right now. Don't worry, you do what I do. If I get down, you'd better get down. And remember, if I run, you stay right with me if you wanna file this story tonight."

I got onto my knees and peered over the edge of the low roof wall. The street below looked like every other street in this neighborhood: demolished. There was debris in the street and the buildings on either side of the road looked as if they had been skinned and I was looking at their skeletons, their guts blown out of them long ago.

Gary pointed. "We'll see the rabbit come around that corner at the end of the block. He's gonna come down the street about halfway and stop until the first tank follows him. The trick is that he has to still present a good target without getting killed. We don't want to spook these guys. I need them to go at least halfway down the street before we can get them with a kill shot. Preferably, we want the lead tank about three quarters of the way down and his buddy about halfway down. Then we can get them both."

The floor shook beneath our feet and then I saw black smoke rise from between the buildings about a block away.

"Do you actually get volunteers to be the rabbit?"

"You'd be surprised. Some of these young guys want to prove themselves. This is a good way to show you got balls to the rest of the group."

"Did you ever do it?"

"Yeah, I had to do it the first time to show these guys it could be done. The driver and I almost got our asses shot off. We got one tank but it cost us both about a half pound of shrapnel each. I'm pretty sure I still have bits of these damn buildings under my skin."

"That's leading from the front."

"It's the only thing these guys respect. You have to show balls or you ain't nothin'. They're fighting for their lives. If you can't give the same amount of sacrifice, they don't want you around."

The ground shook again and the explosion was loud and close. So close it threw up a small cloud of dust from the ground at our feet. Gary's team next door shot him an urgent message on the radio. It was exactly what he was hoping for.

"The rabbit's coming around that corner," Gary said and pointed to the street below.

I looked down, trying to memorize the scene for when I would try to describe it later for my story. In an instant, a small pickup truck with two shooters sitting in the back went flying around the corner and careened onto the sidewalk. I could see the driver correcting through the windshield as he steered the truck back onto the road.

"Dammit, I wish they'd be careful. That's our last truck," Gary said as he watched his men below.

The truck slowed a bit to make sure they didn't fully lose the tank. A second later, the tank came barreling around the same corner in hot pursuit. It crushed garbage and debris under its tracks, knocked over a light pole on the sidewalk, and corrected its trajectory to follow the truck.

The truck driver below saw the tank advancing and gunned the engine as the two fighters in the back fired their rifles at the tank to keep them good and pissed. The driver swerved back and forth in a zig-zag pattern to keep the tank from getting a clean shot at them.

The machine gunner, firing from the position to the right of the main gun on the tank turret, was doing a respectable job making his bullets count. A few bursts managed to hit the truck and made the two gunners in the back of the pickup take cover behind two barrels positioned at the back of the bed which they used as a shield.

"What's in those barrels?"

"Sand. We fill them with sand so the men have something to hide behind if they need it."

I looked down and saw the truck turn down a side street about three quarters of the way down the street. The tank was still traveling at about twenty miles per hour and would be at the intersection where the truck escaped in about ten seconds.

"Are they gonna shoot?"

"Just wait a second. That tanker has to wait for his buddy or he can't follow him. He'll slow down or stop to wait for him and then we'll have them."

Just as Gary said it, the tank slowed to a stop just as the second tank rounded the corner at the far end of the block.

Gary put the radio to his lips, "Hit the far one now," he said into his radio in Arabic.

A few seconds elapsed and a bright flash, followed by a huge dust cloud, erupted from the roof of the building across the street. A few seconds after that, the crew on our roof fired and the sudden blast made us jump.

"Holy shit, that was loud!" Jake yelled, holding his ears.

I looked at him and laughed. I was laughing at Jake, but then thought that it was a little callous to be laughing when I knew Gary's guys had most likely just killed two regime tank crews.

"Goddammit!" Gary yelled.

"What's wrong?" I yelled to Gary.

"The first crew missed. The far tank isn't dead. We gotta go. Come on, we gotta go now," Gary said and grabbed my arm.

* * *

Gary led the way. Jake and I were right behind him, and his anti-tank gun crew of two was right behind us. All five of us clamored down five flights of stairs, dodging broken furniture and piles of demolished cinder blocks, clothes, and appliances. We made it to the ground floor and saw the gun crew from across the street holed up in an alcove waiting for us. I could tell they were well-rehearsed on their extraction plan.

Gary gave them a hand signal I didn't recognize and we all ran down the street in the opposite direction of the burning tank behind us.

"Why are we running? They can't shoot us if they're dead," Jake said as he kept up with Gary and me.

Gary huffed a little as he ran, but turned his head and said, "Two reasons: one, that tank is gonna cook off all of its fuel and ammunition as it burns. It's gonna spit out all of its machine gun ammo and big gun ammo all across this neighborhood. We need to be well-clear of that."

We kept running.

"And the other reason?" I asked.

"That second tank is still out there. It's gonna be pissed and call in all his friends on this position."

We ran down the street a few blocks and then stopped to catch our breath. I heard the cannon shells explode as they began cooking off behind us. We all panted and waited for the tank crew from across the street to meet up with us. We were now a guerilla group of seven.

"Okay, we're gonna go down this street for about ten blocks and we should be okay. That should keep us clear of any counterfire. You guys ready?" he asked, looking at Jake and me.

"Yep, let's get outta here," I said.

We ran about five of the ten blocks and then stopped for another breather. Gary pulled out his canteen and took a few sips and handed it to me. I did the same and handed it to Jake. He gulped a bit and Gary grabbed it away from him.

"Not too much, kid, you'll get cramps," he said and stowed it in his tactical vest. He took a few more deep breaths and gave a thumbs-up to his guys as they were putting their water away as well. They returned his gesture and we moved out again down the road at a slower jog.

After a block, Gary stopped and listened to his radio. He said a few words into it and then replaced it in his vest.

"What was that?"

Gary chuckled a bit. "Those tanker guys are pissed. That was the rabbit, he said that the tank we missed found them and chased them. They managed to lose them because my guys thought they were unwilling to get lured in again. But the tank is very near our neighborhood."

"They aren't coming in are they?"
"No. Not yet. And that's not good."
"Why?" Jake asked.
"Because they are probably staying clear of the airstrikes they just called in."
"On our neighborhood?"
"We'll see," Gary said. "Come on, let's go. We won't know until we get there."

Chapter 41

June 6, 2013

The airstrikes didn't take long to materialize, but it wasn't what I thought they would be. They weren't jets. They were helicopters with barrel bombs right on top of Al-Waer. There was no way of knowing if they would land near our part of the community or not. We just had to get there to find out how bad it was.

We were about two blocks away when we heard, felt, and saw the first barrel bomb impact ahead of us. The explosion felt like it was right around the corner. Black smoke came pouring from down a side street and enveloped us all as we ran. There was nothing we could do but breathe in the thick air. It stuck to our mouths and throats and made us cough up black phlegm. I told Jake to put his scarf up over his face like a cowboy. I did the same just so I could have some sort of filter from all the dust in the air.

We didn't see the next explosion, but it knocked every one of us to the ground. It was close, only about a half block away. Right where we needed to go.

I got to my feet and Gary helped a few of his guys up off the ground. I helped Jake up and was grateful he was okay. Gary appeared in front of me out of the smoke.

"You okay?"

"I think so," I managed to say between coughs.

"You okay?" I asked Jake.

He only nodded as he coughed into his scarf.

"Okay, let's get over there and see if we can help," Gary said and led the way into the dust and smoke that now permeated our neighborhood.

* * *

We heard the screaming before we saw anything. We emerged from the smoke near the clinic and were horrified. Dozens of bodies were strewn about the street and sidewalks. Able-bodied men and women, young and old were carrying people into the clinic. Some were bleeding, some were unconscious, and some were clearly dead.

Jake ran ahead of me and bolted through the clinic door first, no doubt, looking for Amala. I was right on his heels and was not prepared for the carnage. There were men, women, and children crying out with all manner of wounds. I made my way to the makeshift operating room and slipped on the blood-soaked tile floor.

Jake saw Amala working on an old woman's wounds and yelled for her. "Amala!" he cried and wrapped her in a quick hug.

She pushed him away, annoyed. "Jake, I'm working. Go get some gauze in the storeroom," she said and continued working on the old woman.

Jake disappeared into the storeroom and came back with an armful of gauze and put them on a chair next to Amala.

"Unwrap one of those and press it down right here," Amala said to Jake and pointed to the old woman's femoral artery where her leg met her hip.

Jake took a gauze package, ripped it open, and placed it where she said.

"Hold it down hard so she doesn't bleed to death while I work on her chest wound," she said.

I took out my iPhone and snapped a few pictures of the organized effort to save the old woman and the chaos around the table.

"What can I do?" I said, feeling useless and a little guilty.

Amala looked at me. "Stop taking pictures and help triage outside."

No other comment could have made me feel so low. I made my way through the screaming humanity and began assessing the wounded who were waiting for Amala's help. There were several people lined up outside her door, the closest ones lying down or sitting against the wall. Others, with less life-threatening wounds were standing in a line behind them. It looked as though the triage had already been done.

On my right, in a small room off the main entrance, I saw several bodies covered in brightly colored wool blankets, the local symbol of dead bodies. I desperately wanted to see who was under those blankets, but was still feeling the sting of Amala's comment that I was obviously being a nuisance unless I was doing something medical. I looked around and everyone seemed to be taken care of at the moment. I walked farther into the room and noticed a small body under a dark green blanket. It was soaked through with blood from the waist down.

My hands shook as I pulled the blanket from the body's head. I fell to my knees a split second later when I recognized who it was.

"No," was all I could manage to say.

I tried to compose myself after a few seconds. I had to get out of there before Jake saw me, but it was too late; he came around the corner behind me. He saw me on my knees kneeling next to the small body.

"What is it, Angus? Who is it?"

I pulled the blanket over the body's head and stood on wobbly legs. "Um, these people are gone. Let's help the others," I said, taking him by the shoulders and turning him around.

Jake pushed back on me and got around me somehow. He made a beeline for the small body. He pulled the blanket back and stood there for a second. He fell to his knees just as I had, and hugged the little boy's lifeless body. I walked out to see if I could be of any help to the living.

I heard Jake's scream from the sidewalk outside.

"No, Shawqi! No!"

Chapter 42

Al-Waer Medical Clinic
June 6, 2013

I was ready for him when he came out the front door of the clinic. "Jake, come with me. You need to chill out."

I'd seen that look on other journalist's who'd gone around the bend: eyes crazed, irrational, and unthinking. He was reacting with emotion, the worst possible public display of anguish at this moment.

I grabbed him by the shoulders. "You need to fucking chill out, man."

"They fucking killed him. He never did anything to anybody!"

"I know. Come on, walk with me," I said. "Let's go get a smoke."

"Fuck that. I'm gonna kill them all!" he screamed.

I felt a little bad about it, but I pulled back and slapped him across the face so hard it made my hand sting. I didn't want to hurt him but he needed to snap out of it.

My slap put him back on his heels and then he shifted his anger at me. He lunged for me and I deflected his punch. I swung around behind him, pulled both his wrists behind his back, and forced him to the ground.

"Get the fuck off me!" he screamed.

I looked around and every eye was on us, in the middle of the street, literally wrestling with the grief these people had been enduring for years. I clasped both my hands around his wrists pressed to his lower back and his face flat on the street.

"Listen, Jake. I know you're hurting."

"You don't know shit."

I couldn't take this anymore. He needed to know. I lay down on his back and whispered in his ear. "No, you listen to me. I've been living with this shit for a long time. My son's dead, my wife's gone, neither of them deserved it. These people don't deserve it, either. But you need to pull yourself together. It hurts but, goddammit, you will not put these people into hysterics right now. This is not about you."

Jake's body tensed up like he was trying to get out of my grip. "Get the fuck off me!" he yelled again.

I freed one of my hands and pushed his head hard into the street. "You need to calm the fuck down right now."

I held him there for a few seconds and I could feel his body go limp as he began to weep.

"I'm gonna let you up now. Will you be cool?"

"Dammit. Why him?"

I said, "Will you be cool?"

"Yeah."

"Okay. I'm gonna let you up and we're gonna walk down to the end of the block. You up for that?"

"Yeah."

"Okay," I said and released the pressure on him and sat on his back for a second to see what he would do.

He lay there as I climbed off him and got to my feet. He looked up at me with dirt and concrete bits stuck to his face, tears streaming down his cheeks.

"Why? Why the fuck does shit like this have to happen?"

"It doesn't have to happen. But it does happen, every day. Come on, let's take a walk and get a smoke."

* * *

We walked to my usual writing spot at the end of the block, just before the cross street I knew the snipers had in their sights. We sat with our backs against the wall and smoked two cigarettes in a row in silence. I knew he needed some time, so I didn't say anything. He needed time to process what he'd just seen.

I tamped out my second cigarette and offered him a third but he waved me off.

"No, thanks."

"Are you sure? Kurt Vonnegut called smoking the longest form of suicide. You sure you don't want another?"

Jake looked at me with just slightly less crazy eyes than before. "I don't want to kill myself. I want to kill all these motherfuckers responsible for this."

"Well, join the club," I said and got to my feet.

"Really? All you do is watch. You don't take any action. You're just a spectator pushing this shit into the media for a lead story."

Fuck this kid. What did he know?

"The fuck I am, you goddamn cherry. You just saw a glimpse of what I've been experiencing for twenty-five years. Why do you think I risk my life coming here to do this? If we don't witness this and tell people what's going on, who will?"

"That's a nice cover story. How many pictures did you take in there?"

"What?"

"You heard me, you callous fuck. How many pictures did you take? Did you take any of Shawqi?"

"Look, man, you're traumatized. I've been there. You need to remind yourself who you're talking to."

"Fuck that. I want to see your phone," he said and flicked his cigarette butt into the street. He stood up and faced off with me.

"What are you talking about?"

"Give me your phone."

"Fuck you."

He lunged at me, but I sidestepped his assault and sent his momentum into the street. He lost his balance and hit the ground. He looked up at me, surprised.

"You think this is my first experience with this sort of thing? I've been covering this sort of shit since you were in grade school, wondering if your glamour shot was going to get you an audition in the fucking Sears catalog. Why do you think Rafi's at my side? Can you guess?"

He just looked at me from the ground.

"He lost his own wife and his brother to shit like this. This isn't new. Just because you're just feeling it for the first time doesn't mean people need to care. This happens all the time. Not only in the Middle East, everywhere. Have you ever been to Africa?"

"Yeah, I have."

"Where? Not where people are shooting at you. Not Libya or Sierra Leone or Nigeria, I bet."

He just lay there.

"I do this because it's all I can do without picking up a weapon, which wouldn't do any damn good anyway. The work I do shows people that they need to care. If they're willing to listen. If they're willing to feel."

Jake got up and brushed himself off. "This is fucking useless."

"Attitudes like that are why we have a society that believes there's nothing that can be effective. It was journalists who keyed the world in on the ethnic cleansing in Rwanda, Bosnia, and Darfur. We show the world what the world is really like, whether they want to see it or not, whether they want to accept it or not. It's the only thing that drives me. I got nothing else."

We stood in silence for a few seconds. Jake shuffled to the sidewalk with his head down. "Why do you do it when you know it won't do any good?"

"I have to believe that, at some point, people will have to take notice. If I didn't do it, who would? Things would just happen and no one would know or care. That's part of the reason we're here right now. I saw an opportunity to make a positive change in this situation and I jumped on it. Not because it was going to be easy or because it was smart or even that I had it all worked out. I just knew I needed to do something to help these people, these kids. I can see that you feel it, Jake. I'm glad that you feel it. That feeling is compassion, frustration, anger, and love all rolled into one. I couldn't be a fly on the wall and just report what I see anymore. There's value to bringing the story to people, but at this point in my life, I've got to act."

Jake stood there and stared at the ground. We both turned to look up the block as we heard more screaming from the clinic.

"I guess we should go and see if we can help," Jake said.

"This isn't easy, Jake. Believe me, I know," I said and held out my hand. "No hard feelings?"

He looked at my outreached hand for a second and then shook it. "No hard feelings."

"Come on, I'm sure there's something we can do in there," I said and pointed toward the clinic.

"Okay," he said, "but there's one thing I have to do."

I looked at him. He had a glint of the crazy eyes again. He took a couple of deep breaths and bolted into the middle of the cross street before I could grab him. He held up two middle fingers.

"Fuck you!" he screamed to the hidden snipers.

Sniper shots rang out almost immediately. The intersection behind him erupted in bullets as the snipers tried to shoot him. I jumped out into the cross street and pulled him back around the corner. A bullet impacted the road where he stood a moment before.

"What the fuck are you doing?"

He just looked at me and smiled, breathing hard. "If all we can do to fight these guys is show 'em that we've got balls, then why didn't you get a picture of *that*?"

"You do anything like that again and I'll give you back to your buddy Abdul Aziz."

"Yeah, whatever, you know that was fucking cool. Give me another installment on the Vonnegut suicide plan and let's go see what Amala needs."

* * *

Challenge and Response in Syria
Posted to GRL by Angus Conn
Al-Waer, Syria
Filed June 6, 2013

I accompanied two teams of fighters from the FSA on a mission to kill regime tanks. One team set up on the roof of an abandoned building and the other set up across the street. A third group of four men took a pickup truck and shot at two tanks to get them to follow them into a trap.

As the truck remained just out of reach, the team in the truck led the tanks to a narrow street where the anti-tank crews were waiting. One tank took a direct hit and was destroyed. It is unknown whether any regime troops were able to get out of the tank before it exploded and burned. The second tank was shot at but the anti-tank round missed.

The FSA gunners were able to get away and make it back to the neighborhood they used as a staging base but not before the regime hit the area with barrel bombs in reprisal for the tank attack. It is believed that at least one regime tank crew of four was killed in the tank attack with no FSA fighters killed or injured. But the civilians in the targeted neighborhood took the brunt of the casualties. In all, blasts from just two barrel bombs pushed out of the back of regime helicopters high above the neighborhood, destroyed two buildings and killed eleven people, three men, two women, and six children, including an entire family of five as they took shelter in their home.

Chapter 43

June 7, 2013

I sat with Jake as I wrote another story at our usual place at the end of the street where Jake had flipped off the snipers the day before. Jake was scrolling through pictures on his phone. I could see that he stopped on one of Shawqi and was staring at it.

"I get it. These are men fighting for their country, their families, for what they believe in, their way of life. And some of them die. But the kids. Why the kids?" Jake asked.

"That's why Rafi, Bobbie, and I are here. Someone has to witness this and show the world what's going on. Just because it hasn't been the leading story in the states for months doesn't mean kids aren't still dying every day."

"What the fuck is wrong with people?"

"I remember when Alyssa Milano did that fake sex video where the beginning thirty seconds or so looked like she and her boyfriend were gonna get busy on camera. Then she appears distracted by the TV and stops the romance to comment on the horrible things going on in Syria. I was proud of her for her interest and her effort to highlight it, but as you can imagine, the larger message was lost on all the dudes who just wanted to see Alyssa Milano get down and dirty on video. People are just people. It's my job to make them care and your job to entertain them."

Jake put his head in his hands. "My life is meaningless compared to what's going on here."

"Jake, you can't just drop in for a few weeks and then go back to the red carpet like nothing's wrong in the world. But at the same time, you have to turn the grief to something else. You have to channel it."

He pulled his head up and lit a cigarette and smiled. "Just a little while ago, we were on a plane sipping drinks. Well, I was sipping drinks," he said and smiled. "I thought you were kind of an asshole about all this. But you knew all along what we were getting into. How do you deal with all of this? How do you decompress after what you've seen?"

"I smoke a lot," I said and exhaled smoke. "I compartmentalize, I internalize, and then I write it down. I get angry and write. The sort of stuff you're witnessing shouldn't happen to anyone. I don't care what religion or political belief people are, they shouldn't be subjected to this. There can be no justice if there's no accounting. Someone has to witness it and tell. Even if it falls on mostly deaf ears, someone will eventually take notice. They have to."

* * *

Later that evening, I heard Jake's iPod pumping out music from outside the door as I walked by his room. I peeked in and saw him sitting on his mattress with his back to me. He was staring at the floor with his head resting on the palm of one hand and he had his iPod in the other. I just stood there and watched and listened. When the song ended he hit repeat and listened again. I strained to hear what was playing. As soon as I recognized the chorus I got a lump in my throat and my eyes immediately were awash with tears. It was "Have You Ever Seen the Rain" from *Creedence Clearwater Revival.*

I stood there for the whole song with tears running down my face. I watched Jake as his shoulders began shaking; he was crying. The song ended and he played it again. I thought of filming him to capture his pain but decided to let him have his time. I felt like a shit for even thinking of it. I left him alone after he hit repeat again and continued to cry softly. I thought about my son and had to walk away.

Some memories just ruin you.

* * *

June 8, 2013

The next day began clear and hot. Jake and I sat in our usual place at the end of the block. I looked down the street toward the clinic and saw a few of Gary's FSA guys helping a slender man in regime fatigues with his head bandaged out of the clinic.

Gary came walking out after them and sauntered over for a rare opportunity to smoke and chat. Gary was always, "Out with his guys, whipping Assad's ass," as he liked to say. So we didn't see much of him, unless he agreed we could go with him.

He'd been trying to get Jake, Bobbie, and I a way out of the neighborhood and back to safety in Lebanon, but the smuggling routes were all being highly monitored by the regime. They were taking great pains to put a stranglehold on Al-Waer "to make them an example." This only meant that we would have to starve it out in the neighborhood with everyone else until a smuggling opportunity presented itself. We were stuck in Al-Waer.

"How are my two favorite bleeding heart liberals doing today?" Gary said as he joined us for a smoke.

"Hey, Gary. Who's that guy in Syrian camo with a bandage around his head?" I said.

Gary looked down the block and then lit his cigarette. "He's an army defector."

"Really?" Jake said. "I haven't seen the army except when the ISIS guys shot those tanks up."

"Where did he come from?" I asked.

"My guys brought him in a little while ago. They ran into him on patrol. He wasn't armed and had a head wound where someone allegedly shot at him. He claims that he refused to shoot at civilians and his 'superior officer,'" Gary said, accompanied by air quotes with his fingers, "tried to shoot him in the head for treason."

"You think he's lying?"

Gary looked over at him as his guys sat him down and gave him water from their canteens. "I don't know. I trust my men and they say his story checks out, so I guess I have to believe it."

"What are you going to do with him?"

"I'm surely not going to take him with me on patrol."

"Why not?" Jake asked Gary.

"You millennials don't read books anymore, do you? Oh, that's right, you just watch movies," he said to Jake and laughed. "If I'm wrong, he'll probably shoot me in the head the first chance he gets. No, he's gonna stay around here and get himself recuperated. Once he's healthy again, I'll send him out with some of my guys and test his loyalty a little before he's fully integrated."

"Are there rules for this sort of thing?" I asked Gary.

"Nope, just gut feelings. I'm not sure about him, so he's benched until I'm sure."

"Gary, I see you flipping through your phone sometimes. What kind of hardware is that?"

"It's secret government hardware, my friend. That little piece of gear doesn't really exist."

"Yeah, yeah, I know, but can you get a good signal here with it?"

"Are you kiddin'? If you take this to the door on the roof, you can contact someone anywhere in the world. It's a mini-sat phone and data transfer device. They're gettin' smaller and smaller," he said, patting his pocket where he kept it.

"I haven't been able to get coverage to file any of my stories. Do you think I could use that once? I have two or three stories stored up that I could send all at once."

"Do you really think I would let you send your propaganda over this beautiful U.S. engineered weaponry for the twenty-first century?"

"Yes?"

Gary smiled. "Of course I would. It's actually made on contract with a company in China. But we own the crypto. So, your unencrypted drivel will not only land in your editor's inbox but probably the NSA and a shitload of Chinese hackers. But be my guest. I know you can't get paid if you can't file," Gary said as he pulled it out of his pocket and handed it to me. "Don't drop it in the shitter barrels though. I did that once and it ain't user-friendly after something like that."

Chapter 44

June 9, 2013

I watched the whole filthy mess happen right before my eyes. I was on a second-story balcony across the street from the entrance to the clinic, where I was setting up to film an interview, when an artillery strike began. One large explosion halfway down the street started the barrage. Everyone ran for cover.

I looked down from my perch across the street and saw Amala and Jake were outside talking and sharing a smoke. They got up to run inside and take cover. Jake happened to run in before her as she pushed on his back to hurry. The defector Gary's guys had vouched for with the head bandage was waiting for Amala and pulled a pistol. He grabbed her right arm as she got to the threshold of the clinic's front door, pulled her toward him, and shot her in the head.

She fell sideways and lay motionless in the doorway of the clinic. The defector yelled, "*Allahu akbar*," before he straddled her body and put another round in the back of her head just to make sure she was dead.

I saw Jake standing over Amala, not sure what had just happened. He must have come back to see why she hadn't followed him inside. The defector had moved outside and came around the corner and slugged Jake in the face as he stood over her, stunned. I yelled at Jake to watch out, but he couldn't hear me. He never saw the guy's punch coming.

Jake dropped to one knee as the defector tried to pull Jake by his arm and his hair around the corner. That's when the clinic took a direct hit from an artillery shell right in front of me.

The blast knocked me to the ground and re-injured my already sore left leg and peppered me with obliterated pieces of cinder block and glass. I coughed and strained to look down toward the clinic but couldn't see through the dust and smoke. I got to my feet and ran down the stairs and out into the street. I reached the front door of the clinic and saw that Amala's body was still there. Debris and dust made her look like she had been buried for a hundred years and had just been unearthed, except for the pool of blood around her head that was just beginning to absorb the dirt and turn black.

I leaned over her to check and see if she was breathing but half of the left side of her head was gone. I stumbled into the clinic and saw Nagib, Amala's assistant we had interviewed, and her other two elderly assistants were in a heap near the operating table. Nagib's face was so pulverized I couldn't recognize it. I only knew it was him because he was the only one who wore scrubs. I checked both of the elderly assistant's pulses, but they were also dead. I ran back outside and bumped into Jake. He was dazed and looked like he had just crawled out from under a dirt pile.

"They killed her, Angus."

"I know. I saw it."

"And they took him."

"I know. They took Shawqi, too."

"No. Gary."

"What?"

"Gary just came up the street and that motherfucker shot Gary, dropped me, and took him instead."

"Is he dead?"

"No. He was just wounded. He shot Gary in the arm and was dragging him away. I managed to escape, but the guy disappeared in the smoke."

"Fuck."

"These fuckers gotta pay, Angus. They're gonna pay!"

* * *

The dead had been lined up in the same alley Bobbie had been mending clothes with the old ladies in almost two weeks before. Amala and several others who had been killed in the artillery barrage were there, wrapped in blankets. Once I got Jake calmed down a bit, I gave him the task of going to the roof of the building across the street to charge my phone and iPad. I wanted him to send the daily message to Chuck and report that Amala, an American citizen, had been killed here today, so Chuck could get the basic info on the newswire. I also told him to let Chuck know that I'd follow up with a story with more detail later.

I tried to busy myself with helping the survivors clear out the blown-up remnants of the clinic and try to salvage what was left in the rubble. As I was sweeping away the broken bits of glass and masonry from the sidewalk, I heard shouting as two men asked for help in Arabic inside the clinic's foyer. I turned around and saw they were carrying a body down the stairs. The third floor had taken a direct hit from one of the artillery shells and, for the life of me, I had forgotten in all the chaos that Tamir lived on the third floor.

I ran up to help the men carry the rather heavy body down the rest of the stairs and around the corner to lie beside the rest of the accumulated dead. The body was covered in a blanket like the others and had blood seeping through at the head and midsection.

"Is this Tamir?" I asked one of the men in Arabic.

"*Nam*," he said. *Yes.*

I stood there for a moment and looked at the line of eight bodies after the men had walked away. There were five adults and three children, killed by indiscriminant artillery fire from regime guns, Amala and Tamir among them.

I'm looking at the dead soul of Al-Waer lying here at my feet. This place is doomed. I have to save who I can before they're all taken.

* * *

<u>Volunteer Doctor Assassinated in Homs</u>
Posted to GRL by Angus Conn
Al-Waer Neighborhood
Homs, Syria
Filed on June 9, 2013

For two weeks, I had been getting to know Amala. She had left her residency to volunteer her expertise to help the people where her father grew up. She had been working in a local clinic in Al-Waer while the small suburb of Homs was under siege and cut off by the regime. The people there are unable to get to the nearest hospital, so the clinic serves as all things medical for the population of several hundred still clinging to their homes.

I've watched her change bandages, care for the elderly, conduct surgeries, perform amputations, and respectfully wrap the dead in sheets. She was a rock of stability in this small community, giving of herself and asking nothing in return. I watched her treat wounded neighbors, alongside wounded regime soldiers and ISIS rebels.

But not all were grateful for her contribution. Today, I witnessed an ISIS rebel, one who she had medically treated only a few days before, put a gun to her head and end her life. A life everyone here desperately needed to keep living and helping others. I must focus on Amala and her loving contributions to life and the pursuit of peace and not dwell on the negative thoughts that cross my mind every time I think of her. The only negative thought that

I can't seem to purge from my memory is the sick smile the man had on his face when he pulled the trigger and took Amala from us.

The title of civil war literally defines a war where the participants are members of the same community, but has nothing to do with civility. Small battles are won and lost daily by all sides. But the consistent losers are the people of Syria who must live, sacrifice, and die in the horror created by people who claim to be fighting for their best interests.

Amala and her small staff are only the most recent victims of this uncivil war, along with the hundreds or thousands she could have helped but will now have to survive without her.

* * *

A few hours after the barrage had ended, people in the neighborhood were still cleaning up. Everyone was in a daze after the neighborhood realized Amala was dead, Gary was captured, and most of the clinic had been demolished. Bobbie was out chasing another story and managed to avoid the chaos. She joined me in helping with the cleanup efforts once she returned.

She gave me a big hug when I saw her. "I thought I'd lost you again," she said.

I pulled away, put my hands on her shoulders, and stared into her eyes at arm's length. "Do you want to be done with all of this and retire if we can break this siege and get us and these kids out of here?"

"I think I could seriously consider that," she said and smiled.

"Assad's got a tight hold on this neighborhood, but there's gotta be a way to break free. I guess we gotta make it outta here first," I said and pulled her in to hold her close to me again. "And we have to figure out how to get Gary back. He came for us. Jake and I owe our lives to him."

* * *

I limped into the smoke pit where Amala and Jake used to smoke and talk. She told me one day that her time with Jake was the only time she could relax. Most of her waking hours were filled with horror or dread that she had to constantly suppress so she could appear as the unwavering example of constant resolve. Jake was sitting with his head in his hand and puffing on a cigarette with the other.

"How you doing?"

"How do you think?"

"This career isn't for everyone. I know I've been hard on you, but I give you a great deal of credit for being here and wanting to experience it."

"One of these kids told me that he loved me because of my movies. He said that he wanted to be just like me."

"That's got to feel good."

"No. I feel like a fraud. He only knows my movies. He doesn't know me. He doesn't know that I cry in the bathroom at night with a woman doctor, or I used to, anyway."

"You think I don't feel guilty for who I am? You could say that the only reason I'm here is because I despise myself. But I'm here. You need to give yourself a little credit."

"I don't think I can live up to the expectations people have of me. All people see is the exaggerated persona my stardom has advertised me to be. But that's not me. I wonder what my fans would think of me as I'm crying my eyes out in the middle of the night."

"Well, you're right about that. Star power isn't enough, Jake. You gotta back it up with action. You gotta be genuine. Your industry is based on lying to people. You're never who you say you are. You're always portraying someone else. No one knows who you really are." Jake looked up at me as I spoke. "But that doesn't have to be who you are as a person. You have to show people that you're more than your persona. Your industry shouldn't define you as a person."

"Easy for you to say. You don't have people telling you how to be every minute of the day. They keep you in fear of losing the money-making image they've created."

"Fuck them, Jake. You know who you are. And if you didn't know before this trip, you're certainly finding that out now. You need to harness these feelings and make yourself what you want to be. I get jobs all over the world because I make bonds with people based on a handshake backed up with action. You can be whoever you want to be. Just be yourself and the people who actually spend time with you will like you for you, not for your last movie role."

"It's not that easy."

"The hell it's not. You were a superstar to Amala and Shawqi. You gave them confidence and a chance to focus on something else besides the fucked-up world around them. That's where you earn real star power. Cultivate those types of relationships, help people, listen to people, because you want to, not because you think it'll make good press for yourself. Remember, it's not about you. Don't be the story. Find the star power in others and you'll find the real you."

"You sound like you're trying to convince yourself with that speech," Jake said and took a deep draw on his cigarette.

"Maybe I am."

Chapter 45

June 10, 2013

Bobbie came in and sat on the edge of my filthy mattress.

"How are you feeling?" she asked.

"Good, I guess. My left hip still hurts. I was just getting fresh bandages. What's up?"

"I just wondered if you were interested in witnessing the monster you've created."

"What are you talking about?"

"Can you walk okay?"

"Yeah, I can get around."

"Well, we should go up to the roof. I want to show you something."

Bobbie helped me climb the two flights of stairs to get to the roof. We walked out into the fading sunlight at dusk and I limped toward the edge of the roof. I looked down and saw a neat line of neighborhood men in a hodgepodge of clothes, holding their rifles.

"What are they doing?"

"If you look right over there at the end," Bobbie said and pointed to the far end of the line of men, "your boy is giving some instruction."

"What?"

"He's doing pretty well. It looks like he knows what he's talking about. I spoke to him yesterday and he was concerned that most of the neighborhood militia here couldn't hit the broad side of a barn."

"So?"

"Well, since Amala was killed, he's taken it upon himself to help train some discipline into our friends here."

"Dammit, I told him that he couldn't get involved like that."

"I think it's a noble pursuit and he's doing a pretty good job. But I thought you should know because I don't think he's doing this for a hobby. I think he's got a master plan that may be dangerous for all of us."

"Like what kind of plan?"

"I think he's plotting some revenge and wants a little help from his friends."

"Shit, I was afraid of this," I said.

"Do you think you can try to talk some sense into him? The last thing we need is an inexperienced guy going out on a hunting trip and getting himself kidnapped again, or worse, getting these people killed."

"Yeah, I'll talk to him. Thanks for telling me."

* * *

Bobbie helped me hobble down the stairs and out to where Jake had set up his impromptu training range. He was saying things to one of Gary's interpreters who then relayed his words to the line of men holding their weapons.

"Targets," Jake called out.

The interpreter mimicked him and every other man in the six-man line stood and brought his weapon up to his shoulder as if he was going to fire, while the others stayed kneeling on one knee.

Then he yelled to the line of citizen soldiers, "Magazine change."

The interpreter called out the words in Arabic and the men who were standing took a knee, put their rifle butts in their armpits and reloaded their magazines as fast as they could while the previous men on one knee rose and acted like they were firing.

Jake watched each man on one knee reload and then yelled out, "Magazine change."

And the cycle repeated itself.

I limped up to Jake. "What the hell are you doing?"

"What?"

"You're not some sort of military advisor."

"Hey, I've been trained by Navy SEALs and Green Berets, okay? I know what I'm doing."

"Jake, you were trained to look authentic in the movies. This shit is real life."

"I'm tired of you talking to me like I'm a child. These men need some sort of discipline and training. They're ready to take the fight to the enemy and defend their neighborhood. They just don't know how to do it. I thought we already discussed this."

"We did and I told you to stop and focus on why you're here. This is not what I meant by channeling your anger. And you better not be plotting anything special with Gary's guys either."

"Nothing's going on here, Angus. But what if something was? What's so wrong with taking a little heat to these guys who think they own us and these people?"

"Jake, you are not in the CIA and you're not a fucking Navy SEAL or Army Special Forces. I don't care how much training you've got or if you played one on fucking TV. You're a Hollywood actor. You're not even a damn journalist. You're here to see how I do my job so you can portray it in a damn movie. You shouldn't even be here, Jake. And if I had my way from the beginning, you wouldn't be. This sort of shit is going to get you killed."

"You're the only one allowed to get killed for your passion, is that it? Everyone's getting killed around me, Angus. It's about time someone did something about it, rather than just take pictures and write stories about it."

"If you pick up a weapon, Jake, you will die. You will have become a combatant and there will be no going back. You can get prosecuted in an international court of law for shit like this. This is not just getting even or fighting back. We're in this country illegally. If you get caught with a weapon in your hand, you'll be lucky if all they do is shoot you."

"I'm tired of standing by and watching these people get killed. I'm not going to pick up a weapon. I'm just showing them a few things that may keep them alive a little while longer in this shit hole."

"Jake, this won't bring back Amala or Shawqi, or help rescue Gary."

"I know that, Angus. But something's better than nothing and all these people have seen is a whole lotta nothing for a long time. I'm just trying to give them a fighting chance. Don't worry, I'm not gonna go out on patrol with them or anything."

There was nothing else I could say to change his mind. He was going to do what he was going to do. I heard him yell behind me as I limped away, "One more time, targets…magazine change."

Chapter 46

June 10, 2013

I found Jake sitting in the small courtyard where I heard him and Amala talking for the first time. I opened the flimsy door and took a seat on a filing cabinet that had fallen on its side.

Jake looked up. "You here to lecture me some more?"

"No, I want you to interview Bobbie, just like you did Gary, for practice. The only real way to know what it feels like to be in my shoes is to do what I do," I said.

"What do you want me to ask her?"

"Think like a journalist. What do you want your audience to know about her? Where does she come from? What kind of experiences have shaped her in journalism? What got her into journalism in the first place? What is it like being a female freelance foreign correspondent in the Middle East? Do you see what I'm getting at?"

"Yeah, I guess so."

"Okay, we'll do it just like we did with Amala, except I'll work the camera and you ask the questions. She's waiting for us upstairs," I said as I slowly got to my feet

"Okay," Jake said and crushed his cigarette under his boot. "Sorry for before. I'm just pissed at the situation and thought I could contribute something."

"I know. We're all pissed. But our most effective weapon is reporting the truth. The essence of who we are and why we do this as journalists is wrapped up in directing all of our energy, even negative energy, into positive action. That's what we're about."

* * *

Ten minutes later, I focused the camera on Bobbie. She had recently washed her face in preparation for the interview. She had pulled her bronze shoulder-length hair back into a pony tail to reveal the natural beauty of her clean, soft features. Her penetrating blue eyes waited patiently for Jake's interview. She sat cross-legged on the floor a few feet from Jake.

Jake cleared his throat and looked over at me. I gave him a thumbs-up and started recording. Jake turned to Bobbie and gave her an awkward smile. His embarrassment was interesting given his experience in front of the camera. I guess it's all about context. He'd definitely been out of his element for some time.

Jake cleared his throat again and began. "I'm Jake Westin and I'll be speaking with freelance international foreign correspondent, Bobbie Welch. We're in Al-Waer, a besieged neighborhood in Homs, Syria. So, what made you become a journalist?"

Bobbie focused on Jake as she spoke. "I have to tell you a little background before I can answer that question. My father is a Lebanese naturalized American citizen and my mother is American. They met in college when they both went to Columbia University. My father studied political science and my mother studied French. They both eventually worked as professors at the American University in Beirut. I lived in Beirut for seven years when I was three to ten years old. I spent my childhood there. I learned Arabic from my father, French from my mother, and English in school.

"In 1988, when I was ten, my father got a job at Columbia University and we moved to New York City. I spent my high school years there and went to a private college in upstate New York where I earned a communications degree with a minor in French. After college, I worked at an import-export company in Manhattan where I could use my language skills when 9/11 happened. I immediately felt that I could help raise the average American's awareness of the Middle East through journalism."

"And just like that, you were a journalist?"

"No. I was hired as a fixer in Lebanon for about a year where I accumulated a lot of contacts, including Chuck at the GRL. He eventually offered me a job once he saw that I was able to not only function as a fixer, but could also write stories that he could sell to the various wire services."

"Have you always been freelance?"

"Yes. I've been offered jobs at a few major networks along the way, but none of them offered the flexibility I wanted. As a freelancer, I hold all the cards and choose when to play them."

"Where else have you covered stories?"

"I go where I can get around on my own. I am very comfortable in the Middle East, North Africa, and France. I'm viewed with a bit of suspicion in

Israel because I speak fluent Arabic, but the Middle East is where I'm best suited, so that's where I've focused my efforts."

"Do you think people pay enough attention to the Middle East?"

Bobbie smiled, looked at a spot on the wall above Jake's head and considered the question before she answered. "Not for the right reasons. All they see is the bad. And there is plenty of bad. But there is also a lot of good. If the rest of the world could pay attention long enough to understand the big issues and facilitate tangible solutions, the Middle East could bloom into a brilliant flower the world hasn't seen in several decades. I think the average Westerner sees the Middle East as hopeless, but informed awareness can foment solutions if people are willing to see behind the headlines."

"Let me shift gears here for a second and bring the focus back to you."

Nice transition, I thought. *Jake's really getting the hang of this.*

"Do you believe you are treated differently in the profession or by those you interview because you are a woman?"

Bobbie shifted in her seat as she thought of her response. "I do think that I'm treated differently, and not only because some make me wear a head scarf and some don't. But, as a Western journalist, most men I interview treat me as cordial as can be expected in the region. I am respected as a professional and treated as such. But where I believe that I hold the advantage is my language ability and my interaction with other women. The women will open up to me, whereas they wouldn't share most of the things they tell me with a man. Not only because I speak Arabic, but also for the simple fact that I am a woman. So, in a way, I can get just about any story a man can get and a whole lot of stories men can't," Bobbie said and looked over and smiled at me.

I smiled back. I could tell she wasn't exactly comfortable being the subject. It was usually her asking the questions. It was fun to see Bobbie a little uncomfortable for a change.

"Do you believe you are in more danger than male journalists?"

"There is always the danger that violent men will use intimidation and the threat of rape, but I am not easily deterred and, in the end, I have to assess the risks and decide how far I'm willing to push to get a story."

"I've heard the primary rule among journalists is to report the story and not be the story. Can you explain that?"

"Yes. It's the idea that, as a journalist, you are there to show what is going on, not influence events. If you get yourself arrested or shot or kidnapped, you are not effectively able to be an objective witness. No one wants to read the headline, 'Journalist Arrested at Peace Rally.' That takes away from the bigger, more important story, the one you showed up to report in the first place. So the saying goes, report the story, don't be the story."

"How do you justify the risks you take or the danger you expose yourself to in order to get the story?"

"Every story I cover in the Middle East has an element of risk to it. I just have to constantly assess the risks and make the best decisions I can on where to go, who to interview, and what video to shoot to tell the story effectively."

"Are there stories worth dying for?"

She didn't miss a beat; she had obviously thought about this question before. "No single story is worth dying for. After all, you can't tell a story if you're dead, but the mosaic that is created by a collected body of work in the region is worth the risk. If it's between not telling an important story and staying completely safe or exposing myself to the threat of violence or death to add to the whole, I will pursue the story. But I will also focus on mitigating the risk the best I can to make my contribution to the regional narrative."

"What makes the Syrian conflict different than others you've covered in your career?"

"The biggest difference is that there is no safe place. Every day is a gamble. Will we get shot by snipers, bombed by helicopters, blown up by tanks, or kidnapped? The variety of violent unknowns and the extent of widespread avoidable human suffering is what makes this place different for me."

Jake looked into Bobbie's eyes with total concentration. "Do you ever think that you'll stop being a journalist?"

"Globally important stories will be pouring out of the Middle East for the foreseeable future and I'll be here to report them for as long as I'm breathing," Bobbie said as she looked at me.

"Thanks for talking with me, Bobbie."

"It was my pleasure, Jake. Thanks for the interest." She smiled.

I guess I have a bit more convincing to do before she hangs her hat up for me, I thought.

Chapter 47

June 10, 2013

I was sitting on an overturned bucket, leaning up against the wall in my usual spot, and trying to mull over how we could possibly figure a way to find out if Gary was still alive. I had begun an article in my journal but wasn't making much progress. I couldn't take my mind off how we could even begin to try and help Gary.

The hot early afternoon breeze wafted angry voices coming from inside the clinic. I recognized a few Arabic words such as, "worthless," "scoundrel," and "murderer" that seemed to be aimed at a single person. I got up, shoved my journal and my pen in my pocket, and went around the corner to see what was up.

The disturbance had moved inside the clinic, but the voices seemed louder as they echoed off the bare concrete walls. I walked gingerly through the door and saw a few men crowded around a single figure on the floor. I stepped through the doorway, careful not to slip on the fresh blood trail from the man they had just dragged inside.

I peered between the men surrounding and shouting at the wounded man. He was wearing all black and was bleeding from a wound on his arm and leg. His eyes flickered opened and closed as if he was fighting to stay awake. He was going to lose consciousness if he didn't get treated soon. One of the men standing over him slapped him hard in the face and told him to wake up and take his punishment like a man.

I took out my iPhone and snapped a few pictures as the feeding frenzy around the man intensified. I knew I had better get a few shots before I intervened. Just as I took my last shot, I saw Jake in the doorway. He had come to see what the noise was all about as well.

"Get a good shot?" Jake asked.

"Come on, let's get in there before they kill the guy."

"Yeah, that would be terrible, wouldn't it?"

I ignored Jake and pushed my way through the crowd and winced from the pain in my hip. The men around the wounded man were so angry I was surprised they hadn't killed him yet. I looked at the man's face and then realized why they were keeping him alive. He wasn't Syrian. He was a foreign ISIS fighter.

His almond-shaped eyes gave him away. He was probably Malaysian. He likely didn't understand Arabic, which was probably why he looked so confused and maybe because he was in shock from his wounds. The men around him were getting a little more violent. One man kicked him in the ribs and another kicked him in his leg wound. I had to stop it.

"Okay, okay, get him to the doc," I said.

Everyone looked over at me and one of the men who spoke English looked at me as if I were the enemy. "Stay out of this. It is not your fight."

"Where did you find him?"

"An ISIS patrol shot at us from their trucks. We returned fire and killed one and wounded him. He fell out of the truck and his guys left him."

"You can use him. He knows things about ISIS and can help us."

"He does not speak Arabic. We should kill him to show them that their ISIS foreigners are not welcome here."

"If you kill him, you are no better than they are," I said, feeling like a sympathizer.

"I said, stay out of it," the FSA fighter said and kicked the man again.

The ISIS fighter screamed out in pain, looked up at me, and said in English, "Help me."

Everyone froze and looked at me. I knelt down and got in front of the man's face. "Where are you from?"

"Kuala Lumpur in Malaysia."

"What's your name?"

"Sabtu."

"How long have you been here, Sabtu?"

"Six months."

"Where did you learn English?"

"In America," he smiled.

"Where in America?"

"Chicago."

"What were you doing in Chicago?"

"I was an exchange student there. I studied finance. I was an intern fund manager in Chicago and then went back to Malaysia and worked at a bank."

"What are you doing here?"

"Jihad," he said and smiled again.

A couple of the men lifted the Malay on a table and a nurse dressed his wounds the best she could. I gave him some water and Jake pulled me aside.

"I have an idea," Jake said.

"What is it?"

"We need to send Sabtu back and tell him we want to make a deal with Abdul Aziz."

* * *

About an hour later, once Sabtu's wounds had been dressed, Jake lifted Sabtu to his feet and helped him limp around the corner so we could have a somewhat private conversation with him. To everyone else, it looked as if we were going to interrogate or torture him. They exchanged glances and laughed as they saw us lead him away.

We sat him down once we were out of sight of the others and we stood around him. He looked up at us, not sure what to expect.

"We aren't going to hurt you," I said.

"Why not?"

"Because we don't do the things you do to these people."

He rolled his eyes and laughed. I ignored his taunts and leaned down over Sabtu.

"Here's the deal, Sabtu. We are going to show you something and then we're going to let you go. We want you to tell Abdul Aziz what you see and tell him we want to make a deal."

"What kind of deal?"

* * *

I scrolled through my few pictures I had taken of the anti-tank and anti-aircraft missiles on my phone and showed them to Sabtu.

"We will trade everything in this truck for the American."

"How many are there?"

"A dozen anti-aircraft missiles and a dozen anti-tank missiles," I said and pocketed my phone.

"I don't know if Abdul Aziz will do it. He will not believe you have these weapons."

"If he doesn't now, he will when we use them to blow up your house and knock that black flag of yours down. We have a great view of it from our roof."

Chapter 48

June 10, 2013

I sat with Jake on the roof of a building in the neighborhood that had an excellent view of two Syrian Army tanks that had parked there not more than an hour before. I stared at the tanks below with a pair of binoculars as I hid behind an old satellite dish, just as Abdul Aziz had shown us. I kept looking away to scan the big picture below. I was looking for our little runner. I finally saw him as he crept past the corner of the last building at the end of the block. It was just a straight shot of about fifty yards of bad road to where the tanks were parked.

We gave the kid two packs of cigarettes with a note secured to it with a rubber band for the soldiers inside. We really didn't think the soldiers would shoot the kid, but as soon as they noticed him coming up behind the tank, they traversed the turret and aimed the big gun and its smaller machine gun right at him.

"Think we should have gotten someone with an anti-tank missile up here just in case they shoot him?" Jake asked.

"It's a little late for that now. I think he's on his own."

We both held our breath as the kid kept closing the distance with the turret tracking his every move. He walked slowly toward the back of the tank that was tracking him and stuck his face right up to the barrel of the cannon. It was deflected down low enough for him to talk into the barrel at the crew. He said something and then laughed and slapped the barrel as he walked up to the tracks. He was looking for a place to climb onto it when a hatch on the turret opened up and a soldier leaned over the side.

It looked like he was telling him to go away, but the kid was good. He wasn't scared. He waved the cigarettes at the soldier and I could see he was trying to convince him that they were a gift.

The soldier didn't get out of the tank but told the boy to go around and give the cigarettes to the driver. Our kid walked around to the front of the tank and knocked on the driver's hatch. The hatch opened just enough for the driver to see the kid. A hand slid through the crack in the armor and the boy shook the man's hand and then put the cigarettes in them. He was laughing as he did it. And why shouldn't he? He had successfully gotten word to the regime that we needed a little firepower demonstration that evening that just might make his life a little easier.

* * *

Jake and I stood at the end of the neighborhood block and looked at the empty field just across the street. We couldn't go any farther for fear of being shot by regime or ISIS snipers. The sun was low over the horizon, about an hour before sunset, and the neighborhood actually felt peaceful. There hadn't been much gunfire after the firefight that brought Sabtu to our doorstep.

"You go up that hill and tell Abdul Aziz that I want to meet him in this field in about an hour, at sunset. If he wants those weapons, I want his word, from him, that we have a deal. Do you understand?"

"He won't meet with you," Sabtu said.

"He'll meet with me," Jake said. "Tell him that Jake wants to share a cigarette with him and discuss our deal."

Sabtu shook his head. "You guys won't win this thing. It's not your fight."

"Well, it's not yours either, Sabtu. You should go back to Malaysia and track the exchange rate of the Euro to the Yen and let these people work this out on their own."

"I could say the same about you. Why are you here? To watch the Muslims kill each other? I have more of a right to be here than you two. Islam is my religion."

"This has nothing to do with Islam and everything to do with decency," Jake said.

I looked at the Malay. "I'm here to show the world that you guys are making things worse." I took out my iPhone and snapped his picture. "I will make sure I show everyone you are one of the people responsible for this carnage."

"I'm fighting for the legitimacy of my religion. Some day you Americans will feel these people's pain right in your own neighborhoods. When we are victorious here, we will regroup and come for you. If I am martyred for it, then it is Allah's will."

"If you keep pissin' me off, Allah's will may happen right now," Jake said.

"Spare us the propaganda. Just tell Abdul Aziz that we want to make a deal," I said.

"I will take your message to Abdul Aziz and we will probably take your weapons and we will laugh as we use them against you," Sabtu said.

Jake stared at Sabtu. "Start walking and hope that your snipers realize you're wearing black pajamas or your time in paradise may be at hand."

Sabtu looked over at me. "Well, go on," I said and pointed to his hillside headquarters.

"Go on now before I kidnap you and chain you to my lawnmower in Beverly Hills," Jake said.

Sabtu began limping across the street and off into the field beyond.

I looked at Jake and smiled. "Lawnmower in Beverly Hills, huh?"

Jake shrugged. "I had to say something. He was getting kind of cocky."

"Are you sure you want to meet with Abdul Aziz tonight?"

"Definitely."

"You can't kill him, Jake. That would ruin our plan and probably get us all killed."

"I'm not gonna kill him. I just want to look him in the face, tell him that eventually our paths will cross again, and when that happens, I will most likely have the upper hand."

"I'm not sure threats are going to scare him."

Jake turned around and started walking back to the neighborhood. "It's not a threat, Angus."

Chapter 49

Soccer field between ISIS compound and Al-Waer
June 10, 2013

I was furious with myself, but I couldn't let Jake go alone into that field. I knew this was the only shot we had to get Gary back and destroy these ISIS guys. I was supposed to be keeping Jake out of trouble, but instead I was walking into an open field to negotiate a prisoner release for weapons with an ISIS fighter in Syria.

This is not smart. So much for not being the story.

Our former captor and the man who engineered Amala's death and took Gary hostage climbed over a few piles of rubble and walked toward us in the fading light of twilight.

"I think this is him," Jake said as the dark silhouette approached.

"Stay cool, Jake. Think of the big picture," I said.

"I know."

Abdul Aziz approached and smiled as he got close. He wasn't wearing the full black face covering.

"Why are you smiling?" I asked.

"Because it is good to see my old captives are still alive. I have told my snipers to hold fire as we talk. But if any harm comes to me they will kill you both. This is not like the movies, my friend," he said to Jake.

"We're not friends."

"Jake, take it easy," I said.

"We have people watching you, too," Jake said.

Abdul Aziz laughed. "You must remember. I have seen your fighters. They mean well but they are undisciplined and their shooting is very bad, especially in these conditions."

"That may be true, but I can assure you there are a lot of guns aimed at you right now and something will hit you if anything happens to us."

"Okay, so we are here. What would you like to talk about?"

"You have something we want and we have something you want. We should make a deal."

"Okay, what kind of deal?"

"You know that Gary is American, right?"

"Of course," Abdul Aziz said.

"Then you should know that unless you really want to chain him to a truck and send him on his way for target practice and end up like your old boss, we have a better deal."

"What kind of deal?" he said.

"Have you seen the *Godfather*?"

"Of course."

"Then you will understand what I am about to tell you. I am going to make you an offer you can't refuse."

Abdul Aziz laughed. "I like this, Jake. This is fun."

"What we have to offer is even more fun."

"What do you have that we could possibly want?"

"Didn't Sabtu tell you what we showed him?"

"Yes. But he is not familiar with military things. He was an investment banker in Kuala Lumpur a year ago. He didn't know what he was looking at. Tell me what you have."

"We have a truck full of Milan anti-tank missiles and refurbished SA-7 anti-aircraft missiles. Twelve each," I said.

"We will trade them for Gary," Jake said.

"Yes. This is the same information Sabtu told me. But why would I risk that trade?"

"You can keep Gary if you want and see if someone will eventually pay you for him, but they won't. You will wait a long time and get nothing."

"It would make me happy just to kill him. My men have begged me to kill him and put his death on YouTube."

"You can do that, too. But again, you will get nothing. I am offering you something for him right now. And something I know you've had a difficult time getting from anyone. If you are interested in having the firepower to defeat the regime's most effective weapons against you and your group, then we can help with that."

"If you have these weapons, why don't you just use them yourself?"

"You said it earlier, the people in this neighborhood are not soldiers. They don't know how to use the weapons. They would be a waste in their hands. But they would be effective with you and your men. The neighborhood wants the regime gone as well, so they are content to help as long as you remember who gave them to you and go easy on them."

Abdul Aziz stared back at Jake in silence.

"This is an offer you can't refuse," Jake smiled.

"What if I do refuse?"

"Feel free to do what you will with Gary, but we will learn how to use the weapons to make you and your headquarters disappear. I think you know that it would not be good for anyone."

"And if I agree?"

"We will meet again tonight at midnight. We will bring the truck with the weapons and you will bring Gary. Once Gary is with us, you can take the truck to your side and we will be done. We will not shoot as long as Gary is alive."

"How can I trust you? You are an actor. You lie to people for a living."

Jake laughed this time. "There is one thing I can tell you that is no lie. If you do not agree to this deal, you will die."

"This is not your fight, Jake. Why are you here? Go back to Hollywood and entertain us. Let us sort out our problems on our own."

"It doesn't matter why. I'm offering you a chance to further your cause. All you have to do is agree so you can focus on that goal and let these people live and defend their neighbors and families against the regime. The same thing you are doing."

Abdul Aziz leaned in a little closer. "I know you liked that lady doctor. I want you to know that killing her was…how do you say in America? It was just business. If you kill one doctor here, it is the same as killing one hundred men. Those neighborhood people cannot shoot and they cannot help the wounded. They will be overrun no matter what you do. If you are doing this for revenge, you will not succeed."

"Then you have nothing to lose and everything to gain. We will flash the headlights of the truck three times at midnight. When we see Gary right here where we stand, alive, we will move the truck and you can have it once we have Gary and this will be over. If you do not come tonight, we will destroy you. Think about it. I will see you tonight," Jake said and we both turned our backs and began walking away.

"Keep walking, Jake. Don't look back," I said.

We kept walking and Abdul Aziz yelled after Jake, behind us, "I like you, Jake. That is why you are still alive. I will see you tonight," Abdul Aziz said.

"Good job, Jake. Keep walking," I said as I limped alongside him.

Chapter 50

June 10-11, 2013

I looked at my watch; the black numbers showed 11:30 p.m. in contrast to the luminescent backlight. It had been a relatively quiet night. I only heard a little bit of small arms fire in the distance. I waited, in pain, in the small kitchen area where we planned the bakery raid, for Jake to come back and let me know how the setup was going.

I doodled in my journal but couldn't concentrate to put into words just what the hell was going on. How was I supposed to report on this? This was just one of those things that happened and you hoped you lived through it. Just like Gary said, it would make a good bar story that no one would ever believe. There was no way I could officially report any of this, not only because of Gary's involvement, but also because of Jake's involvement and my own knowledge of all of it.

Jake finally came through the kitchen door. His hair was grimy and every exposed part of his skin was dirty, including his face. He had traded his bloody clothes for some that were just dirty. At that moment, his image was a striking contrast to the pretentious kid I met in the airport a month earlier.

"Have you gotten a nap since this afternoon?" I asked.

"How the hell do you think I could sleep after today?"

"Sometimes you have to."

"I'll have to catch up on sleep if we make it through tonight."

* * *

I turned my digital video camera on and adjusted the night vision feature. I shot a small bit of footage of Jake as we waited for the minutes to tick away toward midnight. Everything was set. I was still limping a bit, but I could get around okay. I wasn't sure if I was going to have to run, but I figured I would deal with that as it came. Besides, there would probably be plenty of adrenaline to make up for any loss of full function.

Bobbie told us we were both crazy and decided to watch from a relatively safe perch on the roof with Gary's night vision equipment. She gave me a kiss on the cheek before Jake and I walked outside. I smiled all the way to the end of the block.

I thought back to all the times we had been in competition for stories and vying for the journalistic spotlight over the last few years. It never dawned on me until I looked back, but it seemed like we were always dabbling in a subtle form of foreplay neither of us were ready to consummate.

During our limited time together, we had learned to love the good about each other and accept the bad. I guess that's all you can really ask for in someone. I wish I had learned that lesson long ago. Sometimes it just takes self-imposed difficulty before we allow ourselves to see what the truth really looks like to us. This job has taught me that the truth definitely looks different to different people. I learned that as long as your version of truth isn't detrimental to others, then you should go with that. I felt that Bobbie's version of truth and definition of love overlapped mine enough for us to be happy together.

Living happily ever after will have to wait until I know we'll live through tomorrow.

I looked at my watch again: 11:58 p.m.

"You ready? It's just about time," I said to Jake.

"As ready as I'll ever be."

I panned the camera up to the cab of the truck where a neighborhood driver sat and waited on our signal to hit the lights.

I pointed the camera back at Jake. "Anything you want to say before we do this?"

"Yeah," he said and looked right into the camera. "In a few minutes, I'm gonna show you what star power is all about."

I looked at my watch again: 11:59 p.m.

"Okay, *thalaatha* (three), *eeth-nayn* (two), *waahid* (one)," I counted down in Arabic. "*Noor*!" I yelled to the driver. *Lights.*

He turned them on and off three times. We all watched the ISIS compound on the hill in the distance. I didn't notice any movement. Then, a single flashlight lit up the middle of the field to our front only fifty yards away.

"They're already there," I said as I zoomed the camera onto the light in the distance. "They must be antsy to get their hands on those weapons."

The light in the distance went out as quickly as it had appeared. Jake ran around to the passenger side of the truck and we both hopped onto the running boards. The driver lurched forward from his parking spot and crept out into the dark field ahead.

The truck bounced over hidden rubble and debris as the driver moved forward. I kept the video camera trained on the area right in front of the truck. I told the driver I'd signal him when to stop. I caught some movement just out of range of the night vision filter and then saw a body on the ground flanked by two soldiers holding rifles. The body didn't look to be moving.

I pounded the door of the truck to signal the driver to stop. The truck squeaked to a stop and idled loud in the night. I hopped down and approached the group in front of us. The soldiers couldn't see Jake and me approach and they startled when we appeared before them.

"Is he alive?" Jake asked.

"Of course he is alive," Abdul Aziz said. "Are those the weapons?"

"Of course they're the weapons," I said.

"Tell your man to get out of the truck. We will take it from here."

"Don't you want to inspect the weapons?"

"They are all there, correct?"

"Yes."

"You didn't take a few for your own defense?"

"They'd rather leave the fighting to you," Jake said.

I could see Abdul Aziz smiling in the green light of the night filter. "They are wise. We will take the fight to the regime and establish an Islamic State for them in return. You have done a good thing for these people. You should feel proud."

"I just want to make sure Gary is alive and then I want to get outta here. We're very exposed out here."

"Yes, we are. My driver will take the truck and we will be done," Abdul Aziz said.

"Wait," I said. "Jake, is he okay?"

"He's hurt, but conscious."

"He's conscious?"

"Yeah."

"Why hasn't he said anything yet?"

I heard a ripping sound as Jake removed a section of tape.

"Ahhh. You sons of bitches!" Gary yelled out. "I'm gonna kill every last one of you. You better get your stinkin' hands off my weapons. Those aren't yours. They're mine. Don't give them a damn thing, Angus. These fuckers will use it against us," Gary yelled nonstop.

"You better put that back on him or I will change my mind about this deal and shoot him," Abdul Aziz said.

I heard Gary's muffled voice still talking as Jake replaced the tape over his mouth.

"See you on the evening news," I said to Abdul Aziz.

I followed Jake and the driver as they carried Gary's body, secured with duct tape on a detached car door as a makeshift stretcher. It took us a few minutes to get back to the clinic. Jake and the driver switched positions and rested a few times before we got to the front entrance. The driver used his knife to cut the tape that secured Gary's arms and legs and Gary removed the tape over his mouth once his hands were free.

"I can't believe you freakin' pansies traded my weapons for me. You should have demolished that building with me in it. Somebody would have replaced me. Those weapons in that maniac's hands are treasonous. I should shoot you assholes myself."

"Gary, relax. We all need to go to the roof right now," I said.

"I'm not goin' anywhere but up that fuckin' hill to get my weapons back."

"Gary, you need to go upstairs with us right now. It won't be safe out here in a few minutes," I said.

"Safe? Where the hell do you think you are? Ain't nothin' safe around here."

"Trust me, come to the roof with us. Get some water and then after we show you what we want to show you, you can decide if you still want to go take the fucking hill or not," I said.

"Something fishy's goin' on here. What the hell are you guys up to?"

"Let's hit the roof and you can see for yourself," Jake smiled.

Chapter 51

Al-Waer, Syria
June 11, 2013

Jake got to the roof first as Bobbie helped Gary and I hobble close behind. We lined up well back from the edge so we wouldn't be silhouetted against the sky from below, just in case the government snipers were on their toes. But something told us that they were busy watching a different building.

We heard them before we saw anything. A loud roar erupted to our right and then a deep engine growl from the left.

"Those are tanks," Gary said. "They're surrounding us and you assholes gave away all of our firepower."

"Relax and just watch," I said as I centered the ISIS building in my viewfinder.

We stood there watching the dark outline of the ISIS building on the hill and waited.

"What the hell are we waiting for? Those guys are gonna drive outta there with our shit and we're never gonna see it again until they shoot it at us."

"Just a few more minutes," I said.

"Fuck this, I'm gonna go get my guys and we're gonna fix this. Leave it to a couple bleeding hearts to—"

The night exploded in a volley of tank fire that lit up the night. Flame shot out of each of the two tanks' barrels that had positioned themselves on opposite sides of the far corners of the field we had just come from. The ISIS building on the hill disappeared behind an initial fireball that engulfed the house in a gray cloud, which glowed from the intense heat at its core as it rose into the night sky.

"Holy shit," Jake said.

"How the hell did they know?" Gary said to me.

"We told them."

"How?"

"We had a kid give one of the tank crews a couple packs of cigarettes and we wrapped a note around them with a rubber band and told them when and where they should park to destroy a truckload of ISIS weapons."

A secondary explosion, larger than the initial explosion from the dual tank blasts, shot large projectiles into the night sky. We all hit the deck as an anti-tank rocket streaked past us on the roof, missing Gary by a mere foot.

We slowly poked our heads up to watch the rest of the show. Two anti-aircraft missiles shot out of the glowing rubble simultaneously and rocketed into the sky in opposite directions on wild flight paths. They finally exploded high in the sky, raining flaming debris all the way to the ground. Several more rockets went off in random directions. One anti-tank rocket impacted the building next to ours and started a fire.

"Weapons don't just explode like that, even after a tank shot."

"We siphoned some gas from the truck that held the weapons and soaked a few of the foam cut outs in the weapons cases in diesel fuel. Once they went, the rest went with them."

"Not a bad idea," Gary said and chuckled as he stared at the cloud that used to be the ISIS building in the distance. "Well, I guess if I can't have them, neither can they."

"Yeah, they fucked up. They should have killed us when they had the chance," I said.

We all laughed as we each watched the spectacle and realized that we had singlehandedly defeated the worst neighbors on our block. We watched the dangerous fireworks display in front of us until no more missiles cooked off. I let myself savor the victory for a while as the ISIS building glowed like the embers of a campfire in the distance.

As I stared at the dancing flames that enveloped the monument of our triumph, my mind moved to our next challenge: getting us and the children out of Al-Waer safely.

***

Not long after the ISIS fireworks display, Jake helped the FSA soldiers place Gary on a mattress in one of the rooms and disappeared into another. I limped in a few minutes later to see how Jake was doing. He was snoring so loudly I thought it was a joke. I shut the door and had to laugh. I hobbled down to where Bobbie was staying to see if she wouldn't mind a little company. I fell asleep in her arms and slept better than I had in years.

Chapter 52

June 12, 2013

Luckily, Gary had shown me where he hid his mini-sat phone and data transfer device in the event he was captured. He didn't trust his guys with it and didn't really trust me with it either, but told me he'd rather have an American take it than anyone else. I used it to send Rafi an e-mail asking if he could meet us at the border. He got back to me within an hour that he could, but we would have to arrange getting ourselves to the border on our own. There was nothing he could do; the Syrian forces had continued their patrols around the northern Lebanon border and had intercepted a few journalists and their fixers and turned them around with hefty fines. He told me that he was lucky to get back into Lebanon before they tightened the noose.

He said that if we could get ourselves over the border, he'd be waiting with transportation for three and maybe four people if Gary decided he needed a breather. But I seriously doubted Gary would admit to that. Gary was the type of guy that would only leave if he was ordered to and then he'd do it reluctantly with a boatload of reasons to stay.

I found Jake and Bobbie talking over some coffee in the medical clinic's kitchen area. They both looked startled when I came in.

I smiled. "Sorry, am I interrupting something?"

Bobbie smiled back. "No, we were just going to come and find you. We were discussing logistics."

I poured myself a steaming cup of thick coffee from the camping stove on the counter and blew on it for a second to cool. Ever since we tipped off the regime tanks to the ISIS weapons cache, the snipers had withdrawn. We'd been getting water without getting shot at for almost a whole day. It was glorious to have coffee and actually have water for a whore bath and brushing my teeth.

"Logistics, huh? That's funny, I just read an e-mail from Rafi a little while ago about the very same thing. He says he'll have a ride for us at the border town of Rablah on Highway Four but we have to get ourselves to the border."

The two conspirators were silent for a moment before Jake looked at me. "How many people can he take?"

"He said three, maybe four, if we can pry Gary away."

Jake and Bobbie looked at each other and Bobbie looked at me.

"What the hell is going on with you two?"

"Do you think he can accommodate forty?" she asked.

"What forty?"

"We did a head count and there are thirty-six elderly women and orphaned children still in the neighborhood. And several of them need urgent medical attention. Those, plus us four makes forty."

"How the hell are we gonna transport that many people to the border?"

"Tamir's son was able to fix up one of his father's old trucks from some parts he cannibalized off a few burned-out government vehicles. But he only has one and it'll be maxed out at forty," Bobbie said.

"I had forty *trucks* set to make runs and get the people out and now all we can do is forty people in *one* truck?"

"Angus, we're doing what we can," Bobbie said.

"I know, but how do we know the regime will let us out of here? The long pole in the tent has always been safe passage to the border and then the government allowing people to leave."

Bobbie looked at Jake and he looked back at me. "I think we may have the safe passage thing figured out," Jake said.

He tossed me a brick with the same note we passed to the tankers secured with the same rubber band.

I did my best with the Arabic but read the English translation below it:

Our crew will escort women and children from Al-Waer to the border tonight. Highway Four and Ring Road Intersection at 0400.

"Are you kidding me?" I smiled. "How did we get this?"

"The same tank crew we tipped off about the ISIS weapons trade was willing to pay us back for the kill."

"Why would they want to do that?"

"Gary's radio guy intercepted some radio chatter from ISIS that a few of the ISIS guys survived the tank hit on their house last night. ISIS has apparently sent for reinforcements and talked about having an all-out assault on Al-Waer and killing everyone here for retribution. But they want to capture you, Gary, and me alive. The tank commander is from Homs and wanted to get as many innocents as he could out of here before it was too late. It's definitely time to go," Jake said.

"What makes you think ISIS can rally an assault force soon?"

"Gary's comms guy intercepted government radio traffic that ISIS reinforcements are expected to arrive sometime tonight. After they arrive, they could hit at any time. Even Gary thinks we need to go," Bobbie said.

"What's he gonna do?"

"He said he would stay here with his guys and all the neighborhood men to buy us some time to get away."

"And all we can get is one truck, huh?"

"We can only do what we can do," Jake said. "Do you still have Gary's mini-sat?" Jake asked me.

"Yeah, it's right here," I said and handed it to Jake. "What are you gonna do?"

"I'm gonna go to the roof to get a signal and do my part and get us some transportation set up for forty at the border," Jake smiled.

"How the hell are you gonna do that?"

"You forget, I have star power," he said and smiled.

Chapter 53

June 13, 2013

We spent the rest of the day getting all forty civilians and ourselves packed up and ready for the ride to the border. We fed the children all the food we could find and packed up three jerry cans of water for the trip. I sat in my spot and wrote in my notebook what had transpired since the last time I wrote; just in case something happened to us, there would at least be a record of things up until that moment. I didn't have time to type it out, save it on my iPad, or file it in e-mail, so old fashioned pen and paper would have to be good enough for posterity.

I finished writing and watched the long shadows of late afternoon creep down the street on what I hoped would be my last day in Syria. I tamped out my cigarette and threw it in my butt can. I looked inside the can and smiled. It was about three quarters full of cigarette butts. I snapped a picture of it with my phone to show anyone who'd listen, who probably wouldn't believe me back in the normal world. I smiled to myself as I remembered what Gary told me: "Nobody believes the true shit."

We waited until the last light of the day had gone and the stars were just emerging in the sky as they shined on our journey like a blessing. It needed to be as dark as possible so we could hide our movements the best we could. Despite our precautions, we knew we couldn't avoid roads since our truck was not off-road capable and the children wouldn't have been able to handle the rough trip even if it were. We knew we would have to take our chances at any roadblocks getting from Al-Waer to our meeting point with the tankers. I hoped the tankers were true to their word for an escort.

* * *

Our truck driver saw the first roadblock in the distance. As our truck approached, the turret of the tank slewed over and the big cannon adjusted its position to aim right into the truck. The tank's spotlight cut the night sky like a thick white laser and lit up the cab like the sun. Bobbie and the driver put their hands up and climbed down from the cab.

Three regime soldiers met them and told her and the driver to sit on the ground next to the truck while one guarded them and the other two inspected the truck's load. I carefully climbed down from the back and came around the truck slowly so as not to spook the soldiers.

One of them lit me up with a spotlight and yelled for me to get on the ground. I put my hands up and hit the dirt. The soldier came up to me and put his boot between my shoulder blades and pressed the barrel of his AK-47 to the base of my neck.

"*Sahafiyy*!" I yelled in Arabic. "I'm a journalist."

He just told me to shut up. I craned my neck up to see the soldiers pulling the women and children out of the back of the truck. They were lining them up shoulder-to-shoulder and making them lie face down on the ground. One of the soldiers pulled my attention away as he began going through my pockets while another one held me down. He pulled out my passport and told the guard to line me up with the others.

They dragged me over to the group and threw me next to Jake.

"Oh, fuck man, they're gonna shoot us all. I've seen videos of this. They line you up and shoot you," Jake said.

"Shut the fuck up, Jake. Just chill."

"Fuck that, we're dead."

"No talk," the guard said in English.

One of the tank crew hopped down from the tank and approached us. All we could see was a dark figure, backlit by the tank's spotlight. He talked with the guard for a few seconds but I couldn't hear what he said. The guard handed the tanker my passport. He looked at it and then at me.

He came over and threw it to the ground in front of me. "You are American?"

"*Nam*," I said. *Yes*.

"You are journalist?"

"Yes."

"You come from Al-Waer?"

"Yes."

"Where are you going?"

"To Lebanon."

"Yes, you are right to leave. My men destroyed the ISIS base in your neighborhood. ISIS came back for revenge and killed everyone. The government took back the neighborhood tonight. Many had fled, but many are dead also. But we took back what belonged to us. It is our country, not yours or ISIS. You do not belong here."

"Everyone is dead?"

"Yes. ISIS, FSA, and there were Westerners, too. They were no match for so much firepower. Is this all you could get from Al-Waer? I was told there may be more."

"No, this is it."

"They do not belong in Lebanon. They belong here. They must be tried for their crimes, for killing government troops."

"They're just children. They're orphans. They didn't kill anyone. It was their parents who were killed," Jake said.

"Shut up, that is propaganda," the tanker said and aimed his rifle at Jake. "I should kill you all right now."

His men raised their weapons to their shoulders and aimed them at the group. I just sat there waiting for them to shoot.

"We are saving your future, your children," Jake said.

The tanker lowered his weapon and stared at Jake for a moment. "Our future is ours, not yours."

"We want the children safe so they can return in peace. Do you have children?" Jake asked the soldier.

"Jake, shut the fuck up," I said.

He just ignored me. "These children must live. Kill us, the Westerners, and let them go so they can come back in peace. We only brought them out here because your people told us to meet you here for safe passage to the border. We're trying to help your children."

A soldier came up and handed the tanker my video equipment. He took it and looked at it for a moment. "Is this yours?" the soldier asked me.

"Yes."

He threw the camera on the ground and smashed it to pieces with his rifle butt several times. He saw me cringe a bit, but it was an act. I always have my material backed up. But he didn't need to know that.

"These films are our property, our history. Not yours."

The tanker told his men to lower their weapons.

"Even though you infidels spread propaganda about us, we let you live. You tell that story. Tell them that we let you go to tell the West the truth. Not lies about us, but the truth."

"What truth?"

"That we clean our country of all who do not belong here. ISIS, terrorists, and Westerners. We will lead our children to the border and you tell them that we are not animals. It is a pity you could not bring more out of Al-Waer. But everyone who stayed must have been the opposition. We do not kill our own children."

"The hell you don't," Jake said.

The tanker swung his rifle butt and hit Jake hard on the side of the head. He aimed his rifle at him as Jake writhed on the ground.

I raised my hands and got between Jake and the tanker's rifle and just barely saw in the glare of the spotlight that he was wearing a bloody green bandana. "Don't shoot, we know you. We were there when ISIS shot at you and killed the other tank commander and wounded you."

The tanker with the green bandana looked at me. "How do you know this?"

"They kidnapped us and took us with them to videotape it. We were the ones who threw the satellite dish off the roof so you could see how they were sniping at you."

"Yes, we saw this thing they made. Now we shoot every satellite dish we see, and we do not get shot from roofs anymore."

"We sent the child with the note on the cigarettes about the ISIS weapons on the hill. We helped you kill them. Then we got your brick message. That's why we're here."

The tanker held his aim steady. I sat there waiting for a bullet. In a flash, he swung the butt of his rifle and searing pain shot through my head. Dazed, I crumpled to the ground.

I heard shouting and saw the soldiers start loading crying women and kids back into the bed of the truck. The tanker returned and aimed his rifle at us again as Jake and I lay on the ground, holding our bashed heads. I saw blood streaming down Jake's neck and through his fingers.

The tanker knelt down near me and whispered in my ear, "I gave you the message on the brick because I wanted to meet you and tell you this face-to-face. Go, take these children and you remember I could have killed you. Stay out of our country. This is not your fight."

He waved his hand to his men, who then dragged us to the truck and let us get in with the women and children in the back. The driver followed the tank back to the main road. I looked around at the women and kids. My head was throbbing. I felt where the tanker commander hit me and looked at the blood on my hand. I wiped it on my pants and thought of my old friend hidden in my pack. I reached into my backpack and took out the little gold figurine that had been with me throughout my time in Syria. It seemed there was plenty of good luck left in him to share. I watched the eastern horizon as it began to lighten before the sun as we traveled west to the border. I rubbed my little lucky statuette as we bounced down the road. I had plans to donate the statuette to whatever museum would take him, but he needed to get us across the border first.

I am grateful for the luck but wish we could have saved more.

Chapter 54

Lebanon-Syria Border Checkpoint
June 13, 2013

We drove for about a half hour before the tank stopped and pulled off the road. The tanker with the green bandana stood on top of his tank and waved for our driver to stop. I stood and hung out the back of the truck to try and hear what the tanker was saying. He spoke to the driver and then walked back to talk to me. He pointed down the long road to a roadblock about a half mile ahead.

"Keep going," he yelled. "Tell them we let you live because you have our children."

I waved and nodded my head.

"Don't come back until there is peace or you may not live to see it."

I waved again and sat down in the back as the truck lumbered past the tank. I watched the tanker's dark figure climb back inside, silhouetted by the pale blue sky of the early morning just before sunrise. I watched as the tank turned and retreated back down the road to continue the fight for Assad.

I couldn't help feeling defeated until I looked around at the sleeping figures of the children on the floor of the truck. Some were in each other's arms, others were being held by the women. If I hadn't known better, I might have thought they were dead. But I was thankful that they were just sleeping.

* * *

We approached the roadblock at the Lebanon border. The Syrian soldiers stopped the truck and a soldier climbed up onto the running board to speak with our driver. After only a few moments, he hopped down and came around to the rear of the truck with a few of his men. He peered into the back and saw the truck bed was filled with children and women. He looked at me and motioned for me to get down.

I came down and he asked for my passport. I gave it to him and he studied it for a few seconds and handed it back.

"Where are you from?" he asked in good but broken English.

"We came from Homs."

"I know, but where are you from in the United States?"

"I grew up in San Diego, California."

"Is that near Los Angeles?"

"Yes."

"It is beautiful there. I have been to Los Angeles, just for a short time. I have a sister there."

"We were escorted here by a Syrian tank. The tank commander told us we could take the children to Lebanon."

"Yes, I know. The tank commander is my uncle. We are both from Homs. Thank you for helping our people."

"What are you still doing in the army?"

"I am doing what I can. I am glad to see civilians being protected. I was put here on the border because I would not shoot my countrymen. I was lucky I didn't get shot. I thought of defecting, but I thought I could do some good from inside the regime."

"We saw a lot of Syrian army soldiers that do not think like you."

"I know. There are good and bad everywhere, my friend. The good must start somewhere. I have spoken to the Lebanese guards at their checkpoint just down the road. They are expecting you. Do you know a man named Rafi?"

"Yes, he's my brother-in-law."

The soldier looked at me with a confused face.

"My wife is Lebanese," I said.

I didn't want to get into my life story, so I settled for the simple answer as if she were still alive.

"I see. Then you know more than most Westerners about what is going on."

"Yes," I said simply.

"Thank you for helping us, brother. My uncle wanted me to tell you to make sure you told everyone that we are all not butchers. There are some who are trying to do good."

"I know. Life is complicated."

"Yes."

"Thank you for your help," I said.

He shrugged. "What else can I do? It is my country and my people. I have to help where I can," he said and held out his hand for me to shake. "I am Abu Hamza, from Homs. Do not mention me in your stories, but remember my name. Come back when we kick the bad foreigners out and I will have you as a guest in my home when there is peace."

"Thank you."

"Get these children to safety and I will see you again when there is peace."

I climbed back into the truck and the soldier lifted the turnpike and waved the driver through.

* * *

We drove the short distance to the Lebanese checkpoint and the guards had us all get out of the truck. I helped the children down from the back and hardly noticed Rafi approaching.

"Angus!" he yelled and wrapped me in a bear hug.

"It's good to see family," I said.

"It was not easy convincing people that you were coming. They all had bets on whether you would make it. I'm glad you're here."

"Me, too."

Jake hopped down from the truck after the last child came down.

"Hello, Jake," Rafi said and kissed him on both cheeks. "Good to see you, my friend."

"You, too."

"Our ride will be here soon. Thank you for helping. I don't think it would have been possible without you."

"My pleasure, Rafi. Now that I know what Angus was up to the whole time, I was happy to be of some help," Jake said.

"What are you talking about?" I asked.

"You will see, Angus. Jake and I have a surprise for you," Rafi said.

"I don't think I can be any more surprised than I already am," I said.

I heard the deep thud of the unmistakable sound of helicopters in the distance. I looked around the horizon and saw two dark specks spewing a slightly gray exhaust as they approached from the southwest.

"Oh shit. Is there going to be a problem with Lebanese immigration?"

"No," Rafi said with a confidence I couldn't understand.

"Who do you think that is?" I said and pointed toward the helicopters as they grew larger and louder.

"That's our ride," Rafi said.

"What?"

"Jake paid for the charter. We're flying to Beirut in style."

"Are you shittin' me?" I said.

"What good is it to have money unless you can spend it on a friend's philanthropic project?" Jake asked. "Besides, I don't think I could spend one more minute in the back of a damn truck."

Epilogue

Intercontinental Phoenicia Hotel
Beirut, Lebanon
June 21, 2013

Jake and I sat in director's chairs facing Chip Foster, the world-renowned interviewer of stars, royalty, and fifteen minutes of famers. We sat in the restaurant on the top floor of the Intercontinental Phoenicia Hotel in Beirut where Jake and I began our journey together only six weeks earlier.

A makeup artist put the final touches on his face and cleared the set as Chip grabbed his notes and turned his attention to us. "You guys ready?"

"Sure," I said.

He looked at his cameraman. "Okay, roll it," Chip said.

The cameraman gave him a silent thumbs-up. "Angus Conn, Jake Westin, it's good to have you here."

"It's good to be here," we said in unison.

"Angus, I'll start with you. Tell me how it is you and Jake found yourselves in Syria?"

"I got a call from Jake's agent and he asked if I'd be interested in showing Jake a little about how I do my job as research for his next movie role."

"That's for your next project, *The Burden of Truth*, right, Jake?"

"Yes."

"Where are you in that production?"

"We have a few more weeks of pre-production, but we should start shooting in about a month."

"Angus, was it always your intention to go to Syria?"

"Yes. I was following a story about a Syrian museum curator who wanted to trade his museum antiquities for weapons for the rebels. I had negotiated a deal with the Syrian government to allow dozens of buses to come into Homs and get some children and critically wounded civilians in the besieged neighborhood of Al-Waer out in trade for the artifacts. I originally wanted Jake to accompany me to Beirut and hang tight with my fixer until I got back after a few days to execute what I had planned."

"But it didn't happen that way, did it?"

"No, he pretty much tricked me into taking him along."

"How did you do that, Jake?"

"I told him I wouldn't pay him if I didn't go."

"Yeah, and he hid in my trunk until it was too late to turn back. I was going to miss our contact if I brought him back to Beirut. So, I had to take him along or lose the story."

"Didn't you know it would be dangerous?" Chip asked me.

"Yes, I knew. That's why I didn't want to take him," I said.

"But I made him an offer he couldn't refuse," Jake said and laughed.

This is so surreal, talking about this like it's no big deal, I thought.

"What did you see there, Jake?"

"We saw a lot of civilians dying at the hands of all parties, the rebel groups, ISIS, and the government. It's an understatement to say that it was heartbreaking."

"And how did your plan unravel, Angus?"

"The government changed their minds about the trade and took Jake and me prisoner. Then ISIS ambushed the government truck we were in, confiscated the artifacts, and took us away from the government troops. We managed to escape with some help from the FSA. Jake and I convinced them to return us to the neighborhood where we were staying and we pooled resources to help defend their neighborhood. I have to be honest. I felt pretty defeated at that point, but after what we witnessed, I became more determined than ever to try and get as many children out of there as I could."

"There are rumors that you participated in some of the fighting?"

I looked at Jake as I answered. "No, we just observed and then organized a way to get the civilians out when the rebels learned through their intel sources that ISIS was going to attack the neighborhood and kill everyone."

"How did you make it out?"

"We got a truck and loaded everyone in and were actually intercepted by the regime on the way to the border. We were lucky because the tank commander who stopped us happened to be from Homs and volunteered to escort us to the border."

"Where did you get help in Lebanon?"

"My brother-in-law and Jake chartered a flight of two helicopters to get us back once we crossed the border."

"Incredible. And they just let you leave?"

"Yes, another stroke of luck was that a border guard was also from Homs and let us cross the border with no problems. He told us to tell everyone in the West that there are good people everywhere, even in the Assad regime and if everyone did good where they could, the conflict would evaporate," I said.

"Does that give you hope for the end of the conflict?"

"I think our experience shows that there is definitely hope. But people need to act," I said.

"And how have you responded to that message, Jake?"

"Well, I'm pleased to announce that Angus and I have established a charitable organization that Angus and his fellow veteran freelance journalist, Bobbie Welsh, will oversee full-time, called 'The Syrian Children's Foundation.'"

"And what will your new foundation do that others are not already doing?" Chip asked me.

"Our organization is ensuring that every one of the orphans we rescued will be fed, clothed, housed, and educated at an estate we are currently leasing outside Beirut. We will do this for the duration of the conflict and then fund their return to Syria when there is peace," Jake said.

"What about all the other children in similar situations that you didn't rescue, or need rescuing?"

"We have a facet of our organization that is working with the aid agencies to find orphans in the refugee camps that have no other family who can care for them. When they are identified, we will get them into our foundation and care for them as well."

"There's no way to help them all," Chip said.

"Well, we're doing what we can and we will keep doing it until the money's gone. So we want everyone who knows about The Syrian Children's Fund to give what they can to help where they can. I've also made a commitment to donate my entire salary from my new movie, *The Burden of Truth*, to the foundation. Like I said, we're all doing what we can. That's all we can ask of anyone."

"Well, I applaud your efforts, Jake. But do you believe it can make a real difference?"

"It will make a huge difference for all those children we're able to reach and it will be better than nothing. If we all give whatever we can spare toward any positive goal, the results would be a huge leap forward over the collective way our society chooses to solve problems right now.

"There is no way we can hope our problems will just fade away, or hide from them with constant distraction. It took a few dangerous weeks of being in Syria for me to realize that we all must focus on facing our struggles head-on and strive to make a positive impact wherever we can. The alternative is doing nothing. And the result of doing nothing is more horrible than any of us should allow."

THE END

Acknowledgements

My main intent in writing this book was to raise awareness of the atrocities that have been leveled on the Syrian people since 2011, help garner support for innocent Syrian children caught in the crossfire, and honor the brave men and women who put their lives on the line to bring us the truth in dangerous places around the world. It is my sincere hope that this project will be successful in doing exactly those things.

Many people came together to help me get this story into its current form. The first person I must thank is the Pandamoon CEO, Zara Kramer. She immediately understood the greater message I was trying to convey and gave me the opportunity to share it with the rest of the world. The team at Pandamoon Publishing has my sincere gratitude for taking my words on the page and turning it into the fantastic piece of art it has become. Of course, this includes my editors, Nicole Tone, Zara Kramer, Daphne Tuccitto, and Rachel Schoenbauer, the talented art of Fletcher Kinnear for the absolutely stunning cover art and original map, and Matt Kramer for his art direction, coordination skill, tenacious spirit and infectious enthusiasm for any and all projects thrown in his direction. And, of course, my fellow Panda writers for their fantastic support, they truly come together to make a phenomenal publishing team with hearts the size of Pandas.

Outside the writing and publishing world, I have Jeff Sowa to thank for reading everything I've ever written and his willingness to take the time to give me a no nonsense reader's take on every word of this book. I can't tell you how valuable your time and friendship has been to me, Jeff, from Bremerton to the Meadows of Dan, thanks for always giving me the encouragement I needed to continue.

I also owe an unpayable debt to Dee Gordon, who endured countless hours on the phone sharing the nuances of our respective life journeys, sometimes into the early morning hours to the chagrin of both our wives, and for always reminding me that under no circumstances shall I ever save anything for the swim back.

A few people were vital in helping me take my thoughts and translate them to words on the page. Thanks to Kristy and Ray who invited me into their Napoli home, during my last month in Italy, and provided me a comfortable sanctuary where I could craft the majority of this story while enjoying their pool, unbelievable view of the Mediterranean Sea, and their company and hospitality over phenomenal Italian food and wine.

I must also thank Patrick Spencer, who graciously hosted me at the La Selva Villa, tucked away in a tranquil corner of Tuscany, where I had the privileged opportunity to spend a few glorious uninterrupted days to get the last third of this story on paper. While these locales seem like the wrong venue for writing such a serious subject, they were essential in allowing me the contemplation time to effectively relate such an important topic and I am grateful for time well-spent with wonderful friends.

I thank all of my close friends and family, my mother Carol, my mother-in-law Diane, my sisters Lisa and Dina, and my brother Giovanni, who knew I was writing and gave me needed encouragement even though they weren't exactly sure why I chose the topic.

My most beloved thanks go to my two children, Isabella and Vincent, who sacrificed a bit of play time with dad so I could do my part to help beautiful, innocent children, just like them, halfway around the world. And to my amazing wife, partner, and friend, who allowed me the time, even at inconvenient times, to pursue a passion second only to my love for her. Thank you Bonnie, you helped make this book a reality.

Thank you for purchasing this copy of ***Looking into the Sun*** by Todd Tavolazzi. If you enjoyed this book by Todd, please let him know by posting a review.

About the Author

Todd lived most of his pre-adult life in San Diego, California. He enlisted in the Marine Corps out of high school in 1991 and served as an infantry Marine at Camp Pendleton, California, before he attended the U.S. Naval Academy in 1994. After graduation in 1998, he was commissioned as an Ensign in the U.S. Navy as a Surface Warfare Officer and served onboard a supply ship stationed in Bremerton, Washington, before being accepted into Naval Aviation. He earned his Navy "Wings of Gold" in Pensacola, Florida, in 2002 and flew the MH-53E Sea Dragon while stationed at NAS Sigonella, Italy, and the MH-60S Knighthawk at Naval Station Norfolk in Virginia. Todd married his flight school sweetheart, Bonnie, also a Naval Aviator, in 2003. She also flew the MH-60S in Norfolk, VA.

Todd earned a Bachelor of Science in History from the U.S. Naval Academy and a Master of Arts in Diplomacy from Norwich University where he studied Europe and the Middle East extensively. On his non-flying staff tour, he served with the U.S. Sixth Fleet in Naples, Italy, where he was designated a Naval Strategist and spent time traveling and studying international relations throughout Europe and the Middle East on missions for the U.S. Navy.

Todd has had his short fiction published with both *Potluck Magazine* and *The Subtopian* e-zine. *Looking Into the Sun* is his first novel. Todd is still serving in the U.S. Navy and is currently working on his second novel in his spare time between spending time with Bonnie and their two children, Isabella and Vincent.

Glossary

Alaikum salaam – "And unto you peace" in Arabic. A standard reply to the Nation of Islam greeting, "Salaam Alaikum", which means, "peace be unto you."

Alawite – Also known as Alawis, it is the largest branch of the Shia sect of the Islamic faith (inside a larger group called Twelvers).

Aleppo – The largest city in Syria with just over 2.1 million people.

Allahu akbar – "God is greater" in Arabic. This proclamation professes that God is greater than all things.

Al-Qaeda in Iraq (AQI) – The militant Sunni organization comprised of Iraqi and foreign fighters who are in opposition to the U.S.-led invasion of 2003 and with Shiite Muslims in the Iraqi government.

Al-Waer – A neighborhood in the suburbs of the Syrian city of Homs. The neighborhood housed approximately 300,000 people before hostilities; there are between 75,000 - 100,000 people still living there. It was the last besieged neighborhood in Homs before a truce between the Syrian government and the rebels holed up in the neighborhood was signed in December 2015.

Baalbek – An ancient city approximately 53 miles northeast of Beirut in Lebanon's Bekaa Valley. It has some of the best preserved Roman ruins in Lebanon.

Bekaa Valley – A fertile valley in eastern Lebanon that runs approximately 75 miles from the Syrian border in the north to within 20 miles of the Israel border in the south. It is Lebanon's most important agricultural region.

Corniche – A picturesque seaside promenade lined with palm trees that is situated between the heart of Beirut, Lebanon and the Mediterranean Sea.

Free Syrian Army (FSA) – A group of Syrian Army officers and soldiers who defected on 29 July 2011. The group is officially allied with France, Qatar, Saudi Arabia, Turkey, and the United States who each contribute unknown types and quantities of monetary and material military support. It opposes the Syrian government, ISIS, and some hard line al-Nusra groups.

Homs – The third largest city in Syria with a population of just over 820,000 in 2008. Its numbers have dwindled to around 200,000 since hostilities began in 2011. It is considered the "Capital of the Revolution" after tens of thousands of people demonstrated against Bashar al-Assad's brutality in mid-April 2011.

Islamic State of Iraq and Syria (ISIS) – A Salafist Islamic militant group that adheres to a strict Wahabbi doctrine of Sunni Islam. The group also goes by the abbreviation of the Islamic State of Iraq and the Levant (ISIL). The current leader, former leader of AQI, Abu Bakr al-Baghdadi, continues to employ guerilla tactics and terrorism to expand its influence in Iraq, Syria, and across the wider Middle East.

Jabhat al-Nusra (commonly referred to as only al-Nusra) – A rebel group in Syria spawned by the leader of the terrorist organization Al Qaeda in Iraq (AQI) led by Abu Bakr al-Baghdadi. The group is considered well-armed and well-trained. It was created by former AQI operative, a Syrian named Abu Muhammad al-Julani, in January 2013, and remains a formidable rebel group in Syria. Despite reports that al-Nusra had joined forces with ISIS, al-Julani has denied affiliation with ISIS and it remains its own organization at odds with ISIS.

Latakia – Fifth largest city in Syria with just over 380,000 residents. It is the country's principal seaport located on the Mediterranean Sea. The seaport lies just to the south of the city.

Qasr – A small town in northeast Lebanon less than a mile from the Lebanon-Syria border.

Salaam alaikum – A standard greeting among the Nation of Islam meaning, "peace be unto you."

Shabbiha – Syrian government security forces.

Shia Islam – An abbreviation of Shia-ne-Ali, it is a branch of the Islamic faith that believes the rightful successor of the Islamic Prophet Muhammad was his son-in-law and cousin Ali ibn Abi Talib. Modern Shia Islam is divided into three main groups: Twelvers, Ismailis, and Zaidis (Alawites are a branch of Shia Islam in the Twelver group). Shia Islam makes up the religion of the majority population in Iraq, Iran, Azerbaijan, and Bahrain.

Shukran – "Thank you" in Arabic.

Sunni Islam – Is the largest branch of Islam claiming nearly 90% of all Muslims. Sunnis believe that the rightful successor of the Islamic Prophet Muhammad was his father-in-law, Abu Bakr. This belief is the driving factor behind the animosity between Sunni and Shia Muslims.

Takbir – Arabic term that means Allahu akbar, "God is greater."

Zahle – A small town about 30 miles northeast of Beirut, roughly halfway between Beirut and Baalbek.

52934644R00171

Made in the USA
Charleston, SC
29 February 2016